Ryan's eye took in a scene from a heart-stopping nightmare

The huge mutie rattlesnake was well over twenty feet long, its body as thick as the thigh of a grown man. The setting sun glinted off a metal strip that circled the reptile's throat like a silvery collar. The band caught Ryan's attention, but his instant preoccupation was with Lori, sprawled helplessly in the dirt in front of the rearing, hissing creature.

Ryan braced his G-12 against his hip and aimed at the spade-shaped head of the snake. But his finger held still on the trigger of the powerful blaster.

The giant rattler's stunning speed took them all by surprise. Before anyone could tighten a finger on a trigger, it had weaved its head back and forth and struck.

Also available in the Deathlands saga:

JAMES AXLER

DEATH LANDS.

Ice and Fire

A GOLD EAGLE BOOK FROM

WORLDWIDE.

TORONTO • NEW YORK • LONDON • PARIS
AMSTERDAM • STOCKHOLM • HAMBURG
ATHENS • MILAN • TOKYO • SYDNEY

"Pro captu lectoris habent sua fata libelli," said Terentianus Maurus, around A.D 200. This is particularly true if the reader is my line editor, Cathy Haddad. This book is for her, with thanks for her always positive and friendly support.

First edition December 1988

ISBN 0-373-62508-1

This ae nighte, this ae nighte, every nighte and alle,
Fire and sleet and candle-lighte, and Christe receive
thy soule.

—From the medieval ballad,
"The Lyke-Wake Dirge"

Chapter One

RYAN CAWDOR'S FINGERS flexed, brushing against the polished metal floor of the mat-trans chamber. He was still struggling back from the dark depths of unconsciousness. The tip of his right index finger touched something sticky and warm, a little below body temperature. The finger moved a crabbing inch farther, investigating the substance.

Ryan's one good eye blinked open for a moment, looking down at his hand.

"Blood," he said.

Blood it was—a dark pool of it, nearly eighteen inches across, crusting at the edges. Ryan touched again, checking that he was conscious, feeling the too-familiar stickiness.

The chamber still smelled flat and bitter from the gases released during the jump, and the metal disks in floor and ceiling were creaking faintly as they cooled down.

The armaglass walls were a pallid, translucent gray color. The gateway that they'd just left had been walled in a deep, brilliant turquoise. Ryan remembered that, remembered it because it had reminded him so much of the Indian jewelry of the far Southwest.

He closed his eye again and took slow deep breaths, trying to speed his recovery. The jumps always scrambled everyone's brains, making them feel as if the contents of their skulls had been drained, freeze-dried, sandblasted and then returned. While Ryan had been out, his head had slumped and the patch over the blind socket of his left eye had become uncomfortable. He lifted a hand and adjusted it, opened his right eye and tried once more to focus on the crimson puddle.

Blood meant that someone was bleeding—Ryan could deduce that much, despite the mind tremor of a gateway jump. He blinked and followed the blood to its source.

"Fireblast," he sighed.

Doc Tanner had suffered one of his sporadic nosebleeds during the period of blackout. Blood ran from his hawkish nose, through his grizzled stubble, down the furrows of his chin. It dribbled across his neck and over his stained blue denim shirt, pattering in an uncertain trickle onto the floor.

Trying to collect his thoughts, Ryan looked around the hexagonal room. Despite the bleeding nose, Doc seemed to be all right.

Doctor Theophilus Algernon Tanner looked to be around sixty years old. By one measure of time he was only about thirty. By another kind of temporal yardstick he was somewhere close to two hundred and twenty-eight.

During the 1990s—eight or nine years before the skies had darkened with missiles and the civilized world disappeared forever, American scientists were working on different aspects of a top-secret program, under the umbrella name of the Totality Concept. The aspect that affected the life of Doc Tanner was a part of Overproject Whisper, called the Cerberus Project.

The hidden gateways—mat-trans chambers—were in closely guarded fortresses or redoubts, which were scattered across North America.

But they didn't just transport a man in a flicker of frozen time from place to place. The scientists believed they could also be used to breach the last barrier. Time. And in that misguided belief, they experimented in trawling a human being from the past.

The failures were many, and horrifying. The one partial success was Doc Tanner.

Married with two young children, Doc had been a respected man of science, in the year of Our Lord 1896—

Ryan's reminiscence was checked as the old man coughed, spluttered and wiped a gnarled hand over his chin, bringing it away smeared with blood.

November, two hundred years ago: the young scientist had been tugged forward through time to become the prize guinea pig in Project Cerberus. But Doc had never been the sort of person to sit quiet. After a number of combative years he became so troublesome that the faceless men had a choice. Terminate him with extreme rectitude or chron-jump him again. So Doc had been flung a hundred years into the future. A few weeks later all of the scientists he had left behind perished in the rad blasts of the last world war.

Ryan had known him for about a year. Now Doc's mind was reasonably reliable, but the shattering events of his life had permanently tipped the balance of his brain and he was known to wander mentally.

His girlfriend, Lori Quint, lay stretched out on the floor next to him, her blond head in his lap. Some of his blood had dribbled into her long hair, clotting and tangling. Though she was only seventeen years old, Lori had endured an appalling background of incest and violence. Her affection for the elderly scientist had been appealing, but over the past few weeks Ryan had begun to notice signs that all wasn't well between them. The girl was becoming easily irritated and sulky.

But Ryan had learned from his old friend and boss, the Trader, a great and inalienable truth about women: "What women want from men is what men happen to be right out of," Trader had said.

Sitting cross-legged next to Doc and Lori was the only other person of the group, other than Ryan, who'd ridden and fought with Trader. Now shaking his head to destroy the clinging fog in his brain, J. B. Dix, the Armorer, was recovering consciousness.

Under five feet nine in height, slim built, J.B. was closing in on his fortieth year. His complexion was sallow and unhealthy, and his wire-rimmed glasses were hooked safely in a top pocket of his dark brown leather jacket. His beloved and much-traveled fedora lay between his feet. The Armorer was perhaps the greatest expert on weaponry in all the Deathlands. His preference was for a mini-Uzi and a Steyr AUG pistol. A Tekna fighting knife at his hip completed the obvious fighting gear. But his clothes and combat boots also concealed a wealth of hidden equipment: fuses, picklocks and stilettos; wire and a little plas-ex, as well as a folding sextant.

J.B. was a walking arsenal.

As Ryan looked across the chamber at his oldest friend, the man's gray eyes flicked open. He glanced around at the others.

"Doc got a bloody nose," he said. "Rest look okay to me." The Armorer was never a man to use two words when one would do the job.

There were two other people in the mat-trans room, both of them still unconscious. Next to J.B. in the circle was the youngest member of the traveling group of companions, a lad fifteen years of age. He weighed 110 pounds soaking wet and was five feet four inches tall. His long mane of spun silver hair cascaded across his skinny shoulders like a winter fall of Sierra meltwater. His mind blanked by the jump, the boy looked like a sleeping child, at peace with the world.

To Ryan's knowledge, Jak Lauren had killed upward of a hundred human beings and probably as many muties. When it came to close-quarter butchery, Ryan had never seen anyone to match the teenager. A satin-finish .357 Magnum was tucked in his belt. The torn leather-and-canvas jacket he held in his lap, in camouflage brown, gray and green, had tiny shards of razored steel sewn into it. He also carried several—Ryan never knew how many—leaf-bladed throwing knives. The youngster's ruby-red eyes remained stubbornly closed, though movement of his fingers showed that Jak was coming around.

Krysty Wroth leaned against the armaglass wall, close by Ryan, still in the classic lotus position, the palms of her hands flat upon her thighs. Her fiery crimson hair was bunched protectively around her neck. Krysty's body trembled and she sighed. Then she opened her dazzling green eyes, turned her head and half smiled across at Ryan.

"Don't get easier, do they, lover?" she asked quietly.

"No. Just wish we could learn how to control where we go on these jumps. I worry that one day we're gonna end up in a gateway that doesn't exist, with half a mountain on top of us."

"Reminds me of the time back in Harmony Ville, when I was a girl. Fat guy named Johannus fell clean out the top of a two-hundred-foot ponderosa. Folks heard him all the way down yelling out 'So far, so good. So far, so good.' Know what I mean?"

Ryan had heard the story before, but it still amused him. Each time Krysty told it there was a different location and a different person doing the falling. But it remained a good tale.

Now everyone was coming out of it. Lori rolled on her side, her face a pale yellow, holding her stomach. "I feel sick," she moaned. She raised a hand to investigate her hair. "Oh, blood! Who bleeds? Doc? All going in my buggered hair!" She managed to get to her hands and knees before beginning to retch. It had been some time since their last meal, and there was nothing in her stomach but threads of golden bile.

The noise woke Doc. "By the three Kennedys! What's amiss here? Small nasal hemorrhage, I do believe."

Jak Lauren tried to stand up, steadying himself against the shimmering gray wall. "Head fucked," he muttered. "Hate jumps. Head feels bad."

"Take it easy," Ryan warned.

Lori had stopped retching and had also stood up, picking at the matted blood in her hair. As she moved, the tiny silver spurs on her high red boots tinkled with a thin, clear sound.

Ryan sighed and slowly uncoiled, picking up the Heckler & Koch G-12 automatic rifle from the floor, then checked that his SIG-Sauer 9 mm pistol was safely holstered at his belt. He reached down to help Krysty to her feet, getting a smile of appreciation in return.

J.B. stood up in his neat, effortless way, brushing dust off his clothes. "Don't think I'll ever enjoy these jumps."

Doc was last to his feet, dabbing at his bloodied nose with a blue swallow's-eye kerchief. He leaned on his ornate ebony swordstick, gripping it by the silver lion's-head top. "Upon my soul but I have made a dreadful mess on the floor. Considerable tapping of the claret."

"And on my head, you stupe crazy," Lori moaned. "Got it on my boots." The sound of the leather sole peeling from the metal disks was unpleasantly sticky.

"Sorry, my dearest dove." Doc moved to put his arm around her, but the tall blonde moved away, shrugging pettishly.

"Everyone ready?" Ryan asked. He didn't need to check that both his blasters had rounds under the hammer. They always did.

"Wonder where are now?" Jak said, licking his lips. "Can't smell or taste nothing."

"Know when we get outside." J.B. glanced across at Ryan. "Now?"

Ryan nodded. "Yeah. Blasters ready, people. Krysty, you open the chamber door."

The trigger of the caseless G-12 felt good with Ryan's index finger wrapped around it. True, they'd never yet encountered a gateway where the main control room had been infiltrated, but there had to be a first time for everything.

Krysty brushed the tumbling hair away from her face, gripped the handle and pushed the armored door open.

Chapter Two

"SAFE," SHE SAID.

As was usual in the gateways, the main mat-trans chamber opened into a small anteroom, which was only about twelve feet square and contained no furniture. A row of shelves lined one wall, and a dark green plastic beaker stood alone on the middle shelf. Generally the redoubts that Ryan had seen throughout the wastes of the Deathlands had been surprisingly clean. They were all run by efficient nuke plants and comp-controlled to regulate light, heat, humidity and antistat dust maintenance.

This small room was no exception. Very faintly, far off, felt rather than heard, came the whispering vibration of the main power plant—self-maintaining, ticking away dutifully for a hundred years, still doing the job that its long-dead creators had programmed it to perform.

J.B. followed Krysty, with Ryan eventually bringing up the rear. With six of them in the room it was a little crowded. Jak picked up the beaker and looked inside it. He shook his head and replaced the container on the shelf. "Dry as neutron bones."

From several previous experiences, Ryan knew that beyond the closed door would be the main control room for the gateway. Its condition would probably give them a valuable clue as to the state of the rest of the redoubt. Some had been totally evacuated during the megadeath panic in the last weeks of the year 2000. Some had shown signs of having been left in a tearing hurry in the second week of January, 2001.

"Ready?" Krysty asked.

The heavy door was vanadium steel, with a hydraulic power switch. There was the hissing sound of the motor operating, and the door slid open. The six had traveled together long enough to know how they should operate in a potentially dangerous situation. Krysty and J.B. slithered out quickly, flattening themselves against the walls on either side of the entrance. Jak and Doc, with Lori dragging at their heels, darted toward the nearest cover, which was a line of workbenches. Ryan stayed behind for a moment in the anteroom, ready to provide supporting fire if it proved necessary.

But the room was empty.

The huge double doors that would link it to the remainder of the fortress were solidly closed. Ryan stepped out, easing the door shut behind him. He took his finger off the trigger of the G-12 and let the rifle dangle from its shoulder strap. Everyone else relaxed.

"Lori!"

"What, Ryan?"

The tall, broad-shouldered man strode across to where the girl had draped herself across a padded chair. She glanced up, seeing the flare of anger in his eye, and winced as if Ryan had already struck her across the face.

"Get up, girl," he ordered.

Krysty moved a half step forward to try to intercede.

"Keep out of it, lover," Ryan said, quiet, not even turning.

Lori, eyes glued to his face, rose slowly to her feet. In her heels she came close to his six foot and two inches height. Nervously she lifted a hand to flick away an errant curl from her forehead.

"Don't ever do that again, Lori," Ryan warned.

"Do what?"

"Come out of an unknown door like you were strolling into a high-fash clothes store in a fancy ville."

"I don't know what..." she began, ducking and recoiling as he actually lifted a clenched fist toward her.

Like a wolf checking its leap in midair, Ryan succeeded in holding back the intended blow.

"Fireblast, you triple-stupe bitch! You think this is some kind of game? Bang and you're dead and then we all sit around and share a self-heat? Any team's as good as its weakest member."

"And that's you, Lori," Krysty pointed out.

"Just kept your fucking mouth shutting, Krysty," the younger girl snapped.

"We all have to pull together, my dear," Doc said, trying to placate his teenage mistress.

"You pull yourself, you old—"

Ryan reached out and grabbed Lori by the collar, hefting her so that her toes barely scraped the floor of the control room. "Keep buttoned, girl! You screw up and we all get screwed up. Stay alert when you're supposed to."

"What if I don't?" she sneered, recovering her nerve now she saw he wasn't actually going to hit her.

"If you don't stop playing around with all of our lives? Easy, Lori. We dump you. Just walk away and leave you behind. I figure you might live a couple of days on your own."

"You'd chill me?" She looked around at the faces of the other four, seeking some sign that they disputed what Ryan was saying.

Krysty met her gaze, nodding slightly. J.B. simply stared straight back at the blond teenager. Jak turned his fingers into a gun and pointed at her, drilling her between the eyes. Doc shuffled his feet and looked down at the floor.

Ryan answered her question. "You carry your share, Lori, and nobody chills you. You let us down and then you get treated like anyone outside the group. If that means chilling, then . . ." The sentence trailed away into the stillness of the room.

The tension stretched, against the background of flickering lights, dancing dials and chattering comp-consoles. This was the nerve center of the whole redoubt, where every aspect of the building was controlled. Once, it had all been set running for the convenience of the human occupants. Now they were gone, but it still kept steadily to its ordained tasks.

"Looks like they left in a hurry," Krysty said, easing the moment.

In his blood-blurred anger at Lori's casual stupidity, Ryan had barely noticed what the control room looked like. Now he took a few moments to glance around.

If he hadn't known better, he might have guessed that the workers had only rushed out of the big room minutes ago, rather than nearly a hundred years back. There were a number of Styrofoam cups, and plastic containers that had once held sandwiches, long rotted and gone. Pens and pads lay scattered on the benches, scraps of crumpled paper on the floor. On an impulse Ryan stopped and picked one up from the tiles near his feet, unfolding it carefully.

"Like the Dead Sea Scrolls," Doc said. "Open with caution."

The paper was part of a comp-print, covered on one side with an incomprehensible mass of jumbled figures. He turned it over. There, on the other side, was faded handwriting—a question from one person, with a reply in different colored ink.

My room after last food?

Piss in a hot spot!

Ryan grinned. "Nothing changes, does it?" He crumpled the note to brittle shards and let them filter through his fingers like grains of sand.

They spent a quarter of an hour wandering around the control center. Ryan joined Doc by the main display panels that ran all of the gateway's mat-trans functions. The old man was shaking his head at the coded numbers and letters on the liquid-crystal console.

"Make any sense of it, Doc?"

"No. The men who worked on these were a small and highly specialized team, some of the best brains on all of the Totality Concept. I had heard the odd whisper, of course, around the canteens and bars. But nothing that... If only we could learn how to drive these darned buggies! Least we could get where we wanted and not where they shoot us. All along the disassembly line and back again."

"Place like this—abandoned in a hurry—could there be a manual or something?"

Doc sucked at his peculiarly perfect teeth. "Doubt it, my dear fellow. Software and all instructs would go first of all. Instant self-destruct. Press the button on the can, and it's incinerated and pulverized in fifteen seconds. It's the hardware you can't get rid of so easily."

"Must have been someplace they held copies of all the vital documents and stuff?"

The old man patted him on the arm. "Course there was, Mr. Cawdor. Course. Nearly all missile complexes, military bases, fortresses... all of them. But there was one small problem. As soon—"

Ryan interrupted him. "I get it, Doc. Primary, triple-red targets for the nuking? Missile complexes, military bases and... Yeah, I get it. Mebbe one day we'll find something, tucked away at the back of a file, forgotten. Mebbe."

Doc Tanner shook his head. "We had a saying, Ryan. It'll happen when pigs fly. I haven't seen any airborne bacon for a very, very long time."

There was a printed card tacked to the wall by the exit door from the control room. The letters had peeled, and one or two had fallen off completely. But it was still legible: Warning. On Egress No B12 Sec-

Cleared Documentation to Be Removed Under Pain of Instant Court-Martial. This Means YOU.

Doc nodded. "Brings it back. A sign like that surely brings it back. Once they saw I was a kind of threat to them, they watched me closer than a hawk watches a rabbit. By then all international security had become so compromised and infiltrated that I guess us and the Russkies knew all along what we were all doing and what they were doing. Secrets!" He gave a short, cynical laugh. "Not anymore, there weren't."

Jak coughed. "Sorry interrupt. Hungry. Gotta be food around redoubt left in big hurry. Let's go."

"Sure," Ryan agreed. "Everyone ready? Lori? You ready?"

Her bad mood had blown away like a summer squall, and she favored him with her broadest smile. "Yeah, Ryan."

From their previous visits to the concealed fortresses, they all knew that they now faced one of the moments of maximum danger. The entrance that linked the control room and the gateway to the rest of the redoubt was sufficiently strong to withstand almost any power used against it. It wasn't uncommon for local muties to have broken into other sections of the redoubts, but they lacked the weaponry to force the double doors.

"Three-five-two code?" J.B. said.

"Guess so."

It bore out Doc's comments about how ridiculous a lot of the sec regs had become. In every redoubt they'd entered, the "code" to get in and out of the control section had been numerical. Three-five-two to open it and two-five-three to close it.

Ryan wondered why they didn't just have a pair of buttons marked Open and Close.

The Armorer punched out the triple numerals, standing to one side, his Uzi at the ready, braced against his hip. The other five companions were ranged behind him, ready to pour full-metal jacketed death into anything waiting for them.

Nothing happened at all.

"Dark night!" J.B. exclaimed in a voice of the mildest annoyance.

"Try it again," Krysty suggested.

"Could try reversing it," Ryan said.

"If they've played tricks, it'll take a long time to go through all the combinations of three numbers," Doc said, sighing. "The number of possible permutations is . . . about . . . approximately . . . Well, it's a lot."

J.B. pressed the same three numerals again. "Two's a mite sticky. Ah, that's got it."

Behind the immensely thick walls, huge gears began their ponderous engagement, moving for the first time in all the long, still years. Grudgingly edging the double doors apart, the powerful hydraulics hissed at the weight.

Once the gap was wide enough, J.B. slipped through, eyes searching in both directions down the brightly lit corridor beyond. The rest waited, nerves stretched tightly.

"Clear," the Armorer called. "It's a sealed section. Ends in a blank wall one way, no doors. Other way it curves a little to the right. Then there's a big sec door, a ceiling-to-floor job. No side entrances.''

Jak led the others out. The entrance to the control section was now wide open. This was always a difficult moment, particularly as the controls weren't functioning perfectly. If they left the doors open, then there was a serious risk of other trespassers finding their way in and destroying the gateway, stranding them wherever they were. But to close them meant a similar danger—they might permanently malfunction and keep them locked out for good.

''You got two bad options then pick the least bad,'' had been the advice of the Trader.

Ryan punched in two and five and three. Unhesitatingly the double doors closed tightly shut.

It was a typical redoubt corridor, around twenty feet wide, with a slightly arched roof nearly fifteen feet high at its crown. Strip lighting was set at the line where wall and ceiling merged. Ryan spotted the tiny sec cameras dotted along the roof, their probing lenses turning in an eternal quest. No doubt they were already carrying the pictures of the first intruders for a century to some far-off security center. And nobody would be there to take notice of the invasion of the redoubt.

''Least there's no problem which way to go,'' J.B. said, pushing his glasses farther up his narrow nose.

THE STEEL SHUTTERS had been carefully dropped and locked during the evacuation of the redoubt. The main control was a simple, counterweighted green lever, which had to be lifted to raise the doors above their heads.

It was an unusual setup. The gateway section of the redoubt seemed to be stuck out on an isolated wing of its own, with no other passages opening off the main corridor.

They passed under a half dozen of the metal doors before they began to notice some changes.

"Seismic damage," Doc observed, pointing with his cane at several narrow stress fractures in the ceiling.

Everyone stopped and gazed up, seeing rippled furrows in the stressed concrete. The floor under their feet was no longer perfectly regular. There were chunks of loose grit and larger pieces of stone, some as big as a child's thumb. They also noticed that not all of the lights were functioning. About one sol-strip in five was darkened.

"Nukes?" Jak asked.

"I would hazard a guess that we are still too deep for any primary effects of missiles," Doc replied. "But there is no doubt that the effects of heavy nuclear activity can affect the earth for many miles, exposing frailties in its crust and causing shock waves to run far and deep."

Beyond the next barrier the roof was much worse and parts of the walls had split and fallen. The floor was corrugated in tiny waves. Now three in five of the lights were out.

"Don't much care for the way this is looking, lover," Krysty warned. "I've got a feeling that there's something in this place, 'part from us."

"Something? Or somebody?"

She shook her head, closing her eyes and trying to focus the mutie "sensing" powers she'd inherited from her mother.

"No. Weird...not humanoid, and not mutie, either. Some sort of animal." She shook her head. "No. Not really animal. Just . . . something."

They reached another of the barriers. Jak was leading and he glanced at Ryan, hand resting on the green control lever. Ryan nodded to the albino boy, keeping his own finger on the trigger of his G-12. If Krysty could feel something wrong, then it likely meant something *was* wrong.

"Mechanism rough," Jak said. "Sticking bad." He didn't need to tell the others. They could all hear the grating sound from behind the crumbling walls of the passage.

When it reached about two and a half feet in the air, the door stopped moving, with a final, inexorable metallic jolt.

For a moment, in the stillness, Ryan thought that he could hear something moving on the far side, a faint rustling noise, like a breeze moving crumpled pieces of dry paper.

"A ghastly smell," Doc observed, "like old vinegar. It's most unpleasant."

Jak stooped and peeked under the rim of the jammed door. "Can't see much. Nearly all lights gone. Think there's a fork in passage ahead."

Though bright lights affected the white-haired boy's sight, he saw better in semidarkness than any of the others.

"Must be where this spur joins on the main redoubt," J.B. guessed.

"We might as well go take a look," Ryan said. "I'm getting to feel as hungry as Jak. The living and sleeping quarters are where we'll find any eats that are still around."

"Careful," Krysty whispered, licking her lips nervously. "There's... Just take care through that door."

"Go first?" Jak asked.

"Sure. We're right behind you. Watch what you're doing."

The boy flashed a fearless grin and ducked under and out of sight, closely followed by the rest of the group.

Jak was the first to find the cockroaches—or rather the cockroaches found him.

Chapter Three

THROUGHOUT THE DEATHLANDS there were many varieties of genetic mutations, mostly prompted by the effects of intensive radiation, combined with the use of chemical toxins. Ryan had seen some quite appalling examples of human or semihuman muties, sometimes made worse by each succeeding generation. Animals that bred much more frequently had sometimes mutated to a literally unrecognizable degree. And the insects, with their infinitely shorter cycle of life and reproduction—

The first roach dropped from its perch high in the tumbling wreckage of the old ceiling, landing on Jak's shoulders, its clawed feet hooking into the white spray of his hair. There was precious little light in this part of the passage, and Ryan, seeing the "bug" fall, was puzzled rather than worried. The thing was a coppery-blue color and almost a foot in length.

The boy screamed, high and shrill, echoing through the maze of linked passages. "Get the fuck off!" he yelled, beating at the creature, but it was snagged to him.

"Gaia! This is what I saw!" Krysty exclaimed at Ryan's elbow, the disgust dripping from her voice. "There's hundreds."

"Thousands," J.B. contradicted her.

"Millions," was Ryan's own conclusion.

Everywhere he looked he could see the metallic sheen of cockroaches, scuttling across the ceiling and down the walls, a sinuous, undulating wave of scraping, scaly legs and bodies. Eyes on stalks, seeking out the scent and taste of the intruders.

The insects dropped all around the companions, on top of them. Ryan felt one trying to probe beneath his collar and he shuddered at the obscenity of the thing.

Lori was starting to slide into a noisy panic, drawing in harsh, rasping breaths and letting them out in choked mewing noises.

The combination of the darkness and the endless rustling attack was nearly too much for the friends, even for hardened fighters like J.B. and Ryan.

"Hang on! Everyone, keep control!" Their leader's order held off the fear for a few vital beats of the heart.

Each of them was reacting in a different way. Doc was hopping around, crunching the cockroaches beneath his boots, flailing at others with his swordstick, muttering to himself under his breath, trying to get near enough to Lori to help her, as well.

Lori stood still, hunched over, hands clasped over her face, shoulders shaking in terror.

J.B. responded to the mutie insects' attack by running on the spot to prevent any of the roaches from climbing his legs. At the same time he brushed at his hat, shoulders and chest, sloughing off any attached insects. He was keeping amazingly calm.

As the first victim, Jak had suffered the worst shock. His greatest problem was to get the voracious mutie insects out of his long, fine hair. More and more cockroaches landed on him, nipping at the skin of his neck, biting at one another. From behind, it looked to Ryan as though the young boy were wearing a magical, shifting helmet of some mystic coppery material.

Krysty's hair had coiled in on itself at the first presentiment of danger, forming a hard scarlet knot that repelled the attempts of the cockroaches to get a grip on it.

Until he felt a savage bite on the back of his hand, Ryan wasn't sure how much of a threat the giant mutie insects presented. The pain and the spurt of blood brought home to him with a dreadful clarity that they were likely to be utterly overwhelmed by the roaches if they didn't act swiftly.

"Everyone get in line, follow me!" he yelled. "J.B., you got the hat. You come last. Rest keep on knocking the scaly bastards off the guy in front. Let's move it!"

For the rest of his life Ryan Cawdor would remember the ceaseless sound of the cockroaches being cracked apart under their feet as they walked steadily toward an uphill section of the passage. Ryan had glimpsed another closed metal sec door and built his plan around their being able to reach it, open it and get through.

And find no more roaches on the other side.

"Keep going!" he shouted. Krysty was immediately behind him, batting the scrabbling horde off his wiry mat of black hair, beating them to the concrete floor. Lori, weeping loudly, was performing the same service for Krysty. Doc, half carrying her, was pushing next in line, spitting out words with violent fluency in a language that nobody had ever heard.

Jak was just in front of the Armorer, who was plucking the huge insects from the tangled skein of snowy hair, dropping them and splitting them under his boot heels.

They reached the bottom of the slope, moving at a brisk walk. There seemed fewer of the massive roaches as they climbed upward.

Ryan made the mistake of glancing at the dimly visible ceiling. At that precise moment two of the revolting creatures came flopping onto his face.

He distinctly felt the saw-edged mandibles snap shut on the patch over his blinded left eye, while the other clawed at his lips, trying to wriggle into his half-open mouth. He dropped the G-12, letting it dangle from its sling, and tore at the glittering, hard carapaces of the roaches. The light was less faint, and he could see the eyes on their wobbling stalks, rolling at him on the elongated skulls.

The one on the upper part of his face was easily dislodged, and Ryan heaved it against the wall, seeing it split open, the two halves trailing slime down the pale concrete. But the insect by his mouth was stronger and more persistent, and he feared it might pull off a chunk of his flesh if he tried to rip it from his face.

On an impulse, Ryan opened his mouth wider, luring the roach to scrabble with its feelers, jutting its teeth toward the tempting target of the man's fleshy tongue.

Snapping his teeth shut, Ryan felt the brittle crispness of the cockroach's neck yield between his jaws. Somewhere down in what used to be Alabama, Ryan had once rested in a field containing fresh, morning-cold celery. Now that same sensation came back to him.

He spit out the severed head, feeling the body fall away, its legs twitching in a residual and belated state of panic.

An acidic fluid burned Ryan's palate, and he spit several times to try to clear the bitter taste. He longed for a goblet of crystal water to rinse away the flavor.

Krysty shook her head at what he'd done, whistling softly between her teeth in admiration. Doc was the only other one in the group to have witnessed the mutie insect's death throes. His lined face grew pale, and his eyes narrowed in revolted horror.

"By the three Kennedys! I think that I have never been so close to giving the notorious rainbow yawn."

The attacks eased, and they all managed to reach the top of the steepening slope free of the scuttling creatures. One clung tenaciously to the back of J.B.'s jacket, but Jak knocked it away and stamped on it, bursting the shiny body, leaving a smear of stinking slime.

The evidence of earth-shifting was less obvious in this section of the redoubt. There were more lights, and the walls and ceiling were solid and unmarked. They opened and closed the next steel-shuttered door and passed through into a place where several passages came together. Krysty operated the control level, dropping the door shut behind them.

"Looks like none of our insect friends have found their way into this section."

"I'm hungry," Lori said, dropping again into her little-girl-lost voice.

"Me too," Doc added. "And Ryan there looks like he's about ready to devour another tender young roach."

One of the genuine dangers in a building complex the size of most redoubts was of becoming lost. And possibly even starving to death. Many of the secret military bases had corridors that rambled, twined and interconnected for miles. Fortunately, in the redoubts that had been hastily evacuated, there were generally plenty of colored maps of the "You Are Here" variety.

Once they'd found the first of these locators it was easy to work out their orientation and to seek out which sections of the great fortress had been damaged by the nukings.

"Main food stores were down where the roaches had taken over," J.B. said, pointing at the section colored dark blue. "And the mat-trans gateway is down that long spur, marked off Restricted. There. Looks like it's the lower, western sections that slipped. By the main exits. Getting out of here could be kind of tough."

"What's that?" Krysty asked, pointing at a section tinted light blue. It was marked Cryo Restricted and lay at the northern edge of the complex, close to a set of emergency exits.

"Cryo?" Ryan repeated. "Can't remember ever coming across that in any other redoubt. You seen it before, J.B.?"

"Nope."

"Means freezing," Doc told them.

"Freezing cold?" Lori shuddered theatrically, hanging on to the old man's arm.

"Freezing what?" Jak asked, still struggling to free the tangles from his hair.

"Not *what*," Doc replied. "More like *who*. Around the time I was given the big time-push forward, there was a team trying to freeze folks just before or just after they died. The idea was that the future might have advanced medical methods that could cure whatever it was killing them. Advanced! Hah!"

"Who'd they freeze, Doc?" Ryan asked.

"The good, the bad and the . . . can't remember the last bit. The rich and the famous and the important. Mostly the rich and important. Politicians were tops, because... Which reminds me. Ugly. That was it. The freezing units and the good, the bad and the downright ugly."

"Like to go see that cryo place," J.B. said thoughtfully.

Ryan agreed with the Armorer. "Sure. But first we go eat, and I could do with catching up on my sleep for a few hours."

"Days," Jak added.

"Let's head for the living quarters, then," Krysty suggested.

"Carried unanimously," Doc said, grinning with a wolfish good humor. "And we'll go on the morrow and see if any icemen cometh. Not that they will. Not after all these years."

Chapter Four

WHEN THEY REACHED one of the four sections of living quarters, they found more evidence of the haste of the final evacuation of the huge redoubt.

The long tables in the refectories had been cleared of all the residue of whatever had been the last-ever meal. But there were several dropped knives and spoons on the floor, broken glass and plates telling their own tale of necessary haste.

The dormitories were even more revealing.

Beds were unmade, sheets and blankets piled in untidy heaps. Made of rot-proof poly plastics, they had already lasted a hundred years and would probably last another thousand. Each dormitory held around two hundred beds, with partitions that ran from the floor to within eight inches of the ceiling. Each living space had a locker and small folding table.

Ryan had no doubt these long, hangarlike rooms would normally have been kept immaculate, inspected at least twice a day by pernickety noncoms eager to seek out and punish any deviation from a perfect norm. But the events of those dark winter days in 2001 must have meant anything normal going by the board.

"Lotsa mags," Jak said, flicking through a crumbling heap of brightly colored comics and periodicals. Most of them had names such as *Small Arms Digest*, *Close Killing* and *New War*. It was no surprise to Ryan that J.B. immediately perched himself on the edge of one of the beds and began to flick through the weapon magazines.

In Deathlands it was unusual to find very much printed matter. It had been Ryan's observation that as many as ninety percent of the entire population—not counting muties—were functionally illiterate. Many villes had their own little news sheets, run off on antique presses, while one or two of the wealthiest barons might have working hot-metal presses. It was rare to find anything illustrated that had been printed since the long winters.

"Look, lover," Krysty said, laughing. She held out a frail tabloid, rejoicing in the name of *The Weekly Probe*. Its front pages carried several headlines of varying size: King Charles Starlet Bribe Divorce Scandal, said one. Sadly, someone had cut out the photo from the back page, which had run beneath a screaming headline: My Breasts Are Like Dried Cantaloupes, But My Hubby Adores Them.

"Ugh," Krysty said. "Just touching stuff like that makes me feel kind of dirty." She paused. "Hey, Ryan?"

"What?"

"How long since you had a bath?"

"Round 'bout nine years is my guess, Krysty," J.B. joked, glancing up from an exploded, double-page color drawing of a .32-caliber Korth revolver.

Ryan gave him the finger. "Butt your nose out of this one. I guess the last time I had a bath wasn't all that long ago."

"Give me a date, lover. Back in New England? Doesn't count. Just a dunking in salt ocean. I mean a *real* honest-to-Gaia bath with hot water, soap and all the trimmings."

"Not since..." He shook his head. "Truth is, I don't remember."

"Me, neither," Krysty replied. "How 'about following that green line on the map? One that points to Bath and Shower Facilities. I could really get into some good warm suds."

"Fucking triple ace on line!" Jak exclaimed, smacking his left fist into his right palm in a gesture of enthusiastic agreement.

J.B. nodded, glancing across at Lori and Doc. "You two?"

Lori sighed, hugging the old man's arm. "Little girl'd do nothing for a hot wash, Doc."

"Anything," he corrected.

"How's that?"

"You said you'd do nothing for a... But, let it pass, sweetness. I confess that the prospect of laving my weary soul is too tantalizing to imagine. Will there truly be hot water and all?"

Ryan looked again at the map. He rubbed a hand over the stubble on his chin, feeling the dirt and grease under his fingers, wrinkling his nostrils at awareness of the stench of his own body.

"I don't know, Doc. But there's sure as gren-chill one way to go find out."

Doc whooped, slapping his thigh so that a great cloud of acrid dust billowed from his breeches. "Then let's go and follow the yellow brick road," he shouted.

"Green, Doc. It's a green line on the map," J.B. said.

IT WAS MAGIC.

The shower rooms were only about a hundred yards away from the dormitory, and a recreation room with television, books, ceedees and pool tables opened on the right. Then locker rooms, divided into male and female sections.

"Think I'll come in with the guys," Krysty said, "if nobody objects."

"And me," Lori said eagerly.

Nobody objected.

Ryan sat on one of the immaculately clean and polished benches in the shower room, peeling off his clothes. There were sec locks on the inside of the entrance doors which would hold any attackers long enough for the six companions to get to their blasters.

The bathing complex was divided into smaller sections, each with hot tubs, whirlpools and showers. By common consent, the two couples each went into one section, J.B. and Jak sharing a third.

Krysty had turned on the polished chrome taps to the big tub, testing the water with her hand. It took some time to run warm.

"Sure there'll be some hot left after a hundred years?" Krysty called.

"Nuke power plant's working still. Water in a sealed recycle unit. Should be all right, if you wait long enough."

"Yeah!" she shouted. "Steaming. Have to turn the thermo down or we'll come out pink and skinned. You got your clothes off yet?"

"On the way. There's a fifteen-minute laundro on the wall. Clean and tumble dry. Figure I'll risk my clothes through it while we wash."

He unlaced the combat boots, throwing his socks into the cleaning machine. The skin of his feet was pale and unhealthy, and he realized that it had been a very long time since he'd even had his boots off. One of the problems of moving through the Deathlands was that it was rarely safe to strip off completely, even for a night's sleep. The heavy-duty dark gray pants, slit so that he could pull them over the calf-high boots, came off next, followed by his shorts. The brown shirt was last, chucked into the round, glassed port of the cleaner. His long coat with the white fur trim rested neatly on the bench beside the white silk scarf that had the small metal weights in its ends. The wrist chron was waterproof, so he kept it on. Before moving toward the sounds of splashing and the billowing tendrils of steam, he made sure that all his assorted weapons lay ready to hand.

Stripped naked, Ryan realized that his own personal freshness wasn't all that it might have been.

He caught sight of himself in a full-length mirror by the side of the open doorway through to the showers, paused and looked himself up and down. But not from vanity. He simply looked himself over, knowing that yet another of the Trader's favorite quotes had been something to the effect that the most basic weaponry tool was your own body.

Ryan's thirty odd years of living had been as tough as they could have been, with very little gentle quiet in them. Though he stared critically, he felt he was in good shape: a rangy, muscular body, flat across the stomach, with deep chest and narrow hips; a mat of dark hair curling across his chest, spilling down to tangle around his groin and lower stomach. There were seams and scars all over his trunk, arms and legs, and each of them told its own painful story of bad times from his past.

"Checking the reflec, lover?" Krysty teased, appearing in the mirror at his side. "Making sure everything's in real good working order?"

"Yeah. It's not ... Hey, stop that!"

Krysty giggled and didn't stop. She pressed herself closer against Ryan's body, right hand reaching around his hip.

"I said to stop doing ..."

"Yeah," she said, stepping away from him, head to one side, admiring her handiwork. "Everything's in real good working order."

"What'd you stop for?" he complained.

"You told me to. Know how I always obey my lord and master? Just like my mama always instructed me."

"I'm going in to wash up. If you're not undressed and in the tub with me in about...lemme see. In about forty-five seconds ..."

"You'll what?"

"I'll come and get you, ready or not, and heave you in."

"That a threat or promise?"

"You got forty seconds to find out. Forty seconds and counting."

Krysty made it with six seconds to spare, leaving her khaki overalls in a heap and her dark blue cowboy boots with the silver spread-winged falcons lying crookedly at the side. The cleaner had swallowed her neat bra and light blue bikini pants.

There were automatic dispensers set in the wall, with trim, polished nozzles. Krysty pressed her hand under one and a thin mescal worm of scented soap settled in her palm.

"Come on in, lover. Water's real good. Fireblast! It's been such a damned long time."

Ryan called to her from the sunken bath. He was stretched out full-length, resting his head on the edge of the tub, his thick hair matted and wet. He grinned up at her.

From beyond the next partition they both heard Lori squeal. "It's cold!! Why aren't you turned it up hot, Doc?"

They couldn't catch the old man's reply, as it was drowned out in a hissing torrent of steamy water and a burst of giggling from Lori.

"Sounds like Doc might have gotten himself turned up hot," Krysty said, padding to the edge of the bath, looking down at Ryan's lean and muscular body beneath her in the spray-topped water.

She was partly on his blind side, and he tipped his head to glance up at her, thinking what an amazing physique she had: broad shoulders tapered to a slim waist and tight, firm buttocks; she had the thighs of an athlete, with slim ankles; her breasts were tipped with fire, her nipples hard as cherry stones.

The steam was affecting Krysty's sentient hair, which was uncoiling after the defensive tightness against the cockroaches, tumbling in vivid waves of luxuriant crimson. Ryan noticed that the curling hair at the junction of her magnificent thighs was opening like a soft vermilion fan.

"See what you like?"

He grinned. "And I like what I see. Come on, Krysty." He held his arms up to accept her into the embracing warmth of the steaming tub.

One in the bank of hair dryers wasn't working. And when they tried to shower after their lovemaking in the tub, Ryan and Krysty discovered that half of them were only running cold.

AFTER HIS BATH Ryan took the opportunity to shave off the stubble that seemed almost a permanent part of his life, revealing the livid scar that seamed across his right cheek from the corner of his good eye past the angle of his mouth.

Krysty brushed out her hair, making it crackle with vitality. By the time they'd finished, their clothes were ready, clean and dry, slightly warmed. Ryan laced up his boots, stretched and yawned. "That was *so* good, lover," he said quietly. "All I want now is a decent meal and then twelve hours of bed."

She didn't reply. Dressed only in her bikini briefs, she walked to stand by him, kissing him on the cheek, as soft as the caress of a hummingbird's wing.

J. B. DIX, TRIM AND SPRUCE, had found what had once been the living quarters for some of the administrative officers in the redoubt: separate cubicles, each with double-size beds, and dining areas with tables that seated six. The kitchen units held a better than average range of tinned food. To everyone's relief the stove worked and there was no need to open any of the ubiquitous and disliked self-heats.

"By the three Kennedys!" Doc exclaimed. "But we are surely the most elegant sextet in all of Deathlands. Not to mention the most fragrant."

Jak had appointed himself in charge of the cooking facilities and he was bustling around, helped by Lori. The boy's hair, under the rare influence of shampoo and clean hot water, danced around his narrow face like the fine spray of the ocean thrown on jagged rocks. Ryan found cutlery and plates while J.B. scavenged around some of the lockers in the individual rooms.

"What're you heating up for us, Jak?" Krysty asked, leaning back in one chair, resting the heels of her boots on another.

The boy peered at the faded labels as he slid them into the electric opener. "Tomato soup, oxtail soup and vegetable soup for the start. Potatoes, chicken nuggets and corn. Cherry and apple pie to finish up."

"Sounds real good," Ryan said, licking his lips in anticipation. "Hope it's not gone sour over the years."

"Tins would have blown," Krysty observed. "Should be fine. Oh, but that smells wonderful, guys! I can't wait."

"And look what I found to go with it," said the Armorer, brandishing a ribbed bottle half-full of a dark amber liquid.

"What's that?" Lori asked.

Doc, who'd been fiddling with some sort of electrical control unit in the corner of the dining area, glanced around. "That's Southern Comfort, child. The peach nectar of the gods. Set 'em up, John Barrymore Dix. Best damned barman from Portland, Maine to... to somewhere else. Make it one for my baby and one for the road."

Chapter Five

IT WAS a truly magical evening.

Krysty found some old wax candles in a tiny cupboard marked Emergency Illumination, and they dimmed the overhead neon strips and sat in the soft pools of spilled golden light. The Southern Comfort was as marvellous as Doc had said, brimming over with the taste of peach summers long, long dead and buried in wastelands of glowing ash.

The heated food was some of the best any of them had ever tasted. The soup was a little thick on additives and preservatives, though Lori had succeeded in scooping most of it from the top.

Doc had managed to get the range of concealed speakers around the angles of the room to function, digging out a set of ceedees to accompany the meal. Most of it what he called classical music. Ryan would personally have liked some songs with words, but he had to admit the gentle rhythm went well with the unhurried, peaceful meal.

"This is Vivaldi," Doc informed them, beating time to the music with his fork. "Four Seasons. Lovely, isn't it? There's a Mozart flute concerto next, and then some Gregorian chant. Monastic music." He looked around the table, seeing only a universal blankness. "Well, perhaps you'll like it anyway."

Toward the very end of the meal, as Jak was heating a can of coffee, the sound began to crackle and cut out in one of the speakers.

J.B. caught Ryan's eye. "Got a feeling our arrival here's starting to set some malfunction chains toppling over."

"Could be. Often happens. You find a place untouched since the big fires. I've done it. So've you. Mebbe pick something up and it works. Hasn't been touched in a hundred years. And it works. Ten seconds later it falls apart right between your fingers."

The candles were guttering. Lori had also gone scavenging and come across a box that had once held some chocolate-covered peppermint candy. But it had gone as hard as stone and nobody could eat any. The teenager had been upset by that, leaving the supper table before the others and wandering off to the room she was sharing with Doc.

"My lovely flower sure gets touchy these days," the old man said sadly, more to himself than those remaining. "Must be the generation gap. I daresay there must be something like eight generations between us. I hadn't thought about it like that before."

"Figure I'll go sleep." Jak stood up and stretched like a cat, muscles cracking. "That was one of the best times." He nodded to his four friends and went off to bed, a little way along the passage from the dining area.

Krysty topped up her mug from the pan of coffee that still bubbled on the stove, listening to the melancholy music in the background.

"It's sad, Doc. What is it? Violin or something deeper?"

"Cello, my dear lady. A piece by an Englishman called Edward Elgar. I met him once, as I recall. Slip of a man, yet he burned like a flame. That must have been ... Oh, I disremember."

"You're like a living time machine, Doc," Krysty observed, sitting next to Ryan, letting her hand drop with an easy affection onto his wrist.

"There are times ... have been times, when I have wished only that this time machine could grind to a halt, my dear."

"You got friends, Doc," Ryan said softly.

"I have a wife and I have two children. No!!" The word was almost shouted. "No, Ryan," he continued more calmly. "I no longer have a wife. Emily Louise is dead and buried in the family vault in Deadwood. Mount Moriah, I think it was...up a steep hill, among trees, with a view across the hills. I went there once, with Emily, when we were young and so in love. There was a grave there, a young child's. The stone said 'We really miss our little boy.' Oh, sweet God, how I miss my own little ones! Rachel and Jolyon. Both resting with their Mama. One day, I would wish to be joined with them again, Ryan." Tears began to course down Doc's face, between the newly shaved furrows, dripping off the end of his chin onto the table. "You hear me, Ryan. If it is humanly possible, then I would wish to be buried with my wife and children in Deadwood.

If it still exists. They showed me a photo of the grave once. So I know they are there. Do that for me, Ryan?"

"If I can, Doc. But you gotta know that it's not likely."

"No?"

"Not likely," Ryan repeated. "Chances of us being around that part when you finally buy the farm... Chances are, we'll all have gotten chilled before you. You old buzzard, Doc. You got more years left than the rest of us together."

Suddenly conscious that he'd been weeping, the old man dabbed at his eyes. "Good of you to say so, my friend. But ask not for whom the teller bowls? He bowls for me. I believe that my memory has played some scurvy trick with me. That sounds to be a little awry. No matter. I should go and join my sweet bird with her youth. Good night, sweet friends. May choirs of angels sing you to your rests."

Doc made an unsteady bow and tottered off toward the room he was sharing with Lori, the other three watching him go.

It was Krysty who broke the long, thoughtful silence.

"Bastards who trawled him from his family set up a damned big debt. I just hope they died slow, cold and alone."

J.B. stood up. "Odds are they died hot and fast, Krysty."

"And alone?"

He nodded. "We all do."

With a nod of the head he left Ryan and Krysty, closing the door quietly behind him. The music had ended, and there was only the faint, muted hiss from the speakers.

"You and me, lover," she said.

"Best there is," he replied, leaning back and sighing.

"Handful of jack for your thoughts?"

"Been a great evening. One of the best. That peach drink. Good food. Doc's classic music. Just the six of us. Times we've seen. Places we've been."

"Getting old, lover. A sure sign when you start getting... What's the word I want? Nostalgic. That's it. You can't look back at yesterday, Ryan. Tomorrow's the one really counts."

"Guess you're right. How d'you feel about going to bed?"

KRYSTY FOUND some packets of deconstituted egg and cooked them in powdered milk, adding some shreds of freeze-dried bacon for something that approached an old-fashioned breakfast. They could wash it down with reheated coffee.

"Stove's blinking on and off," she said. "Looks like some of the auxiliary power sources are giving up. Mebbe even the main power. Be bad news for the gateway if it's that."

Ryan brushed his fingers through his hair. "Yeah. Could be real bad. After we've eaten we'll get everyone together and talk about it. Most times we've ended up in a redoubt we take a look outside. Could be for once we should think about making another jump out of this place.''

Krysty sighed. ''Another jump? Need it like a rad shot in the head. Come to think of it, lover, that's just what another jump would feel like.''

Jak and J.B. appeared ten minutes later, followed by Doc. He apologized for Lori's lateness, explaining with blushing cheeks that it was her time of the month and she had stomach cramps.

The discussion didn't take very long. Everyone was interested in going to find the freezing section of the redoubt. There was a general agreement that it was only fairly minor bits of electrical equipment that were failing, most of them coming off unimportant sections of the main power grid for the huge fortress complex.

While the others were eating, finally joined by a pale-faced Lori, Ryan decided that he'd go and freshen himself with another shower.

The immaculate white tiles and the mirrored chrome taps and controls heightened his anticipation of the steaming water.

Fortunately Ryan turned on the taps before he stripped and stood under the needle-jets.

There was a distant, sinister gurgling, amplified by the metal pipes. Ryan quickly stepped back, hand dropping to the blaster on his hip. The noise became louder, an obscene bubbling sound, surging toward the shower room.

''Fireblast!'' Ryan moved away, hissing between his teeth at the appalling stench.

It was a black liquid, streaked with vivid green, like rotting molasses. Oozing from the gleaming metal nozzles, it crept down the walls, staining them with its glossy filth. It flowed over the main control taps before Ryan could get anywhere near them, making it impossible for him to stop the outpouring.

He heard the door open, and Jak called out to him. "You here, Ryan? We...what fuck's stink? You okay, Ryan?"

"Stay where you are, Jak. Yeah. Looks like it's end of the line time for hot showers. Power unit just pulled the plug on us."

Despite the new evidence of the redoubt beginning to run down, everyone agreed that they should at least take a look at the cryo section.

Following the light blue pattern on the fortress map, they headed north, through areas of the huge redoubt that had been more carefully evacuated and cleansed. Only once did they find any region that proved interesting.

"Map said there was a small arms and plas-ex module out this way," J.B. said. "Be good to find it and see if mebbe there's anything left that we could use."

"Always use a few spare rounds for the G-12," Ryan agreed.

A torn poster on a side wall proclaimed that Volvos Are Best—Forget the Rest.

"This way." Jak pointed to a side passage. A neat yellow sign warned all B8 or lower cleared personnel not to proceed farther without signed sec permit. The armored door was half-open. Spray-painted on it were the two words Raiders Rule.

"Gridiron team," Doc explained as they stooped beneath it.

Lights shone brightly ahead of them. Most illumination units in redoubts operated on proximity-trembler systems. Sensors picked up the vibrations of anyone moving along the corridors and would switch on the lights for a couple of sections ahead. So, no matter how quick you were, you could never catch a functioning length of corridor in the dark. To try was as futile as a man spinning around in front of a mirror, hoping to snatch a glimpse of the back of his own head.

The corridor opened without warning into a massive room, at least as large as an aircraft hangar, divided by partitions and pallets like some vast warehouse.

"Black dust!" J.B. exclaimed. The use of this rare saying told his companions how truly amazed J.B. was.

Most of the shelves were full of cartons, tins and boxes of all manner of ammunition and explosives. Spilling out over the floor, the munitions gave every evidence of something near to panic, of people scrabbling to survive despite the odds.

"Let's go, guys," the Armorer said, his sallow face alight with eagerness, eyes sparkling behind the lenses of his glasses. None of the others, except for Ryan, had ever seen him so animated. Ryan had once seen J.B. more excited, but it had been in another time and at another place.

"Could be boobies?" Jak suggested, stopping J.B. cold in his tracks.

"Could be, kid. Sorry. Didn't mean to call you that. Could be, Jak. Good point. But we've never seen nothing in any other redoubt. No, I figure we're safe. Just take a little care, is all."

Mostly they ran into booby traps out in mutie country. Then a lot of care had to be taken about what was picked up or moved. Four of the young blaster team from War Wag Three had gone to buy the farm together, around five years ago, Ryan figured. They'd stumbled into an encampment of stickies, out toward the Darks. One of them had seen a tiny crippled baby, bawling its eyes out and had stooped to pick it up and comfort it. He'd snagged a thin fish line linked to a simple detonator and a pound of plas-ex. It'd taken over an hour to collect the shredded flesh and bone of the four adults and the infant out of the surrounding trees and bushes.

Krysty had plenty of ammo for her own 9 mm Heckler & Koch P7A-13. She wandered around the huge storeroom, hands in her pockets, feeling the cold smoothness of the jet-black stone Apache tear. She watched as Ryan, Jak and J.B. darted around like children in a candy store. Not that Krysty had ever seen a candy store, except in old vids and mags.

Ryan was delighted to find an unopened wooden box of rounds for his caseless rifle. Ammo was becoming increasingly scarce throughout the Deathlands, particularly for rare guns like the G-12. It was a fifty-shot automatic, able to fire on single shot, triple or continuous burst. The rounds had no metal jacket, being molded into the case of the actual propellant. They were 4.7 mm by 21 mm. He eagerly loaded one of the pockets of his coat with the unusual rounds. The SIG-Sauer pistol fired standard 9 mill ammo, which was still being made, in unreliable bastardized forms, in any ville with a decent machining plant.

Krysty strolled up and down the aisles, carefully avoiding stumbling over the hundreds upon hundreds of loose rounds scattered everywhere. There were neatly typed cards thumbtacked to the shelves, telling her what was in the cartons. And what had once been there.

Lists of death-dealing names, some of which she recognized and some she didn't, the endless fugue of the long-gone megacull.

Lori took a handful of .22 rounds for her pearl-handled PPK, and Jak stuffed another couple of dozen .357 slugs for his Magnum cannon into his pockets.

Not surprisingly, there was nothing there that Doc could use in his nineteenth-century Le Mat handgun, with its central .63 caliber scattergun barrel and the nine-chamber revolver barrel, firing straight .36s. So the blaster remained in the hand-tooled Mexican holster rig.

Overlooked on a back shelf, behind some tumbled boxes of Mark Seven ball, J.B. discovered a dark green metal container, stamped in an endless string of white letters and numerals. He hauled it down, letting it crash to the floor, then levered the spring clips open along one side.

"Hey! Come look! Anyone want a real good new blaster? With lotsa rounds?"

Everyone gathered by the crouched figure of the Armorer, peering over his shoulder. He was pulling sheets of brown waxed and oiled paper off a dull black gun.

"Heckler & Koch full- and semi-auto," Ryan said. "Don't know the model. Never saw one like that. Integral silencer."

"And laser-optic sight," J.B. said with a note of reverential awe in his voice. "It's one of the MP-7 SD-8s. Only made a few, according to what I've seen. Supposed to be a good gun for anything up to thirty yards."

"Going to change that old Uzi of yours, J.B.?" Ryan asked, not really expecting Dix to agree with the suggestion.

"Why not?"

"Hey, I was only..."

J.B. picked up the blaster and cradled it, feeling for the button to activate the laser sight, aiming it across the room. Everyone watched the tiny ruby dot of light. "Yeah. Like the feel."

"You fire it from the shoulder?" Krysty was puzzled by the strange double sight on top of the short muzzle.

"No. Not at all. Close quarters you press the trigger and spray. Aimed shots you can use the laser spot. Then hold it braced against the hip and let go. No need to aim from the shoulder. Not with a baby like this."

Without a sign of regret the Armorer laid down the battered mini-Uzi that he'd carried for so long over so many miles, walked away and began to rummage through the box that contained equaloy 9 mm ammo, emptying his pockets of the old bullets.

Jak picked up one of the guns and hefted it, shrugging and putting it back again. "No. Slow down close fights. No."

"Saw some grens racked up over that side," Ryan said.

"Yeah. And some plas-ex. Be right there with you, when I got enough ammunition."

Jak and Krysty followed Ryan across to the far side of the weapons wing of the redoubt, with Doc and Lori trailing behind them.

"Here. Look colors!" the albino teenager exclaimed, standing, jaw gaping, at the serried rows of different kinds of hand grenades.

They were much smaller than the type used in the conventional wars of the twentieth century, only half the size of a baseball, but relatively heavy. Some had two-step button firing pins and some had flip-top detonator releases. All were silver or black, with bright strips of different paints. Labels told what each one was.

"Scarlet and blue is imploder. Met one of those before," Jak said, remembering a close call on the Mohawk River. "How they work?"

"Like an explosion, only it works on a kind of antimatter principle. Sucks things in as it goes off," Ryan explained.

Krysty ran a long finger down the row of printed labels. "Stunners. Burners. Frags. Lights. High-alts.

Shrap. Nerve. Smokers. Grounders. Low-ex. Delays, various. Remotes.''

"Take an implode, stun, burn and frag each. Others are too specialized for us. Basically we'll just want to stop or chill. Nothing else."

They all stashed away four grens. Ryan pocketed a couple of extra implodes for good measure. Lori complained that they were too heavy for her.

"What's the pointing for?" she asked. "Got blasters and they do any job."

Doc shook his head. "I fear that when in Rome... I mean, when in Deathlands, one must look first for survival. Anything above and beyond that is somewhat of a bonus, my dear child."

Lori pouted and swung away, the bells on her spurs tinkling with their usual thin, bright sound. As she stalked off she tripped over some loose ammo, cursed and nearly fell.

She'll break her rad-blasted ankle with those heels one of these days," J.B. stated.

Ryan nodded. "Could be." He looked around. "We all got what we want? Enough to chill a mutie army, I guess."

"After the chill, we can go and look at the freezing," Doc said, smiling broadly. "Get it? That was a joke, was it not?"

"Very nearly, Doc." Krysty sighed. "Very nearly."

Chapter Six

"This is it."

The six had walked briskly through the sweeping corridors of the redoubt. One of the surprises had been that they still hadn't the least idea where in all of Deathlands they were.

The light blue locator strips had brought them to the northern limits of the fortress, which was one of the largest that Ryan had ever encountered. They saw no further signs of life and no more evidence of any seismic damage to the structure.

The nearer they came to the auxiliary exits at the northern flank, the less they saw of any hasty withdrawal. There were few rooms opening off, and all of them had been stripped bare and left utterly deserted.

"Anything else you can tell us about these cryo places, Doc?" Ryan asked, walking alongside the old scientist.

"When I was first trawled, none of us would have dreamed it would become possible to put a human being into a sort of suspended state of animation and then hope to revitalize them. It would have been like the books of Jules Verne."

Ryan had actually heard the name before. "But what about when you were around Project Cerberus in the late nineties?"

"No." A vigorous shake of the head. "You must be aware, my friend, that science had become ever more specialized. I saw and heard...perhaps more than they wished."

"How'd they do it?" J.B. asked, joining them at the front of the party.

"The freezing?"

"Yeah. Ice or what?"

Doc sniffed. "Not ice. Some gas, I believe. Let us see how well my memory can recall..." For a hundred paces or more he didn't speak, forehead furrowed with the effort of trying to remember. "Yes," he said finally. "It depends on the temperature at which the gas liquifies. Carbon dioxide was discarded because it doesn't liquify, just freezes solid at minus seventy-eight Celsius. No good. Nitrous oxide, a scant ten degrees more chill, not cold enough. Then I think liquid nitrogen."

"Colder?" Ryan asked.

"Much. My memory toys with a figure of minus one hundred and ninety-six degrees."

The Armorer whistled. "Dark night, Doc! That's some kind of cold."

"Indeed it is. I have seen experiments. A flower becomes as solid, and as fragile, as spun crystal. Place an apple into liquid nitrogen for a few moments and then take it out and strike it with a hammer. It will shatter into a thousand splinters. But I cannot imagine what human flesh becomes."

They walked on in silence for several minutes, each of them locked into imagining that situation. If an apple became like stone, then how would flesh react to being frozen?

Krysty tugged at Ryan's sleeve, breaking into his thoughts. "Figure we'll find us some freezies, lover?"

"Not likely. Not impossible. If they evacuated the redoubt in a hurry, they might not have been able to take any with 'em. But from what Doc says about it, there might not have been any in the first place. It was all kind of experimental."

"Soon know," she said, pointing to the sign on the wall ahead: Cryo. Medical Clearance 10 or B Equivalent Only Permitted.

"TVs watching us." Jak pointed up at the diminutive cameras that ranged ceaselessly backward and forward.

"Nobody watching them," Ryan said, pushing at the control lever for the single sec door that blocked off the passageway.

"Hear something," Krysty warned, stopping and putting her head to one side, listening intently.

"What?"

"Quiet, lover."

Ryan strained his hearing, thinking he might have caught the faint sound—or imagined that he'd heard—or... "Can't hear anything unusual, Krysty."

"Hissing. Like steam. Far off." Her body relaxed, the tension easing. "Yeah. Thought at first it could have been an armored door opening. That kind of a sound. But it's not. Too steady. Constant pitch to it."

A little farther, around a wide bend, they came across a different kind of a door.

"Airlock," Doc observed. "Guess that makes sense if it's some sort of medical base."

The notice beside the armaglass-topped door ran to about fifty lines, covering all manner of rules and regulations about who could go through and when and with whose permission, as well as details about what kind of protective clothing had to be worn.

"You sure this isn't full of some kind of germy gas or nervers, Doc?" J.B. asked, looking strangely reluctant to proceed any farther.

"No. I imagine it will be quite the reverse, my dear Mr. Dix. Free of all manner of germs or infection. The clothing will be to stop us bringing sickness in, not to prevent us catching it from anyone or anything in there."

Ryan laid his hand on the door and began to push it open. The voice was deafening, making everyone jump.

"Cryogenics command. Unauthorized personnel withdraw immediately! Security will take finality action!"

J.B. unslung his new blaster and leveled it at a bank of linked speakers set in the center of the arched ceiling.

"Unauthorized personnel withdraw immed—"

The integral silencer reduced the noise of the gun's explosion to a polite cough, like a nervous curate clearing his throat in front of his maiden aunt.

"That's telling big-mouth ratboy," Jak sniggered.

"Move it out," Ryan ordered.

SOME YEARS EARLIER, in wind-washed Wisconsin, Ryan had led a hunting party through the ruins of a deserted ville, and they'd come across the tumbled stones of what had once been a large hospital. One wing had been freakishly protected from the worst of the nuke blasting. He still remembered the cold wind blowing along the corridors and the look and feel of the place.

Now, on the fringes of the deep redoubt, there was a similar feeling.

Ryan almost felt that he could even catch the long-gone scent of disinfectant lingering in the dull, repro-cessed air.

"Looks like they cleared up rather carefully here," Doc observed. "Look in here. Everything copybook neat and trim. Like they were hoping one day to come back and pick up where they left off."

It was true. Word processors stood at the ready, under plastic covers; phones waited for the next call; filing cabinets were closed and orderly; an operating room waited for a new patient, rustless scalpels and probes lying in glittering ranks with other nameless tools of the surgeon.

"Gives me creepies." Lori shuddered. "Reminds me of the redoubt I came from. Cold and ... and watch-ing us."

Ryan knew what the girl meant. It was oddly sinis-ter the way that everything in this section was so per-fect. It was almost as if they'd slipped through into a time warp. At any moment a sec man or a doctor or a nurse would walk along the antiseptic corridor and challenge them.

They reached another air-locked door.

Krysty was in the lead, but she faltered and stopped, putting her hand to her forehead.

"What is it?" Ryan asked, moving quickly to her side.

"Don't know, lover, but... Gaia! Something strange is...living and partly living. Dead and yet...not dead."

"Freezies," Doc said. "They must be what Krysty can 'see' in there."

"Could it...?"

She shook her head, the mass of crimson hair dancing across her shoulders like filaments spun from fire. "How the...? I don't know, lover. I just tell you that there's something up ahead of us that's not like anything I ever sensed before."

"Could go back," J.B. suggested, the tone of his voice making it obvious that he wanted to keep going on.

"No. Krysty says that what's through there isn't alive, so it can't hurt us."

"But said not dead, as well," Jak pointed out, lips peeling back off his sharp teeth in a feral grin of anticipation.

"So, let's move on," Ryan said.

There were two air locks close together, each with its own set of instructions about making sure no clothing was trapped in closing doors and not attempting to leave until pressure equalizer had fully returned to zero.

Beyond the second set was an ordinary pair of double swing-doors. Now the humming and hissing sounds that they'd heard from way back had become much louder, as though they were closing in on the heart of a sleeping giant.

Ryan took the lead, pushing the doors open and stepping cautiously through, into a huge control room, much like the one that ran the gateway.

"This is it."

The other five filed in after him, stopping to gaze around at the amazing complex of comp-panels with lights, buttons and switches. The humming was louder.

"Look." Krysty pointed across at the long side wall of clear glass. Behind it, angled on a raised platform, were about twenty silvered capsules, looking like sci-fi coffins.

"Freezies," Doc breathed. "So, the stories were true. They exist, and there they are. By the three Kennedys, they're freezies!"

Chapter Seven

THE CONTROL ROOM contained everything needed to being functioning again immediately. Everything except instructions. The consoles held clues to how they might have operated, but nothing more.

"This one's marked Coolants Input," J.B. called to the others, who were wandering around the room.

"How d'you open up the doors here?" Lori asked, rattling a black handle on the glass wall in front of the capsules.

"Leave it, dearest!" Doc instructed. "We must exercise some care. A rash and hasty move could lead to an unimagined disaster."

"There's twenty-five of these metal boxes, Doc, but it looks like only nine of them are operational. Five got a liquid display saying Not in Use. Eleven got a red malfunction sign glowing, like something went wrong over the years."

"What about those nine?"

"Just a steady green. Lots of dials and bleepers, but they're all static."

"How 'bout unfreezing 'em, Doc," Jak yelled. "See what hundred-year man looks like."

Ryan smiled at the boy's enthusiasm. "What'd happen if we tried to let 'em out, Doc?"

"Who on God's green earth knows, my old comrade in arms? With nothing to guide us, I fear that it would not be a likely success."

"Could try, though," Ryan insisted, fascinated by the thought that the gleaming capsules might contain men and women from a hundred years ago, people with all the scientific knowledge and wisdom that they'd had in those days. Who knew what information they might be able to convey?

"I think not. To tamper with such things, far beyond our wisdom, Ryan... This could be a fearful Pandora's box of evil or disease. How can we take on that weighty responsibility?"

"We got every right, Doc. There's nobody else here but us. I say let's try and defrost 'em."

"The old-timer sighed. "This is madness, my friend. Madness. But we don't even know how to begin to release them from their eternal durance."

"Ounce of plas-ex and they'll pop open like the belly of a drowned dog," J.B. said.

"Here," Krysty called. "Sealed panel says Emergency Mass Release Controls. This has got to be it."

They all gathered around.

The control was on what looked to be the master console. Certainly the chair in front of it was larger and more plush than any of the others. And smack in the center was the panel that Krysty had noticed. It was locked and had an intricate sec key attached to it by a steel chain.

"One key and three locks," observed Krysty.

"Not uncommon, my dear. Many high-security establishments will have a similar system. It prevents a single fit of schizoid psychotic madness. No one person can operate the master key. Or press the red button reading 'Do not pass Go and do not destroy the world.' We'll probably find a time delay on a single key that will shut down the whole override system.''

"So where's other keys, Doc?" Jak asked. "Round here?"

"In the ruins of what was once the Pentagon? Or Washington? Camp David? Nevada? Air Force One? I can tell you, my snow-headed colleague, that those missing keys will remain missing until Gabriel blows his horn. And probably after that as well.''

"Plas-ex time," J.B. announced, fumbling in the lining of his leather jacket.

Ryan was about to warn the Armorer to be careful, then decided to keep his mouth shut. J.B. would be as careful as he could be without needing to be told about it.

He teased out a tiny piece of the gray explosive, rolling it between his fingers. He worked the thin worm of plas-ex into a triangular shape, pressing it to the top of the sec-locked control. He took out a detonator, which was no larger than a thumbtack, and pushed one end into the gray strip.

"Ten seconds," he said. "Ready? Go." The Armorer tweaked the end of the detonator to activate its timing mechanism.

They all ducked behind the desks for protection, though the explosion was barely noticeable.

But it did the trick.

A three-sided section of the cover had been lifted off, exposing a single red switch beneath it. On the console, a number of lights flashed furiously.

Doc laughed. "One hundred years ago, a whole peck of telephones would have been ringing all over the shop. This must have been one of the most secret places on the planet."

"Not anymore. You figure this'll start to thaw out the freezies, Doc?"

"Kill or cure," the old man replied.

"Do it, Ryan," Lori said imperiously.

Moving carefully to avoid cutting his hand on the sharp edges of the torn cover, Ryan gripped the red switch and pulled it firmly toward himself, hearing the solid click of the contact being made, somewhere beneath the top of the desk.

"There she blows," J.B. shouted, taking off his fedora and waving it in the air in a most uncharacteristic display of enthusiasm. Lights flashed above each of the nine silver pods that the companions had assumed were occupied. What looked like steam was released in hissing, blinding clouds, concealing everything behind the great glass wall of the control chamber.

"Coolant release," Doc shouted. "Guess it must have been something like liquid nitrogen after all. It's being vented right now. My stars, but this is exciting!"

"Others opening too," Jak called, pointing to the rest of the capsules, whose lids were visibly beginning to lift.

"What are they going to be like?" Krysty asked nobody in particular.

Doc fielded the question. "Those that have already ceased the cryogenic process will obviously be exceedingly defunct. Dead. Gone before. Joined the choir celestial. Sleeping with their Maker. Resting the rest that has no awakening. Dived into the last great darkness. Savoring the enigma of the journey from which no man has yet returned. Plucking at the harp where—"

"Doc," Krysty interrupted irritably, "answer the bastard question, will you? What are they going to be like? The ones that unfreeze?"

"Ah, yes. Bear in mind that the probability is that they will have been frozen either at a point near death or at a point where a disease had them severely in its grip. Perhaps some illness that had not yet run its course, but for which medical science had, then, no hope of cure."

"Fucking sickies, Doc?" Jak said.

"In a word . . . yes."

"What if it's catching?"

Krysty's question stopped everyone in their tracks. Suppose these illnesses from before sky-dark were hideously contagious? None of them had thought about that.

"Can't be," Ryan denied with a positive degree of false confidence.

She persisted. "Why, lover?"

"Too much risk to anyone here or in the freezing part of the redoubt."

"Ever hear of LIDS?" Doc asked thoughtfully. "Perhaps not. Lethal Immune Deficiency Syndrome. The government suppressed the facts about it, trying to avoid a panic."

"What was...?" asked Jak.

"Your body's resistance to illness vanished overnight. Caught by walking through someone's sneeze. Easy as that. And you *really* could get it from toilet seats. If the nukes hadn't ended civilization, it could have chilled more people than the Black Death."

"What if one of them in those there are got it?" Lori asked, glancing toward the exit.

"As I said. There were many ways you could pick it up. Any sort of contact, no matter how casual, spread the virus, which was always a hundred percent terminal. But it was easily detected, as I recall. So, they'd not have let anyone in here with it. At least I remember from some of the scuttlebutt whispers at the time... Where was I? Oh, yes. When the sons of bitches fired me forward, they were talking about concentration camps and portable crematoria and even IE."

"What was that, Doc?" Krysty asked. The old man's horror tale from the past had caught everyone's attention. Nobody was even bothering to look at the fog-filled cubicles and the ponderously opening streamlined freezing chambers.

"Involuntary Euthanasia. It never got quite that bad, but there was martial law in the air, my friends, and a cold hand around your heart if you tested positive. Bad days."

He shook his head sadly, tapping at the floor with the metal ferrule of his cane. The dismal insight that he'd given into the past of their country held everyone in silence, a silence that was broken by a yelp from Lori.

"Look!"

The inactive or malfunctioned capsules were now completely open. The other nine were still hidden behind the veiling torrents of released coolant.

The blond teenager led the way to peer into the open containers, her spurs jingling merrily as she ran. The others joined her, staring into the padded interiors of the frozen coffins.

Some were quite empty.

Some were not.

"Bones, bones, dried lazy bones," Doc Tanner whispered, turning away with a sigh.

Hermetically sealed for a hundred years, the failures of the cryogenic experiments had become perfectly mummified. The skulls were encased in a tight mask of brown leather, the eyes long vanished into the shadowed sockets. The jaw gaped, held in place only by shreds of gristle, like old whipcord. The bodies had been wrapped in a shroud of thin plasticized cloth that had probably been white but had deteriorated to a patchy yellow. The skeletal hands and feet emerged from under the bindings, hooked and sere.

"Take a look at this double-poor bastard," Ryan suggested. "Seems like he sort of recovered some, when the machine folded up."

Doc was at his side, wiping at the smeared glass. "Lord, Lord," he said quietly. "It puts me in mind of a tale from Mr. Poe, concerning a premature burial of a wretch who... Oh, dear.''

It was a dreadful sight.

The person, male by the short strands of straggling hair that clung to the top of the wrinkled skull, had made a fight of it. The winding-cloth was torn and bunched near the feet. The knees were drawn up and the back arched, the arms lifted, hands pressed toward the sky, as he had attempted to lift the massive weight of the locked lid. The head was tilted, jaw yawning in what must have been the last muffled, choking scream for air, the dying calling out to a world that was already dead.

''I'd hate to get chilled in a metal box,'' Lori said. ''When I'm gone I want it with children all around and friends and a hill covering by heather with the sun and a big watery fall. That's how I'm going to be gone.''

''How long d'you figure the thawing's going to take, Doc?'' Krysty asked, frowning through the glass at the wreathing coils of gas and steam that still encircled the remaining nine cubicles.

''I fear that I have no idea, my dear girl. Time past and time present are both perhaps... What am I saying? No. I can speculate that the full freezing process must have taken many, many hours. Perhaps even days. But we have pressed the emergency button and everything will... I suppose, be much speeded.''

''But it'll still take some time?''

Doc shrugged his shoulders. ''You are as wise as I in this, my dear. We must all wait for however long it takes.''

THE ROOM CONTAINED nothing of interest to any of them, so the next few hours dragged slowly by.

Doc sat in a corner with his back against a wall, Lori's head in his lap. Jak pared his nails with one of his assortment of throwing knives. J.B. repeatedly stripped and reassembled his new blaster, eventually becoming so familiar with the weapon that he could do it with Ryan's scarf knotted tightly over his eyes.

Krysty and Ryan strolled together around the rows of control consoles, her hand resting lightly on his arm. She sang a childhood song that she said had been taught to her by her mother, in Harmony.

"It's an old ballad, from way, way back before sky-dark. About a baron who catches his young wife making love with another man. He bursts in on them—his wife and this Matty Groves—and he's got all his sec men with him. And he threatens him. Says they should have a fair fight."

"Doesn't sound very fair."

"It's not. But he says 'In England it shall not be said I slew a sleeping man.' But Matty Groves doesn't have a chance. He gets chilled, but the wife turns on her husband and says they're all through."

"Sing it, lover."

She did, her sweet voice flooding the room, rising over the mechanical hissing and throbbing of the thawing cryo capsules. The age-old song of passion, betrayal and death caught everyone's interest.

When it was over Doc led a round of applause. "Beautiful, my dear silver-throated Miss Wroth. I had heard the song before, sung by a maiden in the

Ozarks, when I was a callow youth. But not so finely as you have sung it. Bravo, my dear, bravo!"

"Anything happening, Jak?" J.B. asked later, watching the teenager as the youth catfooted along the row of containers.

"No. Can't see. Wait…" He pushed his face against the glass, trying the sec-locked handle. "Still shut tight. But looks like clearing."

"It's about time," Ryan said, levering himself up off the floor, where he'd been resting. He joined the young albino. "Yeah, I can see the lids up. Can't make anything inside 'em, yet. Too much of that mist."

"They going to be skeletons like the others, Doc?" Krysty asked.

"Frankly, ma'am, should any of them actually be returned to some sort of life, I think we might be more concerned about their brains than their bodies."

Doc continued to try to monitor the dials, seeking some kind of pattern that might tell him how the thawing was going.

"Looks to me like a basic draining of coolant, combined with some sort of bodily fluid replacement and reassessment. Blood coming in and the artificially frozen preservatives thawing and seeping out of the system. All sorts of artificial stimulants and nourishments pumping in, as well.

"Any signs of actual monitoring of the vital functions, Doc?" Ryan asked. "Those there?" He pointed at a number of display panels, each showing an unbroken line of pale green electrical light, accompanied by a thin, toneless bleeping.

"Could be. If they are, then we're not going to strike too much gold. I've seen more signs of life in a petrified dinosaur's dropping."

Another hour passed. The nine capsules were all open, but there was still too much mist in the cubicles to see what was happening. And the monitors remained stubbornly unchanged.

"Triple zero," J.B. muttered to Ryan. "Laid the ace on the line, best we could. Still got us a lot of nothing. Time we moved?"

"One more hour. Then we go. Krysty says she can still 'see' something. Like she's never seen before. They gotta come around, don't they?"

The Armorer pushed back the brim of his hat and shrugged his shoulders. "Mebbe, Ryan. Mebbe."

The big digital clock on the far wall of the control room clicked over another forty-two minutes, then things began to happen.

"The line's broke," Lori said, pointing at one of the monitors marked Vital Function 17. A blip had appeared, running slowly along, followed by another. And another. The tone changed to a more insistent cheeping, drawing attention to itself.

"Number seventeen. That one, in the corner." Doc pointed to the booth with that number stenciled above it.

Another monitor came to life, on one of the capsules nearest the main entrance. And a third one.

Moments later the first appalling screams began.

Chapter Eight

KRYSTY SPOTTED a new display that had clicked into life on one of the many desks. It was labeled Time to Manual Override Unit Sec Lock.

Most of the twenty-five numbers were blank, but nine glowed. Of the nine, six were showing a hesitant orange light. Three, including number seventeen, were showing a glittering emerald green, bright as the eye of the dragon.

But everyone's attention had been torn away by the sound of the screaming.

Faint at first, like the first stirring of a summer breeze in the top branches of a mighty pine forest, then louder and more insistent, drawing them to capsule 17.

"Alive." Jak's eyes were wide in amazement. "Moving and 'live."

The silver top had now folded all the way open, and the coolant mists had finally vanished, allowing the companions to see into the lined box.

"We can open it in about ninety seconds," Krysty told them, checking the repeater chron over the armored glass door.

"Dark night!" J.B. said. "It's a woman and she looks like she's already been chilled."

Flat on her back, with a number of thin plastic tubes connected to her arms, was a woman, aged in her sixties. The hair was silver gray, tied in a neat coil. The hands jerked and twitched at the binding shroud in uncontrollable movements. Her brown eyes were open, staring sightlessly upward, and her mouth gaped, revealing pink gums. The screams rose and fell in a steady, racking rhythm, seeming beyond any conscious control of the freezie.

What the Armorer had said was deadly accurate. The woman looked on the brink of the grave. Ryan recalled at that moment Doc's warning that many of the cryogenic experiments had been carried out either on the newly dead or on the imminently dying.

"Forty seconds," Krysty said, raising her voice above the muffled cries.

The freezie's arms were painfully thin, her narrow body showing every sign of extreme emaciation. Her hands were like a bunch of twigs, covered in opaque skin, and her cheeks were completely sunken in, stretched over sharp planes of bone. The eyes were almost hidden in the scraped caverns of the sockets.

"What can we do, Doc?" Lori asked, tugging on his sleeve.

"Precious little, I fear. If only we knew what ailed her we could—"

"Fifteen seconds and we can open up the door and get her out."

"Then what?" Lori was almost crying at the sight of the old woman's obvious suffering.

The screaming stretched on, flat, barely rising and falling. Just a succession of mindless notes. The eyes of the freezie showed no sign whatsoever of any kind of consciousness.

"There's 'nother one coming out!" Jak called from near the entrance. "Man. Doesn't look so close to chill."

"Lock's open," Krysty said, reaching and turning the handle. As the door swung, the volume of the screaming became much louder, like the edge of a diamond saw drawn across a sheet of plate glass.

Ryan sniffed, catching a unique smell that was both sharp and flat at the same time, with a bitter overlay to it. Chemical and unpleasant.

"The wretched woman had recently undergone some drastic surgery to her brain," Doc observed. "See? The sutures look almost fresh."

"What's that mean?" Ryan asked. "What's making her scream?"

"I would hazard that—pure speculation you understand—but I would guess it may have been a terminal brain tumor."

The woman was trying to tear at the material of the winding-sheet, and her head was tossing to and fro. Her breath was fast and ragged, making a pulse at the angle of jaw and neck flutter and dance.

Krysty had gone back to the console that recorded motor functions, gazing at the buttons and punching at one or two.

She shouted to the group gathered around the open door. "What'd you say was wrong?"

"I would guess a tumor, but—"

"Intrinsic carcinoma near parieto-occipital sulcus? If I spoke it right."

"It says that?" Ryan asked.

"Her name's Joan Thoroldson. It also says she's sixty-four. There's been exploratory surgery. Then it says IIT."

"Inoperable, imminent termination," Doc muttered. "She is near death, Ryan, and in the most dreadful agony."

"Can't we..." Lori began, stopping as Doc solemnly shook his head.

"Nothing. Unless we can..." He turned his questioning gaze to Ryan.

"What, Doc? What can we do?"

"We can ease her passing. The swifter the better for her."

"Fireblast! Are all freezies gonna be like this? What's the point of...?"

"If civilization had not plunged a knife into its own belly, then possibly there might have been advances in laser or even in cryo surgery that could have restored her and then immediately excised the cancer that rips at her brain."

Ryan whistled softly between his teeth, trying to control his own disappointment. To spend all this time and to hope that there might be something of value from before the long winters... and to find a crazed, dying old woman!

"What can we do, Doc?"

"Put a bullet through her brain. Stop her suffering, Ryan Cawdor."

The screaming continued, unrelenting in its panting harshness.

"If you don't chill her, Ryan, then I will," Krysty warned.

Inside the capsule, the woman was becoming more and more restless, her hands reaching up to pluck at the empty air, the tubes straining from her yellowed flesh.

"Yeah," Ryan agreed, blinking his one good eye. He drew the P-226 blaster from its holster, pausing for a moment. Then he leaned around the open door, reached in and touched the muzzle of the SIG-Sauer to the shaved side of the woman's skull. He squeezed the trigger once.

With a frisson of almost supernatural horror, Ryan saw the head kick sideways, a chunk of bone exploding on the padded pillow, releasing a flood of watery blood and pinkish brains. The eyes stayed open and the screams continued.

"How can...?" he began, feeling a thrill of something that was close to fear—until common sense reasserted itself. The noise of the screams was from behind him, not from the twitching corpse in the cryogenic cubicle.

"Triple fucking crazie!" Jak shouted. "Look what's doing himself!"

Krysty was still at the console, this time trying to punch up information on capsule number 3. "Henderson Otis. Age twenty-seven. Auto crash-up. Major brain damage."

Ryan, J.B., Doc and Lori joined the white-haired teenager in front of the chamber, standing paralyzed by the dreadful sight inside. Fortunately the sec lock hadn't yet sprung open and Henderson Otis couldn't get at them.

But that didn't stop him from trying.

He had clawed his way upright, tottering on shaky legs that were seamed with fresh scars, wrapped in moldering bandages. The wrap-sheet had been torn and kicked away, lying in a crumpled, bloodied heap on the floor.

All of the feeder and drainer tubes had been ripped from the man's flesh, each one leaving a crimson mouth that dribbled fresh blood. But it was the face—that face and the expression smeared upon it—that held the attention of the five silent watchers.

The accident that had led to Henderson Otis being frozen against the false hope of a better tomorrow had obviously done hideous damage to his skull. Now his face was pressed right against the glass of the door, disfigured with a slobbering leer of bestial hatred. Almost without realizing it, everyone had drawn their handguns, knowing that if the creature succeeded in liberating itself from the armaglass confines, it would surely attempt to rend them all limb from bloodied limb.

The teeth were mostly broken off in jagged stumps, and half of the protruding tongue had been sheared away in the crash. The left side of the skull had been stoved in above the ear, above where the ear had once been. The pale skin showed bruises, deep purple, yellowing at the edges. The left eye was closed, invisible behind a slab of puffy flesh.

As the man scratched at the door, fingernails bent and broken, he made a feline hissing sound through his gnawed lips.

"Another mercy killing?" Ryan said, hand on the butt of his pistol.

"I think there is no possible option for us," Doc agreed.

"Waste of time...recovering a freezie," J.B. commented, shaking his head at the gibbering apparition in front of them.

"Only about a minute before the armadoor opens," Krysty warned. "Best get ready."

But Henderson Otis took matters into his own hands, turning away from them, some rudimentary remnant of intelligence making him realize he couldn't get at the six watchers. Picking up one of the sharp-ended glass syringes that had been either nourishing him or drawing off the preserving liquids, he lifted it clumsily in his hands and glanced over his shoulder at the door, half smiling.

"Thanks, but no thanks," the freezie said, the words quite clear.

With an inflexible determination Otis lifted the syringe and drove it into his own right eye. Ryan winced, Lori shrieked in horror and Doc gasped. The others were silent.

A clear fluid spurted, with the faintest subtle tint of pink. Otis grunted, drawing the spike out and ramming it into the bloodied socket once more. The tendons in the wrists stood out with the effort of pushing it clean through the back of the eye into the brain.

The second attempt was successful. The arms flung wide as though some invisible force was crucifying him. His head snapped forward on the chest, and the corpse slithered to the floor of the chamber. Almost simultaneously there was a loud click of the sec lock opening.

"Rest in peace," Doc said, bowing his head over his locked fingers.

"Amen to that," Krysty whispered. "Come on, lover. Let's all get the fuck out of this bastard boneyard."

Ryan stood quiet, looking down at the wreckage of what had once been a healthy young man, trying to imagine the long darkness of a hundred years that Henderson Otis had endured, against the hope of being awakened, being resurrected and made hale and complete once more. Had there been consciousness at all? Had any part of the brain remained functioning? Or had it been the dim red glow of smoldering insanity?

"We'll never know," he said, answering his own question.

"We going?" Jak asked, shuffling nervously from foot to foot.

"I want to see sky and trees," Lori said her face as pale as milk.

"Sounds good to me," Krysty agreed. "Nothing to keep us here."

"What about the other pods?" J.B. asked. "There's another six or so opening."

"Leave 'em," Ryan said, more loudly than he'd intended. "I don't want to see any more things like that in there."

"Could be that we could do another kindness . . . if any of them are in need of help in passing," Doc suggested.

The stillness was interrupted by the clicking of another sec lock, which made everyone spin around to be greeted by the weak but steady voice.

"What's the year? And who . . . who am I?"

Chapter Nine

"RICHARD NEAL GINSBERG, born March 22, 1970. Occupation..." Krysty turned away from the VDT screen. "Just says that his job was listed and sec-coded with a high B classification. That's all we know."

The freezie was around five-ten in height and seemed to be around 160 pounds. His hair was very dark, cut short, with tight curls. Ryan noticed that his muscle tone was very poor, which could indicate some side effect of the cryogenic treatment, or it could show that Richard Ginsberg had worked in a sedentary job and rarely took much exercise.

He had been sitting up in his polished capsule, peering out through the glass door. Other than the two short questions, he'd said nothing. He simply lay down again as the six friends moved toward him. Then he fell into what seemed a natural and peaceful sleep.

Ryan and Jak had lifted him out, winding the crackling sheet of plastic off his naked body. They lowered him carefully onto the floor and covered him with some blankets that Krysty had discovered in a wall closet. In the cubicle, in a green locker, J.B. found what they guessed must have been the freezie's own clothes—laundered underclothes, a gray shirt with a trim collar, a suit in a darker gray material, light fawn socks and tan shoes in imitation leather. The only other item in the locker was a pair of horn-rimmed spectacles.

Now that they'd actually got themselves a live one, none of the group quite knew what to do with him. In the end they agreed it was best to let him rest peacefully for a while, so that he could sleep off his hundred years of sleep.

"Wish there was more in the computer about him," Ryan said. "Name, age and a secret job. Not much to go on."

"When he comes around he can tell us himself, can he not?" Doc asked.

"Think his brain shitted up," Jak offered.

"I wouldn't be surprised. I trust that none of you has noticed anything amiss, but there are, confidentially, times that I find my own brain becoming a touch fuzzy at the edges."

Ryan grinned at the old man. "We never would have guessed if you hadn't told us, Doc." And now that he'd thought about it, Ryan was amazed at how lucid Doc had been since they'd entered the cryo section.

While they were waiting they checked out the other six capsules that had been activated by the master control. Each of them had been occupied. Five men and one more woman.

What had happened to them gave a dreadful insight into how experimental the freezing process must have been, and how unreliable were the systems that controlled the thawing out.

All of them were dead.

Extremely dead.

Doc's guess was that somehow the controls had malfunctioned, causing a grotesque speeding up of the unfreezing.

The flesh seemed to have puddled off the bones in a sludge of instant decay. The cubicles reeked with the warm, sweet scent of rotting meat.

Fortunately it was possible to keep the capsules hermetically sealed, so that the odor scarcely filtered out into the main control area.

"It's like opening a domestic freezer in the middle of August," Doc observed, "and finding that the power had been disconnected three weeks earlier. Or like poor Monsieur Valdemar, if that was his name."

"Who's he, Doc?"

"Who, Krysty, my dear?"

"Somebody Valdemar?"

"Oh, yes. A character in a tale of grue. A man on his deathbed who is miraculously given the blessing of eternal life. But it becomes a curse as he is permanently fixed at the moment of death. He is finally released from this damnation and his body liquefies and rots to nothing in a matter of moments. Rather like those poor devils in those gleaming coffins. Better they should have passed on in a natural way, I think. Far better."

Richard Ginsberg woke several times, but never seemed to come all the way back to anything approaching full awareness. He opened his eyes and blinked around, showing only a mild bewilderment at where he might be. But he would almost immediately slide back into sleep.

Once he spoke. "Thirsty," he said.

Everyone pulled out small ring-pulls of clean water, and it was Lori who opened one of hers and held it for Ginsberg to sip. He coughed and choked, but managed something that might have been a crooked smile.

"Probably getting dark soon," J.B. said. "Best get him to the sleepers for the night. Be instant chill to go out into strangeness with him. Any trouble and we're all dead meat."

Ryan sucked at a tiny hole he'd recently noticed in a back tooth. "Yeah," he agreed reluctantly. "Rather have moved. We're all ready. But you're right, J.B. It'd be self-death if we tried." He looked at the others. "We're going to where we slept last night. We'll take turns carrying the freezie. Let's go, friends. Let's go."

Ginsberg seemed to be slipping into a deeper sleep, verging on coma. When they got him to the living quarters in the middle of the redoubt, Doc examined him, peeling back his eyelids, finding no response.

"Shock, maybe. He's becoming catatonic, switching off his mind so he won't have to come to terms with what must be a great disturbance. The alternative, sadly, is that the thawing hasn't worked quite as it should...or we have omitted something important. And poor Mr. Ginsberg is, quite simply, dying."

"Nothing we can do. Jak's given him some of that soup. Most dribbled right on out again. We've wrapped him warm and snug. Figure someone should stay with him through the night?"

Krysty's question wasn't answered immediately. Ryan broke the silence. "No. He's next door to us and the partition doesn't run to the ceiling. Jak and J.B. are to the other side. If he makes any noise, one of us'll hear him and wake."

By MORNING, Ginsberg looked close to death. His pulse and respiration had both fallen away to critical levels. His skin felt cold, and he failed to respond to any kind of stimulus.

"Gotta be something we can do," Lori said, standing with the others around the freezie's bed.

"We can leave him to die and get out of this place for a look-see," J.B. suggested.

"Just like that?" Doc retorted, the anger riding at the front of his voice.

"Yeah. He'll be worm fodder in a day. Mebbe less than that. Why wait and watch?"

"Sometimes, John Barrymore Dix, I have serious doubts about the code by which you live. By which we all live. I fear that I cannot—and will not—simply pass by this poor refuge from the past. Walk on the farther side and avert my eyes? No, thank you, my friends. That is not the way of Theophilus Algernon Tanner."

The Armorer took the reproach with a reasonable grace. "You got a point, Doc. Grant that. But if there was close danger here, you still wouldn't see me for dust. And the freezie could go get frozen again. But what can we do for him, Doc? You tell me that, will you?"

"Wish I knew, J.B., I wish I knew. He seems to be gently slipping through our fingers. After all those years..."

A short while later Richard Ginsberg appeared to stabilize. His heart and breathing steadied and even rallied a little. And, beneath the blankets, his flesh no longer felt so bitterly cold.

By noon there was a rekindling of a real hope for him.

"Looks better, Doc," Ryan said.

"I feel now we should try to restore him to consciousness. And try to make him take nourishment."

"How?" Lori queried.

Doc scratched his head. "Excellent question, my sweet passion flower of youth. How indeed?"

"Slap his face a few times, sit him up and pour some hot soup down his throat," Krysty suggested.

"Might kill him," J.B. said. "Then again... might cure him."

"What do you think, Doc?" Ryan asked.

"I do wish that you would all make a little more effort to recall that I may be called 'Doc' but that I know precious little about medicine. I am a doctor of science, and none of my science is of any avail here and now. I don't know, Ryan Cawdor. Why not try it? I doubt it will actually contribute to his death."

Ryan supported the dark-haired man, sitting him up on the bed. Krysty sat at his side, licking her lips nervously, looking at Ginsberg. "He's starting to show a beard. Look. All that stubble frozen for ten decades."

"Get on with it," Ryan urged her.

"Gaia help me," she whispered. "May the force of the Earth Mother act through me to save this stranger from the past."

Ryan noticed how the sensory curls of her crimson hair had retreated in tight bunches, as if seeking to protect her. Krysty swung her arm back, and then whipped it forward, hitting Ginsberg a solid slap across the left cheek. Though Ryan was braced against it, he was still rocked.

"Fireblast! You don't have to force his skull off his spine, lover."

"No point unless I do it hard. Keep him still there."

This time she used her left hand, leaving the vivid imprint of palm and fingers on the pale skin. Ginsberg's eyes jerked open, unfocused, then closed once more. Ryan could feel that the man's breathing had quickened.

"Again," he ordered.

Krysty slapped the helpless freezie's face twice more—a sharp back-and-forth motion, making the head roll from side to side.

This time the eyes flicked open, and stayed that way.

"Again?" Krysty asked, hand lifted ready.

"No," Richard Ginsberg gasped in a weak but clearly audible voice. "Thank you, but no. Not again."

"Welcome to the future," Doc said.

Chapter Ten

CRYOGENICS AT THE LEVEL of federal government was still highly classified at the end of the twentieth century. Carried on in a small number of top-secret redoubts, the experimentation was one of the many peripheral projects linked to the Totality Concept.

Richard Ginsberg had been put forward as a suitable candidate for freezing in the last months of the year 2000, late in October and just ninety days before sky-dark blotted out the United States of America and replaced it with the Deathlands.

Richard Ginsberg, of course, knew nothing of that. He had been locked into dreamless sleep, in his chromed coffin, far beneath the mountainside redoubt.

The last things he'd seen as the anesthetic shut down his mind and body had been the cornflower-blue eyes of Sister Magdalena Cohen, winking at him over the top of her surgical mask—eyes as brilliant as the bright circle of lights that had dazzled him from the ceiling of the operating theater at the Air Force base in Nebraska. Then a face mask came, smelling of a sickly mixture of warm rubber and disinfectant. And the angles inside his own skull folded in on his brain, like a Japanese paper sculpture.

The risks had been explained to him in advance, and he'd also undergone extensive counseling therapy to try to prepare him for his eventual reawakening.

His psychiatrist had gray hair, shaved to a fine stubble, with an enormously bushy mustache that overwhelmed his narrow, foxy face.

"We don't know when you might be revived, Rick," he said. "One month. One year. One century. One millenium. Who knows? I don't know. Nobody knows. All we know is that eventually medical science will be able to cure your illness. Until then you will be ceaselessly monitored."

A thousand years!

"I believe, from the best current information, that research into your ailment points to a cure within five years. Tops."

"FIVE YEARS. Tops," Richard Ginsberg mumbled, cradled in the arms of Ryan Cawdor.

His eyes were still blurred, but now he was able to make out some details. Perhaps if he could be given his spectacles he'd be able to see better. Because what he saw didn't make any sort of sense at all.

There was a tall young woman with very red hair, like molten copper, sitting on the bed by his feet. Ginsberg was recovered enough to know that this woman was called a nurse. She was a future nurse, in an odd dark blue uniform, with a massive, shiny automatic pistol at her hip. She'd been slapping him on the face! What kind of a hospital was this?

"He's starting to come around." Doc leaned forward and stared into the man's white face. "Guess he doesn't know where in tarnation he is. I was like that. It takes time.''

An old man, with a lined face, wearing a denim shirt and a weird Victorian frock coat. Pleasant, deep voice and some very expensive orthodontic work. Ginsberg tried to smile in pride at remembering that word. Must be a surgeon. Eccentric genius, perhaps.

"He's tried to grin," Lori said, looking over Doc's shoulder and beaming at the helpless figure on the bed.

"Nurse," Ginsberg said, with an effort. Pretty from what he could make out. Hair like Kansas wheat and eyes like a Montana skyscape. She looked to be very tall. She moved out of his line of sight and he could hear a peculiar tinkling sound like tiny brass cymbals.

"Lay him down and I'll go heat some soup for him," J.B. offered.

Porter? Middle-aged, eyes hidden behind glasses. But why was he wearing a hat in a hospital ward? And he had a gun at his hip, as well. *And* another slung over his shoulder, making him look like a guerrilla.

"What's . . . I mean, where and when . . . ?" But the connections between brain and speech were temporarily down.

"Just take it quiet," Ryan said, standing up so that he could look properly at the freezie.

Richard Ginsberg freaked out at the sight—a mat of unruly black hair above the hardest, most cruel face that he'd ever seen; one eye that glinted like polished marble, the other lost beneath a leather patch; a fearsome scar that seamed the cheek, tugging at the right-hand corner of the mouth. He struggled to lift his head, checking to see if this man, too, was carrying a gun.

However hard he tried, the disoriented freezie couldn't fit Ryan into his futurist scenario. The one-eyed man looked like a killer. It just wasn't possible to pretend otherwise.

"What soup?" Jak asked, popping into sight at the end of the bed, appearing to Richard Ginsberg like a demented demon from the locked door of a psychotic imagination, a little boy with immensely long hair that was as white as snow and as fine as sea wrack. His eyes blazed like coals in an open hearth.

"Veg soup," Ryan replied, turning away from the freezie for a moment. He missed the fraction of a second when the eyes rolled upward in the skull before the man slipped back into the safe harbor of unconsciousness once more.

While Ginsberg slept on, Doc called the other five together to make a short speech to them.

"My dear friends. Unaccustomed as I am to public speaking, I declare this laboratory to be well and truly... What am I saying? Goodness, but my mind seems to have slipped a gear or two."

"Or three or four," Lori added in a less than kindly tone.

"Our newfound and defrosted companion will require much help."

"If he stays awake long enough for us to help him."

"Indeed. It seems clear that the sight of us, perfectly normal though we might appear to one another, was not quite what the poor man had expected.

I would imagine he had thought to recover in a hospital amidst the best of medical care.''

"Will he not know he isn't . . . he is in Deathlands, then?" Lori asked, and was rewarded with a broad smile from Doc.

"Excellently deduced, my little bitty pretty one. A positive Hercules of the intellect. A veritable Napoléon of . . . No, that's not it. But, Lori is right. This is what we must take care with. Richard Ginsberg will think he has been thawed out to be cured of whatever it is that ails him. In a future world of peace and wonder.''

"What's sickness?" Jak asked. The heating of the can of soup had been put on the back burner until Ginsberg recovered again.

"It was obvious—painfully so in both cases—what was wrong with the other freezies. Here, it is less so. Perhaps leukemia, or some associated blood disease. Looking at him, I can see no evidence of any particular illness. Since he has been frozen for a hundred years, his muscle tone is, understandably, not good. Or, might there have been some progressive sickness there? I have no doubt that he will be able to tell us himself, when he finally recovers. But, I say again, be cautious about how we break the news of the long winters. It could topple his frail hold on sanity forever.''

THE NEXT TIME that Richard Ginsberg opened his eyes, he waited a long time before risking speech, trying to formulate a concept that would explain what he was seeing.

He recognized from the layout of the room that he appeared to be somewhere in one of the large underground fortresses known as redoubts. Reaching that deduction was the easy part. The six people that he saw around him were much more difficult.

It seemed possible that some kind of bizarre bunch of terrorists had infiltrated the complex and were taking him hostage. That fitted the facts as he saw them. He decided that the best opening gambit was simply to tell them his name. Ginsberg opened his mouth, ready to speak.

"Richard Ginsberg."

Shit. Things were even worse than in his worst imaginings. Though he'd opened his mouth, the voice had come from somewhere else, from the sinister fellow with only one eye. He'd said his name for him.

"Your name is Richard Ginsberg, isn't it?"

No response.

"I asked if your name was Richard Ginsberg? Can you hear me?"

"Yeah."

"Yeah, you can hear or yeah your name's Richard Ginsberg?"

"Both."

"Good. We're getting some soup for you and some water. Guess you must be hungry after...after so long."

The tall blond nurse spoke. "I'll be hungry after a—"

"Lori!" the one-eyed man snapped. "Can the talk! Remember?"

"Sorry, Ryan," she said, pouting and grinning like a child caught with her hand in the cookie jar.

Ginsberg cleared his throat and tried again. "You unfroze me?"

"Yeah."

"How do you know my name?"

Krysty answered him. "It's on the comp-console screen. Date of birth. Everything else was classified, and we couldn't access it."

He nodded. "Figures. Did you find any clothes? And my glasses?"

J.B. handed over the spectacles and Ginsberg slipped them on. "Clothes are in the locker."

The freezie blinked owlishly around. The six fuzzy figures now sharpened and became distinct. But none of the bewilderment eased.

"You know who I am. Who on the green earth are you?"

Ryan made the introductions. "This is Krysty Wroth, Doc Tanner, J.B. Dix, Lori Quint. Jak Lauren's getting the soup. I'm Ryan Cawdor."

Ginsberg coughed, struggled for breath for a moment. "Oh, that's... Must be all the stuff I've been full of for... Hell! I guess I have to ask you now. Why push it across the tracks? You aren't doctors and... But you said he was a doctor?"

"Science, son. Not medicine."

The man in the bed nodded. "Right. Got that clear. Now, if you aren't doctors and you all...look the way you do, then I figure something's gone very, very wrong with things."

"Things?" Krysty said.

"Things," he repeated, waving his hands in a vague gesture. "This isn't what I kind of expected, you know. Not guys with guns. I'm supposed to be brought out of it so I can be cured."

"What ails you?" Doc asked, moving out of the way as Jak brought in a bowl of steaming soup.

"Thanks." Ginsberg sat up and took a sip. "Wow! That's hot. And . . . I can't really taste it. Guess that could take some time to return."

"It's tomatoes," Jak said helpfully.

"Could be watermelon for all I can tell, kid."

"Don't call me 'kid,'" the albino boy warned, angrily.

"Sorry. You asked about what my illness was, didn't you? Mind's still fogged. Like a Frisco evening. Funny. I can remember watching the mist come rolling in over the hills into the bay when I was only about nine years old. Now, I can't remember things about what I was doing before they . . ." The words tailed off and he sat, sipping at the soup.

Ryan prompted him gently. "What was wrong with you?"

"Amyotrophic lateral sclerosis," Ginsberg replied, stumbling over the long syllables. "Something like that."

"Sounds real bad," Krysty said. "What is it?"

"It's Lou Gehrig's disease," Doc told her. "That's what it was known as."

"Right!" Ginsberg exclaimed. "You're kidding me, aren't you, Doc? You really are a doctor, and this is some kind of hospital. Right?"

"Wrong," Ryan corrected. "Who's this Lou Gehrig guy, Doc? Some kind of scientist?"

"Ball player. First baseman for the Yankees way back in the . . . way back when. It's a kind of progressive muscular weakness."

Ginsberg gave the half-empty bowl back to Jak. "Thanks. Guess I wasn't as hungry as I thought I was. Yeah, Doc, you're right. Lou Gehrig. When they diagnosed what I'd got, I kept hearing the name. Read up about him, some."

"What's it do, this sickness?" Jak asked.

Ginsberg sighed. "I always thought, when they started to talk about cryogenics, that I'd wake up and some guy in a white coat would pat me on the shoulder and tell me I was cured. Not have some . . . not get asked what my illness was."

"No," Ryan said. "I'm real double-sorry, but you have to know this clear from the start. None of us knows nothing…anything…about your sickness. We can do nothing for you."

Ginsberg took off his spectacles and polished them on the sheet, not saying anything for several moments. He peered at the light through the glasses, wiping away a small smear. Finally he nodded.

"I appreciate your honesty, Mr. Cawdor. Truly I do. When they confirmed the diagnosis of amyotrophic lateral sclerosis, ALS they called it, I'd known something was wrong. My coordination had been off for some weeks. I'd stumble, or I'd drop something. Spill food. I'd played baseball, like Gehrig, and suddenly I started to miss the pitches. Fumble it when I was out in right field. Lots of silly things. I felt tired. Weak.

Wanted to lie down and rest a lot. They did all the tests on me.''

He stopped and put his glasses back on. The others still stood around him, listening to his story, crowding the small cubicle.

He carried on. ''They tried everything. Digitalis. Didn't help. Androstenolone. Same. I was getting steadily weaker.''

''Did they know what caused this sickness,'' Krysty asked.

''Nerve cells in my brain and in my spine were just sort of giving up the ghost. Degeneration is the name. No cure. No hope. Fetch the coolant and pop the boy in the freezer. Thaw him out in a thousand years when we can save him.''

The bitterness reached the front of his voice, and he buried his face in his hands. ''That string of operations and tests and then the actual freezing. Having to say goodbye to all my friends. My parents. All of them. Like I was an astronaut going boldly off to brave the new frontiers. Now I come around and I'm in some military base with a half-dozen people who I don't know.''

Lori sat on the bed and patted Ginsberg on the arm. ''Could be badder,'' she said. ''You can be dead and it's badder.''

''You think so? You get what I got, young lady, and you sometimes think death is going to come in with a blessing.''

''Disease like that goes into remission, doesn't it?'' Doc asked.

"Sure. That's the irony. When I got frozen I was feeling better than I had for months."

The freezie still hadn't asked the question that Ryan and the others were dreading. But all of them were waiting for it.

Ginsberg sighed. "Mind if I snatch some sleep, folks? I feel kind of drained with all this waking up."

"Sure. We want to think about moving outside this redoubt sometime today," Ryan said.

"Yeah." Jak grinned. "Find out where fuck we are."

Ginsberg smiled. "Sure. I understand that you—" He looked suddenly puzzled. "How d'you mean? Did I hear you right? So you can find out *where* you are? How come you don't ... don't know?"

Nobody spoke and everyone tried to avoid catching the eye of the bemused freezie, looking everywhere except at him.

"Hey, come on, Mr. Cawdor! What's going down here? What? And..."

Here it comes, Ryan thought.

"I want to know where we are. What's going on? What year is this? And—" his voice broke like a lost child's "—what in the name of God Almighty is happening?"

Chapter Eleven

THE SIX COMPANIONS stood by the subsidiary exits from the redoubt, on its northern flank. Richard Ginsberg leaned against the wall, breathing hard.

Walking was difficult for him, and the others had taken turns helping to support him. His muscles were painfully weak and wasted. Ryan noticed that the freezie's way of walking was slightly peculiar, each foot lifted rigidly then set down with an unusual firmness. Ginsberg also kept clenching and unclenching his fingers, as though they were stiff and sore.

Ryan had, as gently as he could, given him a spotty version of history from the October morning when Richard Neal Ginsberg had last seen the light of day, up to the present morning, one hundred eternal years later. The freezie had taken the news fairly well in spite of Doc's concern for his sanity.

Ryan sketched in what he knew of the end of civilization, the long winters, the barren wastes and frothing hot spots; the changes in the land and in the climate and the changes in the people.

Ginsberg had asked surprisingly few questions.

"When I saw you all, sporting guns, I guessed something was...bad. Had to be. Course, when I went under, the war talk was louder. Same old faces and voices. Hatred. I was born and raised on growing hatred in...once that...can't remember his name, the Russian leader who talked peace. Once he was toppled—word was the CIA brought him down—it all went downhill."

He'd cautiously asked how many had died in the first waves of missiles. Ryan told him that nobody knew the answer to that. All records were gone, and the months immediately following the devastation were known as "the lost days."

Rick's parents had lived in a neat apartment in a brownstone on the Lower East Side of New York. All that Ryan, helped by Doc and Krysty, could tell was that every city had been hit hard and often. There was a ten-tenth's death rate in all major metropolises, and for people within the heat core, death would come like the snuffing of a light.

"A single microsecond of surprise, and then an infinite merging with the cosmos," Doc had told him.

"What's kind of hard," Rick eventually said, "is the sure knowledge that every person I ever met in my entire life is now dead. Most died within a few miserable weeks of my being frozen. Now I'm here and I'm all on my fucking own! I'm still dying and...and what's the point of it all, huh? What's the point?"

DESPITE URGING particularly from J.B., Rick steadfastly refused to carry a blaster.

"Sorry, John," he insisted. "I'm a little of a peacenik in my own way. I abhor violence. From what you've been telling me, I guess I might have to get used to a mighty different world from the one I knew.

Maybe in some ways, I might like it better. But tote a pistol? Thanks, but no thanks."

What was odd was that he hadn't shown much interest in precisely who Ryan and the others actually were or how they'd gotten into the triple-secure redoubt or how they moved around the Deathlands.

At Doc's suggestion Ryan hadn't pestered Rick about what he'd done back before the megachill. The fact that it had been highly classified meant it could be an area of his life that might provoke a strong and upsetting reaction.

The outside doors of the redoubt swung open on the familiar 3-5-2 code. Jak led the way into the fresh air, the other six following him. Rick leaned on Krysty's arm, bringing up the rear.

"Oh, to see the sun and taste the breeze..." the freezie said, clearly on the edge of tears. "Whatever happens, I've seen this once more." He hesitated. "Why is the sky that strange purplish color?"

"Strange?" Ryan echoed. "It's nearly always that color."

Doc smiled sadly. "It wasn't always so, Ryan. What our new companion says is correct. The skies were always blue when I was a lad. Yellow sun. White clouds. Not the hideous hues of the chem clouds and the dark nuke sky that haunts us all."

"How come you remember that, Doc?" Rick asked. "Nobody's that old."

"It is a tale told by an idiot, Richard. Told by me. Too difficult to comprehend or even to believe. One day, when you are somewhat recovered, I will tell you."

"Speaking of believing," Rick continued. "In your travels, you never came across—maybe in one of these redoubts—anything called a . . . a gateway, did you?"

Before anyone could stop her, Lori leaped in with both feet.

"Course, stupe! That's how we always are getting around Deathlands. Jump and jump in gateways."

Once again nobody looked at the freezie. Ryan stared across a narrow blacktop that vanished steeply over the brink of the hillside. Beyond it was a sweep of valley, disappearing into some thick forest. There was no sign of a ville anywhere.

"Just a damned m-m-m-minute," Rick stammered. "Did I hear you right, Lori?"

"Yeah."

"You guys use gateways? They still work? Sweet... They still work? A hundred years after the bombs and they still work. Wow!"

"What do you know about mat-trans?" Doc asked curiously. "Is that why you were given a high-B sec rating, Mr. Ginsberg?"

"I can't tell you. Freedom of information doesn't apply. Would you be on a need-to-know listing? Of course you wouldn't. You were all dead. I mean not alive . . . when the last need-to-know precaution list was . . . Oh, this is weird, guys. Like dropping a tab of the best Nicaraguan acid. You've been using the gateways! Which ones? Where?"

Ryan suddenly guessed it. "You worked on them, didn't you? That *was* the reason for your high sec rating. You know all about gateways and jumps! Fireblast! You've got plenty to tell us, friend."

J.B. interrupted him. "If we're going to get some miles before dark, Ryan, we'd best get started. Talk can come later."

Ryan ignored the good advice, glaring at Rick. "Is it true?"

"I don't know."

"What d'you mean? You must know what your bastard job was!"

"I think it . . . it might have been something about gateways, but I can't remember. My head hurts, and I'm tired and confused and why don't you leave me alone? Please."

"Please," Ryan mocked angrily. "You could hold the key to information that might alter all our lives!"

"Ryan," the Armorer urged, "it's a good walk down there. And the freezie's in poor shape. Don't want to get caught by dark halfway down the mountain. Come on, Ryan."

"Sure. Yeah, you're right, J.B., I know that. But—" he faced Rick again "—get your memory working and we'll talk later. You got lots to tell us."

IT WAS a difficult journey.

In several places the road had been washed away by torrential rains or shattered by quakes. When they were about a quarter of the way down, J.B. stopped and drew out his tiny pocket sextant, checking where they actually were in the Deathlands.

Rick Ginsberg sat slumped on a huge boulder, head in his hands, panting with exhaustion. The trail was high, and Ryan was conscious of the thin air. His heart was working harder than usual, and any effort was more tiring. There was a marvellous vista to enjoy to their west—the orange sun was sliding down amid a nest of feathery thundertops tinted a light purple.

"What are the mountains, Doc?" Krysty asked, brushing dust from her coveralls.

"Look like the old Sierra Nevadas, from the shape and feel of them. But if we're in the high Sierras, then I'm puzzled at what that is way away to the west. Beneath the setting sun."

"It's a lake," Lori said. "Big, big lake, far as I can see."

Doc shook his head. "Can't be, sweetness. There is no lake of that size hereabouts. We must be a good twenty miles or more away from it and yet it looks utterly vast. Ergo, we are not in the Sierras."

"Wrong, Doc," J.B. folded the sextant and slipped it into one of his infinitely capacious pockets.

"Wrong?"

"Wrong. We're close by the Pacific. These are the Sierras, all right. This is what used to be called California."

"But the ocean never came this close to such high peaks, unless..."

Rick stood up, his pale face beaded with sweat. "You say this was California. That's bullshit! There's no place in the state where you can see the Pacific from..." His eyes, magnified behind the thick lenses, turned to Doc. "Unless... You were going to say... weren't you? Unless the whole..."

Ryan answered him. "Trader'd been here several times over the years, and he told me what happened out west here."

"San something... Andreas, that was it. The San Andreas Fault!" the freezie exclaimed.

"That's the name. Trader said that the nukes came down, thicker than fleas on a gaudy-house mattress. Hit lotsa places along California. Cities and silos. Bases and harbors. Said there was that fault you said. It triggered something way deep under the earth, and the whole mess just opened up."

Krysty backed up what Ryan had said. "There was an old woman in Harmony when I was still a suckler. Said her gran had survived. Bad rad burns, but she'd lived. Been born on the foothills of the Sierras, hundred and fifty miles from the sea. Came around after dark day. The Pacific was lapping at her feet. A lot of the state had gone, slipped into the water and off the edge. She said the waters were clogged with bloated corpses for many months. The smell drove folks away—those that lived. Not many."

"Los Angeles gone? San Diego? San Francisco? All gone?" Ginsberg sat down in an ungainly heap, like a rag doll left to its own devices. "Then it's true, what you told me. Not something spawned in my brain. I'm alive and it's happened, and I'm going to die. I'd hoped..."

"Man who starts thinking of hope has given up thinking how to live," J.B. said. "Seems to me, freezie, that you're too bitching sorry for yourself for a grown man."

"You don't understand," Rick said wearily, barely holding back the tears. "This *isn't* my world!"

"It is now," the Armorer replied. "And we're all wasting time."

RYAN HAD EXAMINED the massive sec doors to the redoubt very carefully before the group started down the blacktop, checking that there hadn't been any serious effort to force them.

Any signs of bad damage often meant a potential threat from local muties. But the doors were untouched, with just the usual evidence of weathering.

They found one possible reason for this when they were a couple of miles down the track. There had been a huge earthslip and the remainder of the road, clear into the forest, was gone.

Now there was just a great expanse of scree, dotted with scrub and sparse thimbleberry bushes. A tiny stream meandered through it, opening up its own little valley between the loose stones. There was about a half mile of nothing before the first shadowed trees. The forest covered a sizable piece of land, eventually filtering down into a terrain of semidesert, dotted with sagebrush and mesquite.

"Get warmer," Jak observed, wiping his forehead with the sleeve of his camouflage canvas jacket.

"Soon be evening, Ryan," J.B. said. "We're making slow time with the freezie. Best we can hope is to reach the wood and make a night camp there."

"Sorry to slow you all down. It would be better if you left me. Better you never reactivated me. Best would have been if you'd walked on by and—"

"Rick?" Ryan said.

"Yeah?"

"Shut your damned mouth!"

"Yeah. Sorry."

"NO FIRE," J.B. ordered.

"It'll be coldest!"

"No fire," he repeated.

But Lori was equally insistent. "I don't want cold!" She stamped her foot, the spurs tinkling prettily.

"The forest is exceedingly dry, my dearest little moonstone, and the brush beyond looked like positive tinder."

"What d'you know? You got thick old skin to kept you warmer. Not like me!"

Doc shrank from her venomous anger, shaking his head. Krysty felt sorry for him and stepped into the argument.

"Don't be a stupe, Lori. You know what a danger a fire could be out here. Wind'd raise it in minutes. Not worth it."

"Bring muties," Jak added.

"You're all against me! Always fucking mob up on me. Not fair," she yelled, her voice swallowed by the dark trees surrounding them.

Nobody took any notice, except for Doc, who took a hesitant half step toward the sulking girl. He stopped abruptly when his eye caught Krysty and saw her shake her head.

Rick had taken no part in the conversation. As soon as they had stopped in a small clearing he'd laid down on the soft, dry bed of dead leaves and fallen into a deep sleep.

The six companions took turns keeping a sec watch. It would have been utterly absurd to think about the freezie keeping guard. Ryan was already having serious reservations about Rick Ginsberg, a weak, enfee-

bled and miserable depressive whose mind was fragile.
The only thing that was in his favor was the news that
he had once worked in some capacity on the gateways.

That alone justified the trouble of keeping him with
them.

But only for the time being.

The night passed by peacefully.

Chapter Twelve

AFTER A SPARSE BREAKFAST from self-heats and ring-pulls of water, everyone sat around for a few minutes, resting, preparing to move on. Ryan was next to Rick, and he realized the freezie was muttering to himself, something about "tomorrow."

He listened more carefully.

"All our yesterdays have lighted fools the way to a dusty death. Life's a tale told by an idiot, filled with sound and fury and signifying . . ." Ginsberg stopped.

"Signifying what?" the one-eyed man asked curiously.

"Nothing, Ryan," Rick replied with a deadly bitterness. "Absolutely nothing."

Lori's good nature had returned, and she led the group, dancing, light-footed, between the gnarled trunks of the mature live oaks. The bells on her spurs jingled merrily, and she sang as she ran, an old hymn that Ryan had heard in some of the fundamentalist Christian villes.

"Watch your step, precious," Doc called, but the girl ignored him, blond hair flying behind her.

Rick seemed in better health and spirits, walking without the aid of a walking staff that Ryan had cut for him with his panga.

"I used to like hiking," he said. "Until I got ill. It became harder going then."

"How d'you feel?" J.B. asked.

"Better." He grinned. "A whole lot better. You know, the air tastes cleaner. Perhaps I'm imagining it, but it does. Fresher. I suppose all the industry being blasted in the war helps that. No more sulfur, acid rain and holes in the ozone layer that used to worry everyone in the...in the old days."

"Your muscles feel stronger?" Krysty asked, brushing an errant crimson curl back from her eyes.

"Yeah. I think so. You know, I can't remember. Funny. I think a century of freezing's addled my brain. There are things I can remember vividly and some that have gone. I can't visualize my mother's face. Silly, isn't it?"

Ryan shook his head. "Doc has the same kind of trouble, Rick. Tell me something you remember well. Anything?"

"Moments in never," he replied. "I can...when I was about fourteen, going to New York with my father. We'd gotten tickets to see the Giants play the Forty-Niners. And we had a day in Manhattan. We went to an art gallery, which had lots of glass and open spaces. Wonderful paintings by Georgia O'Keefe, Hopper, Wyeth and...so many. All nuked. What a... But it wasn't that. It was a warm October day and we wanted something to eat. We were around Fifth and Fiftieth, by the old Saint Patrick's Cathedral."

"Reaching the edge of the tree part!" Lori called from some distance ahead of them.

The others were entranced by Rick Ginsberg's story. He was like a living time machine, painting a picture of a long-ago scene that none of them, except Doc, could imagine with any kind of reality.

"We decided to get some fast food. There were lots of burger stalls and fries. But there was an old Chinese guy who had a stall with pictures on the side—whatever he was selling. I can still see it, and almost smell how good it was—fried shrimp, crab and fish with some rice and a soda. We sat on the steps and watched New York flow by us. I felt real close to my dad at that moment. I don't think I'll ever forget it. Even if I live to be a hundred."

Jak sniggered. "You're more hundred now, freezie. Lot more."

Rick didn't rise to the bait. He simply nodded at the boy. "True enough. So don't be so rude to your elders!"

The albino threw him the finger and darted off to join Lori at the fringe of the desert brush.

Now they were at a lower level, and it was possible to look back up the mountain slope. They could see the scar of the scree-fall, but no trace of the hidden redoubt tucked under the lip of the peak above.

"Think there's a ville over there," Krysty said, pointing across the expanse of orange-gray sand. "And I can smell... not sure what."

Ryan stopped, still just within the shade of the forest, and took several deep breaths. There was something. Very faint but...

"Gas!" he exclaimed. "It's gasoline! Fireblast! If we can smell it such a long way off, then it must be a big field. Or a store so big that . . . If there's gas, then there's wags. Am I right, J.B., or am I right?''

"Could be. Sure is strong. This gas country, Doc? California?''

"Never used to be, but I suppose that the shifting of the great plates of the earth could push oil-bearing strata for hundreds of miles.''

"If you got jack, you're fine,'' Ryan said, "but if you got gas, then you're even better.''

Ginsberg sighed. "What's transport like? If gas is that rare and difficult?''

"There's some. Most villes have stocks. There was a huge store that the Trader found, about two hundred miles north of where Boston used to be. But it got blown. Now there's wags. Transport and war wags. Kind of rough.''

"Trains?'' the freezie asked.

J.B. answered him. "Sure. Often get trains of wags rolling together. Safer that way. Hold off the muties.''

"No. I mean trains, like Amtrak. On rails.'' Seeing the blank looks, he said, "No, I guess there aren't any. How about planes?'' Again, he answered his own question. "Stupid. If there's no trains and there aren't many cars, there sure as little green apples aren't going to be any airplanes.''

"Wrong,'' Ryan replied. "I've never seen any flying wags, but the Trader saw one, once. Out East, he said.''

"Flying?'' Rick asked.

"Crashing,'' the Armorer said with a short, dry laugh.

"That's what Trader said. Got hauled out some old shed. Already gassed up. Baron's oldest son said he'd try it. Up, up and...down again. Body finished in one field. Head in another. Never found the legs, way I recall it."

THOUGH THE LAND had looked fairly even from high above, it was actually seamed with innumerable narrow ravines and dry riverbeds. Doc surmised that this was all a result of the unimaginably catastrophic forces that had shifted the land a hundred years earlier. Since the old Golden State had always been a place of earthquakes and landslides, it wasn't surprising to see the flat desert ripped and patched.

Krysty's feeling that there might be a ville on the far side made them cautious about approaching carelessly. Also, there were sinister tracks in the soft red dust.

"Sidewinder," Jak suggested, pointing to an odd swirling pattern in the sand. There were also peculiar marks, as though large wag tires had been rolled ceaselessly around.

The light breeze through the shoulder-high scrub produced a constant dry rustling that would cover the approach of any creature. Ryan felt the short hairs raising on his nape.

"Bad place," he muttered, almost to himself.

But Krysty, at his side, heard him and nodded. "I got that feeling, too. Best we get across it as fast as we can."

"Not easy, towing the freezie. The way he looks, a half mile'll put him down and out."

"Could go back, lover?"

"Yeah. Nobody ever gets anywhere by going back, do they? Let's go on."

Once they had plunged into the sagebrush, dotted with elegant saguaros, it became difficult to see more than ten paces ahead. The switchbacking terrain was exhausting, even for the hardier members of the group. For Rick Ginsberg, the effect was devastating. After less than twenty minutes he collapsed, eyes rolling up into their sockets, a thin froth dribbling from his cracked lips.

"Cruise up Mulholland after dark and just watch the lights," he mumbled.

The other six gathered around him. Lori dropped to her knees, breathing hard, wiping dusty sweat from her forehead, brushing away her tangled hair. Doc also knelt down.

"By the three Kennedys! This heat quite debilitates one, does it not? I fear that our frozen comrade is not quite up to it. Should we not return to the redoubt and jump elsewhere?"

"I'll give him some water," Krysty said, kneeling beside the prostrate man.

Ryan looked around. They were in a shallow saucer-shaped depression, but ahead of them the land seemed to be rising. "Jak?"

"Ryan?"

"Go up and see if you can get high enough to check how far to the edge of this desert."

The boy returned in less than five minutes, his white hair tinted pink with the fine sand. He jumped down the last bit of the slope.

"Not far," he said.

"Hour? Two?"

"Three. With freezie...? Ten hours. Mebbe more."

Rick was, once more, asleep. Krysty looked up from giving him a drink, her green eyes meeting Ryan's stare unflinchingly.

"Nobody said it'd be easy," she whispered accusingly. "Man's sick, tired, been lying with a dark mind for a hundred years. What'd you expect, lover? Got to be slow with him."

"I know it."

ODDLY IT WAS Doc who first heard the distant sound.

He stood up, putting his hand to his ear, listening hard. Apart from the dozing freezie, the others all looked curiously at the old man.

"What is it?" Ryan asked, his ears filled by the noise of the wind hissing through the scrub. He could just catch the sounds of a chem storm, rumbling and crackling, miles to the east, beyond the mountains.

"For a moment I thought I could hear the sound of... But that is midsummer madness. The folly of an old fool, they always say, you know."

Ryan was about to relax again, deciding it was one of Doc's fantasies, when he heard it, too. When all of them heard it.

A distant, regular humming noise, like an errant wasp, buzzing across the desert, coming from where Krysty claimed there might be a ville. The sound was growing louder.

"Mighty big insect," J.B. observed, cradling his new blaster, and looking anxiously up at the cloud-speckled sky.

Rick opened his eyes and gazed blankly upward, blinking through the pebbled glasses. "What's...? It's an airplane? By God, but it's—"

"Everyone down," Ryan shouted, setting an example by diving beneath a stunted clump of ocotillo. Krysty landed at his side, with J.B. beyond her. Ryan could see that the others were also taking cover.

The noise was louder, hiccuping occasionally, rasping and whining. He peered up through the sparse protection of the brush.

And saw it.

The freezie had been right. It *was* a plane. Two wings on each side, with circles of red, white and blue painted on them; a stubby body, with twin cockpits. It was about a hundred feet above the ground, swaying from side to side, the racket now quite deafening to the people below it.

It had a single revolving propeller set on the point of its nose. Blue smoke coughed from the engine. Ryan could make out only one flier, his round, helmeted face hidden behind an enormous pair of glinting goggles. As far as he could make out, the flying machine carried no blasters.

It dipped and swooped overhead, carrying on toward the lower slopes of the mountain. Jak started to get up, then ducked down again. "Coming back," he shouted.

It passed about two hundred yards to the south of them, again apparently not noticing them. Finally the plane vanished away across the desert in the direction it had originally come from. As the sound faded, everyone stood and dusted themselves off.

"I've seen pix of old planes in vids," Ryan said, "but not one like that. Looked real old."

"Bless my soul," Doc said. "That was a Sopwith 1½-Strutter, or I miss my guess. I studied the first World War during my imprisonment by the Cerberus dogs. Yes, indeed. A trusty biplane. A Sopwith 1½-Strutter. Such a coincidence after we'd been talking about if there were any planes left in Deathlands."

Rick stood up, looking shaken. "What kind of world is this?" he said slowly. "It's a crazed mix of the past, my present and your future. It's all bloody madness."

"Yes," Ryan agreed. "It is."

It was now obvious that there must be a ville beyond the arid wasteland, so they pushed on at top speed, taking turns helping the frail man.

Each dusty arroyo was like the next one and like the previous one. Small clusters of cactuses with steely thorns made walking difficult. Despite Jak's estimate of how far away the edge of the desert was, the hours drifted by and it didn't seem to get much closer.

"Looks like a trail here," said Lori, who'd been leading the way, stumbling and cursing in her spike-heeled boots.

"Hold up," Ryan called, joining her and taking the lay of the land. They were in a broader-sided valley, and the bottom did seem to be trampled flatter. He knelt and examined the earth closely, seeing marks of some kind of wags. J.B. and Jak knelt beside him.

"Two wheel wags," the Armorer observed. "Look at the pattern. Not four-wheelers."

"Watch your step," Krysty warned. "Good place for an ambush."

"Can we rest?" Rick panted. His neat jacket and pants had been torn by the thorns of the innumerable cactuses and covered in a patina of orange dust. Blood dappled the man's hands where he'd fallen, and his face beneath the mask of dirt was pale and lined. He seemed to have aged ten years in the past twenty-four hours, and Ryan yet again pondered on their wisdom in reviving him.

Everyone looked at Ryan, who shook his head. "No. Got to keep moving. This place has taken us the better part of a damned day already. Sun's getting low. Don't want to get caught out by night. By the signs we're not far off where this ville might be. We'll keep going on."

Rick shrugged wearily. "For this I slept a hundred years? Momma was right. I should have stayed home and become a doctor. Very well—" he waved a hand to Ryan "—lay on, my trusty thane of Cawdor. And cursed be him that first shall cry—"

He was interrupted by a piercing scream from Lori, who had ignored Ryan's instructions and gone ahead around the corner. Overlaying the scream was a noise that sounded like a dozen raging chain saws.

Ryan's reactions were the quickest, and he burst through the narrowing rocks, around the bend in the trail.

He faltered as his eye took in the horrific scene of a heart-stopping nightmare.

Chapter Thirteen

A DIAMONDBACK RATTLESNAKE lay coiled in the desert sand, its layered rattle vibrating furiously. The reptile's forked tongue flicked in and out of its mouth, tasting the air around it. The long teeth, angled back, emerged from just below the maxillary bone of the upper jaw. Its slitted eyes remained motionless on either side of the flattened skull. It was well over twenty feet long, its body as thick as the thigh of a grown man.

It was, without the least shadow of a doubt, the largest mutie snake that Ryan Cowdor had ever seen.

The setting sun glinted off some sort of metal strip around the creature's throat, like a silvery collar. It caught Ryan's eye, but his instant preoccupation was the girl sprawled helplessly in the dirt in front of the rearing creature.

In her haste to be first, Lori must have almost run over the top of the giant rattler, stumbling across the bony tail.

The snake's gaping jaws were wide enough to engulf Lori's entire skull, and a tiny glistening bead of poison hung from the needle points of the fangs. It had reared up, at least six feet high, above the screaming girl, its shadow across her body.

Ryan's H&K G-12 was up and ready, braced against his hip, aimed at the spade-shaped head of the reptile. But his finger held still on the trigger of the powerful blaster.

"No!" Doc shrieked from just behind him, his voice so unexpectedly loud that Ryan nearly let rip with the automatic.

"Why not?"

"It'll fall on her and the child'll be instant grave fodder."

It was unmistakably true. The rattler was so gigantic that it hung over Lori, menacing her, its head weaving slowly to and fro. The warning rattle of its tail continued unabated.

The girl seemed almost paralyzed, like a rabbit in the lights of a night wag. She was on her back, legs drawn up, one hand lifted as though she could simply push away the monster snake. Her mouth was open and she was crying out, a string of pleading, helpless words.

"Could try and take its head off?" J.B. suggested.

The rattler was about thirty yards away from the group, its eyes registering their presence. But most of its attention was fixed on the blond girl beneath it.

"Hell of a chance it'd chill her before we could chill it," Ryan replied.

Rick Ginsberg had joined them, panting hard, one hand clamped to his side. His eyes were round with disbelief. "Is that...? You never said a word about sci-fi monsters, Ryan. It's a dream. A nightmare! It'll kill the girl, unless..."

"Shut fuck up!" Jak snapped, hefting one of his throwing knives, gripping it by the weighted hilt. "Could hit eye, Ryan?"

"No," Doc said despairingly. "A clean kill or drive it away."

For several racing heartbeats nobody moved or spoke. The snake's head kept up its hypnotic swaying, and Lori began to weep uncontrollably.

Ryan, keeping his voice low, spoke to the others. "Got to go for the head with blasters. All at once. Should manage to splatter it apart."

"I forbid it, Ryan," Doc whispered, his left hand playing nervously with an errant strand of hair. "The risk is too great."

"You got a better idea? If not, then we'll do it like—"

"Help me, please," Lori called, her voice barely audible above the harsh noise of the snake's rattle.

"Yes," Doc said suddenly. "Distraction. I'll distract the beast and you can then do the shooting part."

Without another word, the old man was off and running, waving the walking cane in his right hand, fumbling as he ran with the silver handle, discarding the ebony case to bare the steel rapier blade within it.

"The double-stupe old...!" Ryan exploded, taken by surprise. "Get ready to try and chill the mutie!"

Everyone drew their own blasters, ready to open fire at Ryan's order, aiming at the blunt, questing head of the rattler.

"Come, thou mighty worm, Ouroboros!" Doc shouted, trying to attract the bright, soulless eyes from

Lori toward himself. He leaped into the air and brandished his sword.

Slowly, incuriously, the snake peered down at him, its rattle slowing to a menacing, vibrating hum. It lifted its head even higher, retreating a little, the smooth coils of muscle tensing.

"Going t'strike," J.B. warned.

Lori had fallen silent, looking around at the bizarre capering figure in his stained frock coat and cracked knee boots. The sword flashed crimson as it caught the last rays of the dying sun. Doc darted in and thrust at the nearest part of the giant snake, bringing his rapier back dripping dark blood. But the rattler didn't move its head, and its eyes were unflickering.

Ryan had leveled his G-12, aiming at a point a hand's span below the jaw. He could actually see the tiny ruby glow from the laser sight on J.B.'s new MP-7 SD-8, an inch or so higher than where he was aiming. Jak's Magnum and Krysty's P7A-13 pistol were also focused on the creature's head and neck.

"Ready," Ryan whispered.

"Avaunt, creature from pitchiest night!" Doc yelled, encouraged by the success of his first assault.

The mutie rattler's stunning speed took them all by surprise.

Before anyone could even tighten a finger on a trigger, the snake had weaved back and then struck, its head a blur of movement.

By the sheerest fluke, Doc happened to be waving his sword in the beast's general direction, even though he was looking down at Lori. The snake virtually im-

paled itself on the tip of the rapier, jerking it from
Doc's hand. The force of its attack knocked Doc
flying to the dirt in a tangle of arms and legs. But the
prick of the steel was just enough to deflect its snapping lunge at the old man.

Frustrated, hissing in fury, its tail swinging with the
rattle back in overdrive, the mutie monster straightened up, ready to strike at the man and woman in its
shadow.

Ryan wasn't about to take any more chances with
the enormous reptile. "Now!" he yelled, squeezing the
trigger of the blaster. Set on continuous, the G-12
poured out a devastating stream of lead, accompanied by J.B.'s gun on triple burst. The snap of
Krysty's handgun and the boom of Jak's powerful
cannon counterpointed the rippling roar of the rifles.

The head and upper throat of the great reptile simply disintegrated under the impact of thirty or forty
rounds of ammunition. Blood sprayed, and a heavy,
black ichor oozed from the mutilated skull of the
creature. Its body began to thrash about with a fearful violence, kicking up blinding clouds of dust. Doc
and Lori vanished behind the red-orange veil of sand.

"Let's get them out!" Ryan ordered, dropping his
gun and darting forward, aware of the other three at
his side. He noticed from the corner of his eye that
even Rick Ginsberg had joined in, hobbling on his
rough stick.

Lori had begun to scream again. Ryan found her
first and heaved the girl to her feet, discovering that
she was in shock as she collapsed helplessly to the dirt.
With a grunt of effort, he managed to lift her onto his

shoulders, carrying her away from the appalling noise of the monster's death throes, the demented clicking of its rattle.

Doc managed to move out on his own, clutching his arm where he'd jarred it in the fall. He had to wait until the writhing began to ease, which allowed him to go look for his swordstick. While Jak looked after Lori, calming her, the others went to examine the twitching corpse of the mutie rattler.

Its head was pulped and both eyes were gone. The main fangs had snapped off into short, splintered stumps, from which threads of poison still oozed into the dirt. The remainder of the body was moving slightly as the nerve endings began to close down on any messages.

"What's that on its neck?" J.B. asked, pointing at the silvery collar that Ryan had glimpsed a few speeded seconds earlier.

Krysty leaned over the immense body, avoiding the rattle that still vibrated with no more noise than a child's toy. "It's locked on," she said. "It'll take some cutting to get it off."

"What's the lettering say?" Ryan asked.

"A name. Can't..." The girl wiped blood away. "Yeah. Azrael. And the number twelve. That's all. Gaia! You figure it's someone's pet?"

"Could be." The Armorer turned to Ryan. "Remember that baron up north...one that had an extra pair of residual hands?"

"Yeah. Oh, sure. He had a mutie maggot as his special pet. Slept in a big wooden bed with silk sheets and got fed like a baby."

"It's a nightmare." Rick shook his head. "I know that now. You're all figments of my imagination. Inside the coolant capsule I've gone stark mad. Yeah, as mad as a hatter. Hatters were mad because they used a lot of mercury in the process of making hats. Fumes rotted their brains. Mad hatters. That's me. Rattlers as big as a semi. Maggots as pets. Redheads with pistols. Albino kids with Clint Magnums. One-eyed men and . . . I can't stop talking. Why's that, Ryan?"

"Because you're in shock, Rick, and you're kind of not used to the Deathlands and its pleasures yet. That'll come."

"Terrific. I can't wait. I'm just not coping . . . know what I mean? Momma always said I was a born underachiever."

Lori was still shaking. "I'm wanting to fuck out of this," she said, voice shrill and high.

"You're all right now, my delicate little Meissen shepherdess."

"No thanks to you! Nearly killing me with jumping in and shouting at the mutie bastard. Stupid yellow old triple-crazy."

Doc's face fell. "I confess that my efforts were not quite as successful as I had hoped, my dear child, but I truly did my best."

"Not best enough, and I'm not your fucking child! You made me rad-sick!"

Ryan felt the old glow of scarlet anger begin to blaze. Something that he'd learned, painfully, to control over the years. He was aware of the flush of heat that brightened the scar across his face, and his fingers clenched with the surging rage. In some ways it was a pleasant, reassuring feeling that swamped everything else. To slap Lori Quint across her petulant, pretty little face and knock her on her ass in the trampled dirt would be a good thing.

"Good thing," he muttered.

Fortunately—at least for Lori—Krysty Wroth had been with Ryan long enough to recognize the flaring danger signals.

"No, lover," she said, taking a half step that put her between Ryan and the trembling blond teenager.

"Doc risked..." Ryan began, gritting his teeth so hard that it made his jaw ache.

Krysty held up a hand, facing Lori. "You live around the Deathlands and you get to see a lot of shit behavior. Every now and again you see someone do something really brave. What Doc did to try and save your miserable skin is one of the bravest things I ever saw. A little steel needle against that mutie monster there!"

"Grace under pressure," Rick added, trying to wipe sweat and dirt off the lenses of his glasses.

"I've heard that," J.B. said. "Read it someplace, years ago."

Krysty ignored the interpretations, glowering at Lori. "You hear what I'm saying?"

"Yeah. But it was Ryan and you lot chilled the snake."

"You'd have been dead if Doc hadn't jumped in when he did," Ryan said, finding that the tide of his anger was ebbing slowly away, leaving him feeling irritable and dissatisfied.

"Drop it, my loyal comrades," Doc whispered. "The child's overwrought and doesn't mean what she says. She could do with a rest. We all could."

"Don't want another night out in the open. Not with rattlers as big as war wags sliding around the brush. We gotta push on toward the ville, wherever that is. The smell of gas is stronger, and there was that air wag. We got to be close."

Ryan knew what he'd said was right. J.B. backed him for moving on. But the reality was that Lori and the freezie weren't in good enough shape to keep on trucking through the fading light.

So they compromised. They had seen that the edge of the arid mesquite region was fairly close. It was agreed that they would trek on for that and then find a place to camp, posting guards against the hazards of the night.

RYAN CURLED UP alongside Rick, hoping to find out a little more about what the freezie had done in his highly classified past.

"Wanna talk, Rick?" No answer. "Rick? D'you wanna talk some?"

The faint snoring and the heavy, regular breathing answered the question.

A violent chem storm raged during the night and some chunks of nuke debris came shafting from deep space, the detritus of the abortive Star Wars project of the 1980s that had finally circled back to its home planet, burning up in streaks of brilliant magnesium light.

The wind brought the heavy odor of gasoline from the greener land that lay ahead of them for the next day.

Ryan fell asleep thinking about a ville that owned so much gas. And so much power. It could be one hell of a place.

Chapter Fourteen

RICK GINSBERG DREAMED during that second night of his awakening.

During his student days at UCLA, he'd dropped some "farmies," as the new hallucinogenics were known. They took you one step sideways from reality, but you still kept in touch. Unless you got an "olly," as bad trips were called. He couldn't remember why they were known by that name. Something lost in the mists of the past.

Ever since he'd blinked his sticky eyes open in the chemical cold of the cryo center, Rick had felt like he was in the middle of the worst olly that anyone had ever known. His brain simply would not keep still. It had no stability. No sense of what was "then" or "when" or "now." During the brief battle against the huge thrashing snake, it had been like a psychodream. The six men and women were now his comrades. Maybe they were his friends. He sure as green earth hadn't ever had any friends like Ryan and the others before, assuming they weren't a figment of his own fervid brain.

That confusion ran through the muddle of his dreams.

A rabbi was talking to him, both of them sitting on bright green transparent chairs that floated in a huge swimming pool, the walls making everything shimmer and echo. The rabbi was fully dressed, but Rick was in a torn suit.

"The question, my son, is this," the rabbi said, smiling with an infinite wisdom. "Are you a man dreaming that you are a butterfly? Or are you a butterfly dreaming that you are a serpent? That is the eternal riddle, wrapped in mystery, shrouded in an enigma. What is the answer, Richard?"

"I am, therefore I stink."

"Wrong. Why do you flagellate me like this? What have I done to deserve it?"

The rabbi segued into his mother, weeping as she leaned on the enormous walnut sideboard that Uncle Maurice had given them.

Rick moaned and rolled over on his back, starting to snore. Ryan reached and nudged him into a half-waking movement, edging him into another dream.

Now he was in a dusty cornfield with his cousin Ruth. But Ruth had a tumbling mane of bright crimson hair, and she was leaning over his naked groin, her lips brushing at his swollen erection. In the background Rick could hear a brass band playing the theme music from *Paladin*.

"This is biblical evil," he said to Ruth, and she stopped, looking up at him, lips full, ripe and glistening.

"No. It's easily done, Richard. You just pick someone and then you pretend that you've never, ever met."

The freezie sighed, his hand fumbling toward his own cock, but the next dream interrupted him.

He stood outside the big brownstone block where his parents had lived, the one that a famous film star, Marilyn Monroe, had once lived in, they claimed. The sun shone very brilliantly and he could hear traffic on East River Drive, horns sounding and the far-off wailing of a fire siren, like the death wail of a demented dinosaur.

His mother and his father and all four of his grandparents stood in a formal row, all wearing Victorian clothes. Frock coats and frilled gowns. They were all nodding to him and smiling, as if he'd done something very clever.

His grandmother, Agnes Laczinczca, beckoned to him, crooking her finger. The bezel of the intricately cut diamond ring flashed.

"When you go to the store, Richard Neal," she said, "you must make sure you are wearing your overshoes."

"It won't rain," he squeaked.

"Not for the rain, babushka. To stop your feet rad-rotting when the missiles come. They'll kill us all. Mr. Kurtz, he already dead."

"In another country, Grandmama," he said.

"Shut noise and eat self-heat," Jak said, shaking him into a muscle creaking wakefulness.

"EVERYONE READY to go?" Ryan asked. "Cans buried out of the way? Good."

They didn't tidy up after themselves out of some inherited desire to maintain the environment. There were some kind of muties, particularly packies, that would follow anyone traveling through the Deathlands, trailing their discarded cans or packets.

"I'm feeling a bit better," Rick told them. "Not so stiff."

"You could use some new clothes," Krysty observed, pulling at a loose thread that dangled from the shoulder of the freezie's suit.

"Yeah. My Fifth Avenue's smartest doesn't stand up well to Sierra rocks and desert cactus. Should have bought a heavier duty cloth."

"Mebbe find something in the ville. Find something to trade."

"What's the money in Deathlands? Guess my American Express gold card isn't going to say more about me than dollars ever can. I heard you talk about 'jack.' What's that?"

"Jack changes from ville to ville. Lotta barons stamp their own coins. Print notes. Mostly only used in that ville. Some big barons got together and agreed their jack could be used in each other's villes." The Armorer thought for a moment. "Your times...jack was the same all over the country?"

"Right. A dollar was a dollar. That reminds me. When you found my clothes, did you find a wallet?"

"What's a wallet?" Lori asked.

"A kind of bag for your money, cards and driving license and... And my Filofax? Hell's bloody bells! My Filofax has gone! I can't live without my fax. What am I going to do? Come on, guys."

All of them, even Doc Tanner, gazed blankly at him. Jak asked the question for them all. "What's fullafacts? Some blaster?"

"No. Nobody could live without one in my day. And mine's gone forever."

"What was it, Rick?" Ryan pressed, fascinated by this glimpse into the lost past.

"Kind of a book that contained the names and addresses of my friends, phone numbers, appointments and all kinds of vital stuff."

"Why did you need a book to be telling you whose your friends are?" Lori asked.

"Because...I guess... I don't rightly remember that, Lori. And since there's now only six friends in the world, I don't need their addresses or names, do I? Guess not."

"DARK NIGHT!" J.B. exclaimed. "The smell of gas is getting double-strong. Got to be pumping it. Not just a big dump."

Ryan agreed with him. Faintly, carried on the wind, he thought that he'd caught the sound of drilling rigs. When he'd driven once across the east-west blacktops of what had been Texas, he'd seen the wrecks of the old oil pumps, perched across the dead prairies like the skeletal remains of ancient birds.

Jak, who was scouting at point, called back to them. "Blacktop here. Looks used. Kept good. Safe come on."

It headed in from the northwest, in the rough direction of the Pacific, looping to run eastward, toward where the scent of gasoline was strongest, toward where they could, at last, make out the smudges of buildings.

"There's a sign," Doc observed. "Perhaps we might go to peruse it."

Snakefish. Population two thousand and growing all the time. Gas sold and traded. Outlanders welcome.

Under that last part, someone had added, in a maroon acrylic paint: If they behave good.

"Better make sure we behave good." Rick grinned. "Looks like some things haven't changed. Strangers are fine, as long as they walk the line."

"Wrong," Ryan said. "Not many villes welcome outlanders. Doesn't matter how they behave."

"Xenophobic capital of Deathlands, you mean?"

Ryan didn't understand him, so he didn't bother replying.

"Someone's coming!" Krysty said suddenly. "Wags. That way." She pointed to the east.

They could hear a thin keening, humming sound, which was far off, but approaching fast.

"Air wag?" Jak asked.

"No. Different sound. Some kind of gas wag," Ryan replied, head to one side, considering what their best course of action might be.

"Two-wheeler," Lori said unexpectedly. "Had vids back in my redoubt. Keeper used to look for them. They was some of his faves. They was about two-wheeler wags. That's what the noise is being."

There weren't many two-wheel wags around Deathlands. They used up precious gas and you couldn't carry supplies on them or mount a blaster. A man on a two-wheel was about as vulnerable as a skinned armadillo.

"Lot of them," J.B. observed, as laconic as ever. "Take us some cover?"

Ryan looked around. The desert stretched behind them, dry and faded, the brush high enough for them to hide. But if they were tracked, then their chances would lie somewhere between zero and one on a scale of one hundred. The thought of what a single match could do with a breeze behind it was terrifying. Ryan had seen some bad fires in his life and didn't much want to find himself at the center of another one.

"We'll stand," he decided. "Keep ready, but nothing unless I give the order. We're travelers. Wag broke down three days ago, far side of the mountains there. Keep it vague."

The buzzing sound became louder. Krysty saw them first, with her heightened mutie vision. "Group close together," she said. "Around a dozen. Lot of sunflash off metal."

It wasn't long before they could all see them, riding down the center of the blacktop, where the white line would once have been.

"Keep together," Ryan warned quietly.

The motorcyclists came closer, and they could all see the morning sun bouncing off steel and polished chrome. They were riding in an arrowhead formation, and their leader held up a gloved hand when they were about a hundred yards off. He slowed, and the rest of the group swerved to left and right, ending up in a half circle around the seven friends, about twenty paces away from them. The riders kept their engines revving, twisting the throttle grips, giving Ryan and the others ample time to look them over.

Automatically the one-eyed man weighed the newcomers up as potential enemies. The odds were they wouldn't prove friendly: eleven, all males, aged from about eighteen to forty-five. Most were overweight, which was unusual in the Deathlands. Many were bearded and had long hair, tied back with ribbon. All wore heavy boots and blue denim in varying stages of filthy decay, with badges and patches painted or stitched on.

But the important items were the blasters. Most had either hand-built pistols, based on old Saturday night specials, or weapons with parts grafted together from other old blasters, .32 the most common caliber. Two had sawed-off scatterguns of uncertain vintage slung from their shoulders. Their leader packed a Smith & Wesson Model 29, with a nine-inch barrel, .44 caliber. From the battered appearance of the piece it looked like it had been used to hammer in nails and stir a caldron of mutton stew, neither of which would stop the killing punch of the blaster, if the man carrying it knew how to use it.

None of the bikers made any obvious threatening moves. Hands rested near holstered pistols while eyes raked the companions. The leader finally lifted a hand again and everyone cut their engines. The sudden stillness was deafening.

The two groups stared at each other for several long seconds, nobody wanting to break the silence. Finally Ryan spoke.

"Nice two-wheel wags," he said.

"Not wags, you straight double-stupe mother! They're our choppers."

"Choppers?"

Rick took a hesitant step forward. "Either my brain has now completely fallen apart in little splinters of sugared candy, or..."

"What?" Krysty asked.

"Or these guys are real, live Hell's Angels."

The man with the Smith & Wesson heard what he said. "One of you's got some sucking brains! Yeah! We're Hell's Angels. Snakefish Chapter of the California Motorcycle Gang. We call ourselves the Last Heroes. Riding the road and keeping the good word alive for today and forever."

"What's a Hell's Angel?" Lori asked, sucking at her thumb in a coquettish baby gesture.

One of the other riders answered her. "Yea, though we walk through the valley of the shadow of the dead, we fear no evil. Because we're the most evil mothers that ever walked through the valley of the dead."

Ginsberg nodded. "I did a sociology thesis on these guys. Well, I mean, not these guys. These guys weren't going to be born for fifty years when I wrote 'The Social Phenomenon of the Motorcycle Gangs: Macho or Myth?' I decided that they were about ninety-nine percent myth."

"What you saying about us, you four-eyed straight mother?"

Ginsberg stepped closer. "You've got the colors and . . . chopped hogs. Sissy bars. It all comes back to me, Ryan," he said excitedly.

"How come you know so much? You ain't from around these parts. You seen other chapters of righteous brothers, someplace else?"

The long-barreled Smith & Wesson was sliding slowly from the tooled holster.

"No. I read about you back in—"

"Enough, Rick," Ryan interrupted quickly. "Let's cut the talk. We're traveling through. We lost our wag three days back. Heading for Snakefish. There going to be some sort of problem here?" Ryan's hand rested on the butt of his automatic rifle.

"Problem, straight? Outlander comes in looking like he's in charge of a gang of mercies. Snakefish doesn't like mercies."

Ryan figured they could take all eleven out, but not without a minimal body count against them.

"Mercies?" Rick whispered.

"Hired blasters," Krysty replied. "Short for mercenaries."

"Wrong. We aren't mercies. I asked you once. I'll ask you one more time. Do we have a problem here?"

Now the Smith & Wesson was jerked clear of the holster. The leader of the cycle gang smiled at Ryan, showing a mouthful of broken teeth. "Problem? What the fuck do you think?"

Chapter Fifteen

"I THINK if there was a problem, there'd be some blood spilled," Ryan replied calmly.

"Could be right. Not mercies, you reckon?"

"No."

"What d'you want in Snakefish?"

"Bed and food for a couple of nights. Then I guess we'd be moving on."

"We're sec patrol for the ville."

Ryan nodded. "Figured that."

The Smith & Wesson was put back in the holster.

"You got names?"

Ryan introduced his six friends. The leader of the bike gang looked like he was concentrating hard. "You got all those?"

"Sure. Don't read or write much, but I got total recall." To prove it, he repeated the names of the group faultlessly.

"You got names?" J.B. asked.

"Yeah. I'm Zombie. Little guy with the beard's Priest. Fat brother's Riddler. Rat next to him. Mealy next."

Ryan looked at the faces behind the names, faces you saw in a dozen villes across the land. He'd read some about times before dark day, and had seen some faded vids. Old photos. Here they were. The same faces from the old pix. Brutish, redneck faces. Good old boy, shit-kicking faces. Narrow eyes that would never look friendly and would often look coldly vicious. Most had their names emblazoned across the backs of their denim jackets: Harlekin, Dick the Hat, Vinny, Freewheeler, Ruin, Kruger.

After the introductions there was an uneasy silence, which was broken by Doc.

"I would be most awfully grateful, gentlemen, if you could see your way clear to conveying a tiny piece of information. What's the distance to the nearest metropolis?"

"What?" Zombie gaped.

"How far t'ville?" Jak translated.

"Why dinne say so?" mumbled the Angel called Rat. "Stupe-straight!"

"Mile an' half," Zombie told them.

"Gas smell is strong," Ryan said. "You got a big plant in town?"

"Just outside the ville in an old fun park."

Rick Ginsberg coughed. "I used to be interested in theme parks and funfairs. Magic Mountain, Six Flags, Elitch Gardens and... what was this one called?"

"Sierra Sunrise Park. You know it?" Zombie looked suspicious.

"Heard of it. Built very late in the nineties. Nothing special."

"Special! It's where our chapter has its home!" exclaimed the rider called Dick the Hat. Since he rode bareheaded the name was something of a puzzle.

"Yeah. Last Heroes redoubt. You stay a few days in the ville, you could come see it," Zombie offered, addressing his words specifically to Lori.

Who grinned at him.

"Who's the baron?" Ryan asked.

"Baron Brennan, Edgar Brennan. Old guy. Been baron more years than anyone can remember."

Rick had another question. "Where did you get the choppers?"

"Me and some of the other righteous brothers came here around three years back. Kind of traveling on. Found a big old warehouse, way out beyond the edge of town. Part where folks said it was a hot spot. We got us a geiger. Warm, not hot. Orange, not red." Zombie laughed. "Folks been scared for nothing. It had been HQ for a chapter before the winters. Found it all. Hogs. Colors. Manuals. Rules. Kruger's best at reading so he told it all. We liked it. Good way of living. All rebels."

"What are you rebelling against?" Doc asked curiously.

To his surprise, the bikers answered him in chorus: "Why? What ya got?" Then they laughed at some obscure private joke.

Zombie, shaking with amusement, tried to explain. "There's this old vid, mostly rotted. It's about some real old chapter of brothers, way, way back. And someone asks that question. We all kind of know it by heart. You know."

"Sure. So, we'll meet up in the ville?"

"Yeah, outlander. We'll do that. And you better walk right or we'll bust your asses. Blasters or not. Right?"

"Hey!" said Riddler, the fattest and oldest of the gang.

"What?"

"How'd they get through the rattlers? They was lucky, Zombie."

"True, Riddler, true." He stared at Ryan. "You see any real big mutie snakes back in the brush there?"

Before anyone else could butt in, Ryan answered him quickly. "Snakes? No. Would've run a mile if we had."

The president of the chapter nodded solemnly. "Been your best bet. Touch one of those beauties and you count living in seconds."

"How come?"

"Baron runs the ville, right? He thinks he does. But Snakefish is built on religion. Snake religion and old-time religion. When you get to the ville you'll meet up with the Motes. Marianne and Norman and their boy, Joshua. That's where the power is in Snakefish. You know that and you walk right. Right?"

Ryan and his companions nodded dutifully.

Having butchered one of the ville's favorite pets wasn't likely to endear them to the folk who ran Snakefish.

At a signal from Zombie, the bike engines coughed into life, spitting great clouds of blue-gray smoke into the cool morning air.

As the Angels vanished into the distance, weaving from side to side of the blacktop, Rick sat down on the verge, whistling his surprise and relief. "Those are heavy dudes," he said. "You hear the way they talked? Like actors in some B-grade movie. Like they learned all that crap about Hell's Angels. But those bikes!"

Doc coughed again. "I have seen and read a little about these gangs of hoodlums. If they are the sec force, *and* if there are some religious leaders running the show, perhaps we should seriously consider returning immediately to the redoubt."

"Those bikes," Rick continued, ignoring Doc's suggestion, "are worth an arm and a leg. Well, back in my time they would have been." Zombie had the big Harley-Davidson, the Electra Glide. And some of the others had true classics, as well: a couple of British Nortons and a Triumph; an Indian Chief and a BMW 1000. Rick saw a 650 Yamaha, and the little guy with the scar on his arm had a beauty. It looked rusted and battered, through the chrome, but was still Bultaco Metralla. "You guys can't believe what some of those...I mean..." He shook his head in amazed disbelief.

Ryan was still thinking about what Doc had said. His own experience had been that the worst kind of ville was one where some sort of freak religion ran the place. Some cults had all kinds of taboos, and a man never knew he'd crossed one of them until he felt the knife opening his stomach.

"Thought about asking who ran the air wag," J.B. said. "Then I figured it could be best to keep zipped. Like on the snakes."

"Sure. You think we should head for the ville or back to the redoubt? If we didn't have the freezie in tow I'd say move back over the desert and into the gateway.''

The Armorer took off his glasses and squinted through them, wiping away specks of orange dust. ''Freezie'd never make it back up. Take two, three days. Guess those sec boys could be to the ville and here again in an hour. With more guys with blasters. Like you said, Ryan. Be some blood spilled.'' He perched the glasses back on his pale, sharp nose.

Krysty hooked her arm through Ryan's. ''My vote's for the ville. Not that I reckon we've got all that much choice. Do we, lover?''

''No. Snakefish, here we come.''

''WHAT'S THIS PARK PLACE the biker was talking about?''

Rick considered Ryan's question as they walked together toward the distant ville. ''Sierra Sunrise Park? I'm no authority on places like that. I only visited a few. I liked the white-knuckler rides, roller coasters and stuff, loops and spirals. Montezuma's Revenge. Demon's Triple. White-water rapids, flumes. Colossus. Giganticus. There was a ride at Sierra, but I can't quite... No. The name's gone. Sorry, Ryan.''

''Gas stinks,'' Jak exclaimed, hawking and spitting on the worn roadway.

''Ville must be rich,'' Lori said. She'd been oddly silent since the Angels had left them, walking on her own in long, swinging strides. Doc was panting, trying to keep up with her.

''I got me the feeling that those long-haired sec bastards don't much take to their baron,'' J.B. observed. "Place where we all have to walk soft and careful." He looked at Lori. "All of us."

Zombie and his gang were waiting for them when they finally reached the end of the main street of Snakefish, California.

Chapter Sixteen

"BARON WANTS to see you. We told him you came from the outlands. He asked if any of you was muties. Told him you didn't look like it, apart from that Jak Lauren. The kid with the snow hair and fire eyes. Never seen any norm like him."

"Don't call me 'kid,' you—"

"No, Jak," Ryan said with a biting voice of authority. "He's not a mutie. Comes from a family out east where they all had white hair. Nothing unusual about it."

Zombie shrugged. "Couldn't care a flying fuck, myself. Seven of you aren't going t'take over Snakefish, so where's the harm?"

They walked a little way into the ville, down a wide street. J.B. nudged Ryan and whispered, "Neutron."

"Gotta be."

The buildings looked like pix in old magazines, books and films. Since half of the old state now lay somewhere beneath the lapping waters of the Pacific Ocean, the nuking must have been both spectacular and total. The shops and houses looked to be in remarkably good condition. That meant the region had received neutron bombs, which effectively took out all human and animal life but left most structures standing.

There weren't many people around, and quite a few of the buildings were empty and boarded up. But Zombie hurried them along, the rest of the chapter flanking them, making it difficult to see too much of the ville.

In some villes the sight of a group of outlanders would have produced far more curiosity. And, often, hostility. But here there was a feeling of relaxation. Despite the bizarre escort on the polished and gleaming old two-wheel wags, Ryan felt reasonably secure. There were smiles and nods. Curtains twitched in some windows. It was weirdly like entering a time slip, back before sky-dark.

Rick had begun to mutter to himself again, looking around, stumbling in the ruts in the road. He shook his head in disbelief and confusion.

"Snakefish, California. John Doe, Main Street, Anytown, United States. Ice-cream parlor over there. Sixty-four flavors. Drug store. Book shop. Flagpole down the way, outside the town hall. Whoops, I nearly... I've gotta complain to the highways department. Too many potholes... too many to fill the Albert Hall. This is then, but that was now. Or now is then. Todays are the tomorrows that I worried about a hundred years ago." He turned to Ryan with a look of desperate, strained intensity. "I'm not crazy, am I, old friend? New friend? All this is like it was. Not like it is. Is it? Is it like this now?"

"Some places. Not many. This is one of the neat-est, cleanest villes I've ever seen. Doesn't mean it's safe, though."

The freezie wiped sweat from his forehead, calm-ing himself. "I know. A man may sit at meat and feel the cold in his groin."

"Sure."

"Beware the smiler with the knife beneath his cloak, Ryan."

"Oh, I always do, Rick. I always do."

Zombie slowed his hog in front of the building with the white-painted flagpole, from which a faded Stars and Stripes fluttered proudly in the pallid sunshine. The rest of the bikers ranged themselves alongside him in what looked like a carefully rehearsed maneuver.

"Baron's hall. He knows you're coming in with us. Just go on in."

A carved wooden sign told them that the building was Snakefish Town Hall, built in 1967 and reconsti-tuted in about the Seventieth Year after the Great Madness.

"I like that," Doc said. "Great Madness. I couldn't have put it any better myself."

They stepped across the sidewalk, up a path that ran between two beds of flowers. Pale yellow rosebushes. The grass had the regular green that came from steady watering. The smell of the roses did valiant battle with the sickly odor of the gas-processing plant they had glimpsed beyond the far end of the main street of the ville.

"This is crazy," Rick mumbled. "I feel like I'm a kid and I'm going to register at the town hall. This is crazy."

Double doors, painted white, swung open at the head of the flight of eight steps and a woman appeared. She was a little over average height, around thirty years old. Black hair bobbed at her shoulders, held in place with a dark purple comb. She wore a black jacket over a cream blouse, and pale fawn riding breeches were tucked into a pair of highly polished, knee-length black leather boots. She smiled at the ragged band.

"Welcome to Snakefish," she pronounced. "Baron Brennan's expecting you. Do come in."

"Who are you, lady?" J.B. asked.

"I'm Carla Petersen. You must be Mr. Dix, from Zombie's description."

Ryan glanced across at the Armorer. It must have been the reflected glow of the soaring sun, but he had the momentary illusion that his old friend was blushing!

They walked through the doors into the coolness of a wide hall with a sweeping staircase that curled up to the second floor. An elderly man in a dark blue uniform with gilt buttons was dozing at a desk near the door.

The woman led the way, heels clacking on the mosaic picture that showed, as far as Ryan could make it out, a girl carrying a sheaf of wheat, rising from the sea with a smile of simpering idiocy on her rosy, dimpled cheeks.

"You lost your wag, I believe, Mr. Cawdor?" Carla Petersen said, pausing on the wide landing for them to catch up. Rick trailed at the rear, panting with the effort of climbing.

"That's right. Three days, up in the hills."

"Where were you coming from?"

"South."

"And you were going . . . ?"

"North."

She smiled with a touch of frost. "Not a man to give too much away, are you, Mr. Cawdor?"

"Man who gives everything away finds he has nothing left for himself."

"True. Very true. Now, just along here. The third door."

Every now and again, throughout the Deathlands, Ryan had stumbled on places where neutron bombs had left buildings virtually untouched. The town hall of Snakefish was like that. Cold stone. Benches padded with worn green leather. Doors that had frosted glass in their top halves. And names painted in almost illegible gold leaf, with their jobs.

"Milius Haldeman, Registrar. Rowena Southwell, School Inspectorate. Crawford Fargo, Highways. Angus Wellson, Divorce Counselor."

She heard him reading the doors. "So many names and civic appointments, Mr. Cawdor. All dead these hundred years. The baron only uses a small part of the hall now. With around two thousand souls in the ville, the administration is kind of low-key."

She paused in front of a door, much like the others. Except that the gold paint was fresher. Edgar Brennan, Baron.

A voice responded to her brisk knock. "Come in, come in, said the mayor looking bigger and bigger and in did walk . . ."

Doc caught the wary look of bewilderment on everyone's faces. "Quoting an old poem," he whispered, "not mad."

The office of the baron was huge, with floor-to-ceiling windows on one side that opened onto a balcony and overlooked the desert. There was a threadbare strip of carpet covering a floor of wooden tiles. A massive bookcase ran the length of the wall on the left. But the glass doors were cracked and the shelves only held a half-dozen tattered and spineless volumes. There was a variety of unmatching chairs and a sagging sofa. The room was totally dominated by an enormous mahogany desk, which was buried with piles of paper, folders and files. It was just possible to make out the shadowy figure of Baron Edgar Brennan of Snakefish, lurking behind them.

"Greetings, gentlemen. And ladies. Come in, come in and sit down. Down."

Carla Petersen ran rapidly through the introductions. As with Zombie, Ryan was impressed with the way she remembered all of their names. The only one that she seemed to falter over was J. B. Dix.

They sat down, finding places among the chairs. Miss Petersen perched on the edge of a small table near the window, next to J.B.

"I would sit down as well, but I think I would vanish," Brennan said. "I'm a little deficient in the department of leg length."

Ryan had thought that the baron was already sitting down.

"Lost their wag three days, Edgar. Looking for food and lodging for two or three days before they move on."

"Lost their wag!" Brennan toddled around the desk and leaned against it. "To find a wag is lucky. To lose one smacks of carelessness. How come you lost your wag? Your wag?"

Ryan was so fascinated by the strange appearance of the Snakefish baron that his mind wandered off the question. "Lost...? Oh, a fire. Lectric short. Fire in the night. Burned out. In the hills."

"Didn't hurt any snakes, did you?"

"No. No, we didn't."

"Good, good, good."

Edgar Brennan was around four feet ten inches tall, a rotund and yet oddly dignified figure. He wore a shirt of dazzling white and a paisley cravat knotted around the throat. He looked to be somewhere in his late sixties. His pants were neatly pressed, his shoes polished to a mirroring gleam. As far as Ryan could see, Brennan wasn't carrying any kind of blaster, which made him kind of unique among barons of Ryan's acquaintanceship.

"We have a few rules hereabouts. Nothing too strict, I hope. Do you have a supply of jack? If you are outlanders here, I expect not. Expect not."

"Trade ammo," J.B. said. "Or mebbe we could work off a trade."

Miss Petersen leaped in. "That would be fine, Mr. Dix, just fine. This ville runs mainly on its supplies of gas. We are not a poor ville. Somewhat the reverse."

"Generous, I would hope. Yes, generous." Brennan's round little face creased into a smile. He gave a throaty chuckle. "We will lend a hand to any weary traveler, will we not, Carla?"

"We will, Edgar, though..."

A small cloud sailed into view and settled itself in a tiny furrow between the baron's eyes. "Yes, there is... Mustn't upset the... But a token of food and lodging for Mr. Cawdor and his comrades? Surely no objection to that." A sudden thought struck him. "Not mercies, are you? Mercies?"

"No," Ryan said simply.

"Where is Layton?" He turned to his visitors. "Layton is my nephew. My heir. I have never married, and he is now my only living relative. A series of accidents have... Accidents. Yes."

"Layton's out having lunch at the Qiksnak, Edgar."

"Course. Thanks, Carla. I didn't realize how time was passing. Passing. Lunch. Three eggs over easy with a double ham and hashies. Double slice of Mom's apple pie to follow. My nephew is a well-grown lad, folks. But kindly and brave. Only person in Snakefish who'd take up the air wag when it was found. Uses too much precious gas, but..." He smiled the smile of an indulgent uncle.

"Perhaps our visitors would care for something to eat?" the woman suggested, standing and moving toward the door of the office.

"Course, course, course. That's a three *course* meal, you see." He waited for the ripple of polite laughter at his small joke. "Give them each enough jack for a couple of days, Carla, my dear. They can stay at the Rentaroom. Have it charged to the civic friendliness fund."

His assistant hesitated. "There'll be a service, tomorrow, won't there? Might be best if they all turn up. Otherwise..."

"Otherwise the Motes could name them undesirable and then it would be a short walk into the sagebrush and a short encounter with Azrael and his brothers and sisters. Yes, they must attend. Tell them about it, Carla, there's a dear."

Outside the building everyone heard the angry whining of the two-wheel wags racing past. As the sound began to fade, a cloud of dust rose toward the window, pressing against the glass as though it sought admission.

"Come this way, folks," Carla directed brusquely.

"Thanks for the meeting, Baron," Ryan said. "And thanks for the kindness."

"Welcome, welcome, welcome." He beamed broadly.

OUTSIDE THE COOLNESS of the shadowy building, the sun struck like the slap of a glove. Doc coughed, doubling over, eyes popping like the stops on a mission harmonium. They waited for him to recover his breath a little.

"Sorry, my dear friends. A small piece of California dust found its way down into my aged windpipe, I fear. I'm better now."

"Breaking down, Doc," Lori said, but it was said affectionately, and she took his arm and kissed him on the cheek.

Carla attached herself to Ryan, glancing around to make sure that J.B. was also close to them.

"Rentaroom's cheap and clean. Not many visitors come to Snakefish. You'll have to check in any blasters, but not handguns. Never seen anything like that rifle, Mr. Cawdor."

"It's a G-12 Heckler & Koch. Fires caseless rounds. Saves a lot of weight and waste."

"Leave it at the desk. And that cannon of yours, Mr. Dix."

"Sure thing, Miss Petersen."

"Carla, please."

This time Ryan was absolutely certain. They were in the shade, but J.B.'s face definitely flushed.

"I'm J.B., short for John Barrymore. You can call me John, if you like, Carla."

"John!" Jak exploded, overhearing the conversation.

"Yeah, John! You want to make something out of this, kid?"

The Armorer stood, braced, his whole body fighting tense as he faced the boy. Ryan knew better than to interfere with J.B. on a matter of blood.

"You don't call me that," Jak said quietly, his right hand slithering toward the back of his belt, where he kept one of his throwing knives.

"Then button up about my name, Jak. Take my meaning? Just . . ."

The teenager grinned suddenly. "Sure, J.B., I understand. Real good."

"My goodness," Carla said. "That seemed to be rather a nasty moment."

"Just play," Krysty replied. "You get used to their ways."

CARLA LEFT THEM in the lobby of their small hotel, having made sure the rifles were checked in safely. Before going she'd called the seven friends around her for a last, urgent word.

"The baron is a beautiful old man, but his grip is not what it once was. There are those in Snakefish who whisper that he is too generous with the ville's gas. Too easy in trading with other villes in the area. He knows of the talk, but believes that his nephew will take over from him soon."

"What about the bikers?" Doc asked. "Those angels from hell?"

"They're the ville's sec patrol," she admitted, "but their hearts aren't with Edgar. They're allied with those who bring true power."

"The Mote family," Ryan asked.

"Yes." She dropped her voice even quieter, glancing around to ensure nobody could overhear. "Guard yourselves against the Motes, outlanders. And when you attend their service, take the greatest care. The greatest. If they perceive you as any sort of threat they can be quite ruthless.''

''I don't suppose there's any chance of something to eat now, is there?'' Rick asked plaintively. ''I'm famished.''

''Of course. Through that door into the eatery. Now I must go. Remember what I said. Take care with the Motes.''

Chapter Seventeen

"YOU CHOSEN?"

"Sorry?"

The thin lips parted for a moment, then snapped shut once the sentence had been hissed out. "You been saved?"

Ryan shook his head. "Don't think so. How would we know?"

The narrow face of Ruby Rainer, owner of the Rentaroom, broke into an approximation of a beatific smile. "I guess you'd know. You ever feel an inner heat?"

"No, not often. Except..." He looked across at Krysty, who struggled to conceal a giggle.

"I have," Rick said. "And I've seen light in the darkness. Warmth in the middle of winter. Floods during a drought. Manna in the wilderness. And salvation in the darkest night of the soul. Amen to that."

"Amen," Ruby added, clasping her bony hands to her even bonier bosom. "I'm well pleased to see that at least one of you outlanders has some spark of the Lord's blessings lighted within the lamp of his innermost heart."

"Hallelujah, sister," the freezie shouted, clapping his hands together. "And...?"

"Yes, brother?"

"Was there not some talk of a dessert to follow that admirable bowl of spiced stew?"

"Oh, oh, yes. Course. Pecan pie or some iced cream with strawberries."

She got orders for five pies and two helpings of the fruit with iced cream. After the dessert Ruby served them some acorn coffee, ground fine, with added herbs. "Best y'ever tasted," she boasted as she poured each of them a brimming cup.

Rick sipped suspiciously at his, pulling an appalled face. Fortunately Mrs. Rainer had left the dining room and didn't see, or hear, him.

"She call this coffee?" he asked.

"Yeah," Ryan said. "I've tasted better, but I've surely tasted worse."

"I recall once eating in a restaurant in some place like Bucksnort, Idaho. They served me a soup that was their special delicacy. I learned afterward it was made from dogs' spleens, with mustard added. Up till now that was the most foul thing that I ever tasted. Up till now..." He gently replaced the cup on the table.

After the meal Rick said he'd like to just go up to his room and rest. The others agreed that they'd split up and walk around Snakefish, checking the place out.

There was a minor spat when Lori tried to insist that she be allowed to go on her own.

"I'm not a shit-assed girly! I'm older enough to go without you having to hold my hand all the hours, Doc."

Ryan settled the argument. "Listen, Lori. Right now you're behaving like a double-stupe snotnose! In a strange ville like this nobody walks these streets alone. Not Doc. Not you. Not me. Stick together in pairs. Safest. Meet back here for the evening meal around six.''

''But I don't . . .'' she began, stopping herself when she saw the look of flaring anger on Ryan's face.

They went in the usual pairings: Lori with Doc, the sunnier side of her nature reappearing; J.B. and Jak wandering off together, intent on a recce of the gas-processing plant. And Ryan with Krysty.

''Snakefish,'' she said. ''Prettiest little ville in the west.''

It was just like walking into one of the small towns that Ryan had seen in old mags and vids. The lack of nuke damage was staggering. The sidewalk was clean, the shop fronts mostly looked like they had been painted fresh in the last month or so.

Uniquely there were several wags parked along the side of the street. Four pickups, one ordinary passenger vehicle, a blue VW and a panel van with a badly painted picture of a leaping salmon on its side.

''That's what living on top of your own gas supply does for you,'' Ryan said. ''That's why they all look so damned jack-heavy. Everyone wants gas. You got it and you name your own price in the trading stakes. Good place to be.''

They browsed along the sidewalk, staring in at the windows of the stores, amazed at the variety and quality of the various goods offered.

There weren't too many folks out and about— mainly women, with a few younger children. Everyone was polite and friendly in a distant, formal kind of way.

There was a sign in one window that read: Snakefish jack, one dollar to one dollar. Outsiders' jack, one-fifty to one Snakefish. Trade by agreement. Sorry, no credit. Don't even ask.

"Shows you how solid things are here," Ryan observed. "Two local dollars to three from outside the ville. Good trade rate."

Occasionally, if you found some isolated community that the nukes hadn't reached, you might find faded signs from before the big fires. In Snakefish it was different. The buildings were untouched, but everything they sold was new.

Practically everything. One establishment was retailing blasters. And most of those were rebuilds and recons from before sky-dark, like the handguns carried by the Angels.

The shop owner was a sharp-faced young man, and he came out to his doorway when he spotted them looking in his window.

"Hi there. You admiring the display? Some real good blasters there, huh?"

"No," Ryan replied, seeing no reason to lie about it.

"What? How d'you—"

"Cheap shit. Recons look like they'd blow your hand off first time you squeezed the trigger."

"I'll have you know that I engineered them myself and I—"

Ryan cut through the bluster. "Then you ought to try one out. Put the muzzle in your mouth and let the hammer down."

Krysty's fingers on his arm told Ryan that she thought he was going too far.

"They aren't that bad! Anyway, what are you carrying, stranger?"

Without speaking, Ryan unholstered the 9mm SIG-Sauer P-226 and showed it to the dealer.

"Hollow tooth! That's one . . . I could do you a real good trade on that, friend."

"I'm not trading, and I'm not your friend," Ryan replied.

"Two hundred Snakefish jack," the gun dealer offered eagerly.

"No."

"Three hundred?"

Ryan shook his head. "Not selling."

"Four hundred and any blaster out of my stock, and that's my last and best offer."

"I told you . . ."

"Let me see it?" He held out his hand. "I'll give you a great deal, or my name's not Honest John Dern. Gimme."

"Two people get to hold this blaster," Ryan said coldly. "Me, and the man that chills me. Nobody else. Right?"

"Right. Sure. If you change your mind . . ."

Krysty was laughing as they walked on. "Can't blame the stupe for trying, lover."

The wind had veered, and the smell of gasoline had weakened considerably. Ryan and Krysty quickly noticed that nearly every store and house in the small township seemed to carry some kind of a snake emblem in a window. Sometimes it was ornately carved from a twisted piece of wood, sometimes a more symbolic shape of plaited string or wool. Most of the totem figures carried a silver collar around the throat.

Apart from the town hall, the largest and most elegant building in the ville was at the farther end of the street. Through a coat of fresh paint it was still possible to make out the name: Rex Cinema and Video Palace. But it was put into the shade by the blaring and colorful lettering across the front.

Come One. Come All. Worship at the Shrine of the Blessed Serpents of the Apocalyptic Gospel of the Martyred Marcus the Peripatetic.

Beneath it was a sheet of card, under clear perspex, which listed the days and times of the services. There was one due the following morning at seven o'clock.

"Early bird gets the snake," Krysty observed.

"Unless it's the one we got first. Baron seemed to think we should go."

"Then we should," she agreed.

The last notice was on a wooden board, screwed to the front wall of the building: Guardians of the Sepulcher of the Sacred Snakes. Norman Mote. Marianne Mote. Apostolic Apprentice, Joshua Mote.

Beyond the old movie house the ville ended. The road just faded out into the semidesert, vanishing into a deeply rutted dirt trail.

They turned and looked behind them, from Main Street to the desert beginning, just past the elegant town hall. Snakefish wasn't more than a couple of straggling blocks wide.

"No gaudies?" Krysty said questioningly. "No drinkers, either?"

"Nope. Not like Mocsin, or some of the real heavy frontier pest holes. This is all clean and decent."

"Yeah. And they worship snakes, lover. Don't forget that."

Doc and Lori were just coming out of a clothes shop as Ryan and Krysty walked past them. The store was called Handmaid and featured a marvelous patchwork quilt in the window, made of hundreds of tiny pieces of colored satins and silks.

"Spend any of your Snakefish jack, Lori?" Krysty asked.

"Nice skirt in there, but old miserable Doc said it cost too many."

"It was beautiful," Doc admitted ruefully. "Segments of lace, some old and some new, all stitched together, and it was kind of transparent. I fear that it cost more jack than we got in total and I decided that the garment would have lasted about zero seconds in the brush."

"Wouldn't have worn it out in sand, would I?" she pouted. "It was so pretty, Doc. I don't wear anything pretty now."

"One day, my dearest and most cuddlesome little dear one."

"Dear one, dear one, dear one," she mimicked, half-angry. "When's that?"

"Tomorrow. Always tomorrow. But one day, I promise you, Lori, it *will* be tomorrow. I shall allow you to make an honest man out of me."

She flounced away from him, head in the air, leaving Doc with Ryan and Krysty.

"Should tan her ass, Doc," Ryan suggested.

Doc sniffed. "She's just seventeen, if you know what I mean, and the way that . . . I'm sure that used to be a song, once. Or I'm a poet and I don't know it. No, the girl's growing up and she's growing away. You can't cage the wind, Krysty. And I would never try."

"Want to walk back to the rooming house, Doc?"

"Thank you, Ryan. Good friends are a consolation against the grievous rigors of this parlous world. And I do appreciate your great kindness toward me. But I must walk that lonesome highway by myself."

"Keep away from the snakes!" Krysty shouted as the old man wandered slowly away.

ONE PLACE that fascinated Ryan was a store selling memorabilia. Predark was its name. The window was dusty and the interior badly lit, despite the ville's electrical power, all of it provided by a huge gas-fired generator on the edge of town.

"Let's go in."

There was a brass bell above the door, and it tinkled like Lori's spurs as they pushed it open. It was a warm day, with dark chem clouds stippling the tops of the Sierras. Inside the store it was humid and quiet, the silence broken only by the ticking of a tall grandfather clock in the corner.

"Good afternoon, strangers. Come into my little cave of riches with a good heart. Be at peace with all men. Gentle be the selling and the buying and could you shut that coil-bound door?"

The last seven words were uttered in a raised voice laced with anger.

Krysty hastily pushed it closed, making the bell jingle once more.

"Keeps out the scale-blasted flies, you understand. Can I help you outlanders to any small curio or other?"

"This stuff all come from before the long winters?" Krysty asked, brushing the dust of the street from her long, fiery hair.

"Indeed. Much of Southern California took the big plunge into the Cific, down the Andreas. Lot of neutrons around here. My father and me been collecting since then. I pay packies to go scouring the old gulches and ghost villes."

At last he stepped out from the darkness, sliding through a curtain of clear glass beads that clicked softly.

The man was in his late fifties and wore a loose shirt, hand-woven in varying shades of purple and green. He sported old-fashioned glasses with lenses tinted a very deep blue, and he held his head on one side like a querulous parrot.

"I do not see well. An accident in a warm spot that became hot without my noticing it. Corneal damage, I believe. That is why I keep my humble establishment a touch gloomy. It pains me less."

"Mind if we look around?"

"Course not, Mr. Cawdor."

"How'd you name my name, Mr...?"

"Zombie and his two-wheelers help me in finding items for my store. He described you very well. My name is Brennan. Yes, the same as Baron Edgar. He is my brother. His nephew, Layton, is my grandson."

It seemed like he was going to go on and say more. Maybe a lot more. But a shadow fell across the window and he turned like a startled hare, taking three steps back to the shelter of his beaded curtain.

"It's all right," Krysty reassured him. "Friend of ours. Rick Ginsberg. Hey, Ryan. Looks like he's been laying out some jack on clothes."

The bell chimed thinly as the freezie entered the shop cautiously. "That you, guys? Thought I saw you from the bedroom. I changed that old suit for something more practical. Laid out most of my cash...I mean jack."

He was wearing a pair of faded Levi's, tucked into ankle-high hiking boots with studded soles, a washed-out work shirt in light brown and a heavy-duty quilted jacket.

"How do I look?"

"Hell of a lot better, Rick," Ryan said. "Could find the going warm in that coat. But, yeah, make life easier for yourself when we get moving again."

"Mr. Ginsberg," the shopkeeper said, "I'm Rufus Brennan. Welcome to my store. Browse around and hope that you will be guided to what is right and fitting for you."

"You never owned a jewelry store down near Fisherman's Wharf in San Francisco, did you?" Rick asked.

"No. Those names are not familiar to me. Why do you ask?

"Just the way you do the sales pitch. But let it pass."

"Let's look around some," Ryan suggested. "Then we can get back and see how J.B. and Jak have been doing. You feeling okay, Rick?"

"Sure. It's just that seeing all this stuff from... We'd have said most of this was plain junk. But it's a time warp. Walking down the street here with the houses and the stores...similar but not the same. No, not the same at all."

He took off his spectacles and began to polish them furiously.

Predark wasn't a very large store, but it was crammed with all manner of memorabilia. One corner was filled with childrens' toys and games. Creatures with names like Care Bears and Dumpyloves, and comp-controlled dolls that would do everything except make people love you. There were plastic figurines that you could move and place into stiff poses. They all had incomprehensible names such as Hutch and Fonzy and Indiana and most seemed to come from places with strange, Oriental names.

There were all sorts of souvenirs. Ryan guessed people must once have collected them to remind themselves of places they'd visited. Disneyland was one that he'd heard of. Tuckaluckahootchie Caverns was one that he hadn't.

One table held a dozen different kinds of telephones. Ryan picked up one that was made to look like a droopy white dog. "You got working transceivers in the ville?" he asked.

"No. Few years back my brother tried to get one installed. Not much interest. Folks figured that Snakefish is such a small ville you could lean out on your porch and shout to most everyone that you wanted."

Krysty was fascinated by an intricate metal tool with prongs, spikes and cogwheels. "Gaia! What's this do?"

Rufus Brennan sniggered. "That used to have a little box, but it was all raggedy. But I know what it was—for coring an avocado—and if you twist that button it will remove the seeds from grapes. Kind of useful, isn't it?"

Krysty laughed, tossing her hair back. Even in the gloom it danced and burned with a living fire. "Useful? I'd rate it about level with a glass scattergun on the useful scale."

"Hell's bloody bells!" Rick exclaimed from the side of the store, where small ornaments and books were piled.

"What've you found?" Ryan asked.

"My past, Ryan. This book. Poems and short stories of Edgar Allan Poe. I had this given to me as a school prize when I was about eleven, around 1981. Scared the shit out of me with its pictures and the creepiness of—"

"Did your friend say he was eleven years old in 1981?"

"No," Ryan said. "He didn't. And if you started talking around about how he did, then it might not be a great idea. Man could get himself hurt with bad hearing. You understand me, Rufus?"

"You can put the blaster back, Mr. Cawdor. I understand you. But if anyone else around the ville misheard when your friend was born it might be harmful. Do *you* understand me?"

For a moment Ryan considered icing the store owner. Questions about Rick would lead to questions about the rest of them. Where have you come from? Where exactly did you leave your wag? How did you get here?

Not the kind of questions that outlanders welcomed in a small ville, however friendly some of its inhabitants might be.

He looked at Brennan for a dozen heartbeats. "Yeah. I understand. Guess we might both take some real good care."

Krysty tugged at the sleeve of his jacket. "Ryan! Look!"

Rick Ginsberg, the dusty, leatherbound book open in his hands, had sat down on the floor. His eyes were wide and staring, and gobbets of tears coursed down his cheeks. Ryan could see he had been looking at an illustration of a large black bird. Rick's lips were moving and he kept repeating the same word.

"Nevermore," he said. "Nevermore. Nevermore."

Chapter Eighteen

IT WAS A COLD EVENING in Snakefish.

Only Doc and Lori had eaten in the dining room of their boarding house. The others had taken their suppers upstairs on trays, all sharing the room where Rick lay in a frightening, almost catatonic trance. He still held the Edgar Allan Poe book. Ryan had tried once to remove it from his hands, but the freezie had wailed like a lost soul and tried to bite him on the wrist.

There had been little time for Ryan to debrief J.B. and Jak. Rufus Brennan had been the soul of kindness and discretion, helping Krysty and Ryan to carry the weeping man across to the Rentaroom, bustling him up the stairs before too many prying eyes could see him.

There was a log fire laid in the grate, and the Armorer had used a pyrotab to get it blazing, filling the curtained room with bright, crackling heat.

Despite that, Rick didn't seem able to stop himself from shivering. His fingers opened and closed and his teeth chattered together. They'd decided to leave on his newly purchased clothes, piling on a couple of blankets for good measure. Doc had asked Ruby Rainer to send up an enamel pot of hot, sweetened tea, explaining that their friend had suffered something of a shock and needed to be kept warm.

The woman had been eager to help, offering her prayers and wondering whether the accident might prevent poor Mr. Ginsberg from joining everyone at the service the next day.

After she'd been ushered from the room, Ryan turned to J.B. "Find anything out?"

"Sure. Friendly folk. Talk to you about everything. Just as long as it's the weather or are we comfortable with Ma Rainer here. Soon as you ask them anything about how the ville's run and how the gas is produced and processed and traded..."

"And mouths clam like snap trap," Jak concluded, locking his fingers to demonstrate what he meant.

"See the plant?"

"Sure, Ryan. No guards. Drillings are all to the east and north. Brought in tank wags. Pumped and then purified. Stored in all kinds of barrels and tanks. Kind of careless. So much gas there that a single burner gren would set half the country on fire."

"Saw bikers again. Zombie and others," Jak said. "Said could ride with 'em. Mebbe after snake service tomorrow. Seem okay."

Ryan glanced at the Armorer, seeking confirmation of the young boy's judgment of the Last Heroes. But J.B. pursed his lips and said nothing—which was as good as saying everything.

At that moment their attention was taken by Rick.

The freezie had begun to talk in a quiet, confidential sort of way, but in a voice quite unlike his natural

PLAY THE
LUCKY CARNIVAL WHEEL

scratch-off game
and get as many as
FIVE FREE GIFTS...

HOW TO PLAY:

1. With a coin, carefully scratch off the silver area at right. Then check your number against the chart below to see which gifts you can get. If you're lucky, you'll instantly be entitled to receive one or more books and possibly another gift, ABSOLUTELY FREE!

2. Send back this card and we'll promptly send you any Free Gifts you're entitled to. You may get brand-new, red-hot Gold Eagle books and a terrific Surprise Mystery Gift!

3. We're betting you'll want more of these action-packed stories, so we'll send you six more high-voltage books every other month to preview. Always delivered right to your home before they're available in stores. And always at a hefty saving off the retail price!

4. Your satisfaction is guaranteed! You may return any shipment of books and cancel any time. The Free Books and Gift remain yours to keep!

NO COST! NO RISK!
NO OBLIGATION TO BUY!

tones. It was a thin, piping little voice, like a young child's. And there was even the hint of a childish lisp to it.

"I'm eleven years old in three weeks. My full name is Richard Neal Ginsberg and I was born March 22, 1970. I live in New York City, which is in New York State, which is the best of all the United States of America, the land of the free."

There was a peculiarly monotonous quality to the speech, as though Rick had learned it by heart and was pattering through it.

"I have a pet turtle who's real old and lives all the time with his head buried in the mud of his tank, and his name's Tricky Dicky. I guess he's real boring. My Dad's name is Jack Ginsberg, and he worked as an accountant in a big office on Sixth Avenue. Mom's name is Naomi and she doesn't do any work. She's like a housewife."

"Little prick," Krysty whispered. "I read about that sort of male attitude. Doesn't do any work!"

"I play softball and I watch football and I like the New York Giants best of all. When I grow up I'm going to be a quarterback and pitch for the Yankees and maybe also work as an accountant. I haven't decided yet but I'm real good at math."

Doc and Lori came into the room, closing the door behind them. They stood at the foot of the bed, listening to the ramblings of the freezie.

"Looks fucking stupe," Lori said. "Look at his eyes all staring."

"I fear our newly thawed comrade has regressed to his childhood," Doc observed sadly. "It was always something of a gamble. I had been delighted with how well he had coped with his blind leap into our future. But now I see how fragile his hold on our reality is."

"Reality sandwiches," Rick said, a tremulous sickly smile clutching at the corners of his bloodless lips. The fingers of his left hand played with the frayed edge of the gray blankets while his right hand kept its deathly grip on the leather-bound volume of Poe.

"What if I deck him, Doc?" J.B. asked. "Short right cross to the point of the jaw. Could snap him out of it?"

"Could snap him further into it," Ryan said dryly. "How about if we get some sleepers from the woman? Feed him some of those and mebbe he'll be fine when he comes around?"

Rick seemed able to hear what was being said and somehow translate it into fragments from his past. "Round and round the little wheel goes and where it stops nobody knows. Not me and not my mom or my dad. Nor my beloved grandmother, Agnes Laczin-czca. She's a wise woman. Witch of the west. She lives somewhere over a rainbow in Kansas, bloody Kansas." A cunning smile flitted across his face. "Shouldn't say that. Bloody. Get my mouth washed with soap and water. Bloody bastard. Fuck and prick." He giggled.

"Got do something, Ryan," Jak said. "Crazy as sun-blind gator."

"Yeah," Ryan agreed. "Sure. Do something. Anyone got any ideas?"

"Rambo. Bimbo." Rick sniggered. "Dumbo Crambo. Wilco. Dildo."

"I could... I've never really tried to do it for anything like this, but Mother Sonja taught me ways of using the force of the Earth Mother for healing. Setting a mind to peace. I could try."

"Try it, lover," Ryan said, kissing Krysty on the cheek.

"Rest of you go out. Got to have privacy and quiet for this."

Doc nodded. "It could work. In my day I was known as something of an apostle of alternative medicine."

"Out, Doc," J.B. said, leading the way. "I'll give you a game of Kiowa if we can get a deck of cards."

The others followed, with Ryan bringing up the rear. Rick was still chattering away to himself on the bed.

"The premature burial. That was always my fear. My terror. To slip into a coma and yet not be dead. Folks not realizing that I still lived. Breathing slow, but living." The voice had changed, had lost the infantile flatness. Now it held more of Richard Ginsberg's normal tones. But it was oddly without inflection, as if the words were strung together by a computer, with no sense of emotion at all.

"I'll go, lover," Ryan whispered. "Next door. You want any help, just bang once on the wall and I'll be in here."

"Sure. Could take some time."

The freezie's words danced over and around them, plaited with an old, sad madness.

"The box closing. Eyes shut but still seeing. The softness of the silken shroud embracing the cold skin. The lid lowering. A loose thread of cotton trailing against the corner of your mouth. Tickling you, for all eternity. A spider, buried with you, seeking somewhere to spin its web and lay its eggs." A shudder racked the man's body. "In your ear, burrowing inward. Gestation. Birth. A thousand tiny spiders, eating inward. Into your living brain. Living and feeling but paralyzed and helpless."

The door shut behind Ryan, and Krysty sat on the bed, reaching to hold Rick's palsied left hand in both of hers. "Be all right," she said. "Quiet and easy, brother. You got so much pain inside you, Rick. Gotta let it out of you."

"Locked in the box. One time around then they put the lid down on you. John said that. John Stewart. Said that. He didn't know what it was like. My body trapped me. Locking and tensing and falling and the tiredness. Bells of hell, the tiredness. I wanted to rest and get away. That's why I agreed to let them do it to me. Knew it wouldn't work. Didn't care. The gateways being used for war. Instant soldiers here and there. Oh, fuck! I hated that. Lock the lid down on the box. Goodbye to pain forever. Then they woke me up. Woke me healed and new. Not now. Not ever. Nevermore. Nevermore."

Krysty systematically began to clear her mind, using the techniques that her mother had taught her, long ago in the ville of Harmony.

When Krysty was under great stress she was able to harness the Earth power, giving herself a cataclysmic strength for a few moments. But using it drained her for hours after. This was different—the healing way had nothing to do with dissolution.

She focused on a sky of untouched blue, a river foaming over silver rocks, imagining the water washing away all pain and anguish. She gripped Rick's hand more tightly.

"I hear the slamming of the lid. My heart beating, louder. How can they not hear it? My nails break against the implacable dark wood. Blood warm down over my palms, my wrists. Muscles straining, helplessly and utterly without hope. Oh, the tigers that come in the dead of night! Help me, help me. The sibyl said she wished only to die."

Ginsberg was talking more and more slowly. Krysty was weeping, not aware of her own grief, tuning in to his bone-cold sorrow, trying to tap it and divert it. She looked for sparks of light within the bleak world that might illuminate and carry hope.

"Come out of it, Richard," she said, lips barely moving.

"Trapped in my crippled body in a twisted, demented time," he moaned, fingers tightening on her hand.

"No." She drew on some lines that her mother had made her learn. "There is a wind on the heath, my brother. Life is very sweet. Who would wish to die?"

"Everyone I loved is dust," he said quietly, the words hardly disturbing the warm air in the small room.

"We all will be, Rick. One day. You and me and Ryan and everyone. Today's baby is tomorrow's dust. Live while you can, Rick. Live and live and live."

His eyes had been staring at the roughly plastered ceiling. As Krysty looked at the freezie, his face grew calmer. His gaze dropped, settling on her face. His breathing steadied, and there was something like the frail ghost of a normal, sane smile.

"Krysty Wroth, I believe?"

"Richard Neal Ginsberg, isn't it?"

"Guess it is."

"Good to have you back," she said, feeling the strain of drawing the demons from the helpless man's soul.

"Didn't much care for the places I've been. Too damned dark."

"It's dark out, Rick."

"Light in here. Light and warm, Krysty. I feel real tired."

"Yeah. Me too."

RYAN HAD BEEN SITTING with the others, relaxing, half-asleep.

After an hour had slipped by he sighed and stood, stretching, feeling the muscles around his ribs tightening as he moved. "Just going to take a look," he said.

As he stepped into the corridor he nearly jumped out of his skin. His fist clenched and he began a lethal, crushing blow to the bridge of the nose, checking his punch in time, inches short of the sharp, quill-like nose of Ruby Rainer.

"Shedskin!" she exclaimed, stumbling back, hands waving at the air. "You were going to hit me, Mr. Cawdor!"

"No, ma'am," he replied. "If I'd been going to hit you, then I'd have done it. Not a good idea to creep up on a person like that, Mrs. Rainer. Could lead to a nasty accident."

She recovered a little, brushing at her print apron, running a finger along the top of the bannister rail, checking it for dust. "That girl, Rosemary! She never cleans up... But that wasn't what I came up to see about."

"And what was that?"

"Is Mr. Ginsberg recovered? I hope he'll be at the seven o'clock service on the morrow. It would be *such* a disappointment if he missed it."

"Just going to check. I hope we'll all be there."

He watched her go slowly down the stairs before he eased open the door and peeked in. Rick Ginsberg lay fast asleep on his bed, breathing peacefully. Krysty slept at his side, holding his hand.

Ryan smiled and very quietly closed the bedroom door.

Chapter Nineteen

"Blessed is the worm!"

"And blessed are the scales thereof!"

"Blessed be the fang!"

"And the hollow needle!"

"Blessed is the crushing and the coil!"

"And blessed are the rattle and the skin of the great worms!"

"The Lord loves the worms of the earth and all that crawl and sting."

"As we do also love them!"

"The poison shall harm only the ungodly and the righteous sacrifice!"

"And the innocent shall walk untouched through all the lands of Canaan."

"As it was in the beginning, before sky-dark and long winter, is now and ever shall be. Our world, never ending. Amen!"

"Amen," came the echoing chorus from the huge congregation that brimmed along every bench and pew in the Temple of Snakefish, formerly the Rex Cinema and Video Palace.

One of the twin guardians, Norman Mote, had just finished the introductory call-and-response part of the

7 a.m. service. Marianne sat at his side, with their son Joshua, the apostolic apprentice, next to his mother.

At a rough count, Ryan reckoned that virtually all the adult population of the trim little ville was there, crammed together, cheek by jowl.

It was swelteringly, sweatingly hot inside the building.

Ruby Rainer had shouted up the stairs, a few minutes after six, asking if they wanted some fresh-baked cornbread with eggs and grits before coming along to the service. They had all accepted, though Rick made heavy weather of the meal.

The freezie was looking better, like someone who had been through the fire and come out the other side purged and cleansed by the experience.

He'd walked with the others along the bustling main street to the church, helped by an old bamboo cane with a curved handle, which had been a gift from their landlady. "It was my late husband's," she'd said. "He got it from his uncle, who found it in a ruined shack up beyond the north-forty well. You're welcome to take it, Mr. Ginsberg."

Ryan had rarely seen so many people gathered together in one place.

Baron Edgar Brennan sat in the front pew, on the right with his brother Rufus. An enormously fat young man sat next along. Ryan figured he must be the nephew, Layton, pilot of the air wag. He was dressed in a suit of dark blue leather and was so large that it looked as though the bench seat might tip up if anyone else stood. The last of the worshipers in that privileged pew was Carla Petersen, who had changed her riding breeches for a pleated skirt, but was otherwise wearing the same clothes as when they'd met her in the town hall. She had turned around as Ryan led his group in, favoring them with a smile. A smile that seemed, to Ryan, to be directed rather more at J.B. than at the rest of them.

There were no children in the congregation. No one showed undue interest in the outlanders as they were shown to a bench on the left, about halfway from the front.

Zombie and his biker brothers acted as stewards, marshaling everyone into their seats, making sure that there was no smoking. They eventually lined up near the altar, looking like sec bouncers at a particularly unsalubrious gaudy house.

Ryan had been particularly interested in seeing what the Mote family looked like. Before the festivities had begun, during the period of waiting for their arrival, he had studied the inside of their strange church.

There was a large balcony toward the rear, which had been extended more recently to run around both sides of the old theater. The altar was on a dais, between old and faded curtains decorated with huge, golden tassels. The chairs for the members of the Mote family were more like thrones, covered in gilt and crudely carved in ornate, writhing snake shapes. The rear wall, behind the platform, was obscured by a bright mural.

"Delicate, isn't it, lover?" Krysty whispered, seeing where Ryan's eye was focused.

"Sure. Like having a war wag run over your face is delicate."

The painting centered on an absolutely massive mutie rattler. Bigger by far than the one that they'd butchered out in the desert, it had a silver collar with the name Mote blazoned across it in scarlet. In its jaws was a diminutive figure that was kicking its legs. There was a 3-D holo effect built into it that made the head swing hypnotically from side to side and the tiny feet wave helplessly.

Around the edge of the picture were a number of oil-drilling rigs, vanishing away into a distance that was blurred by a poor perspective. At the very edge there was a crude version of the Sierras, snowcapped, tumbling out of the mural.

The colors were extremely basic—glaring greens and crimsons, with sickly yellows and a sky of an eye-blinking and unreal blue.

Ryan's ruminations stopped suddenly when he realized that the prayers were over and Norman Mote was about to speak.

He stood a little above average height and weighed about two-forty. He looked to be in his mid-fifties, the mane of sculpted hair a uniform silver gray. His suit was also in light gray, skillfully cut to conceal his spreading waist and stubby legs. He had the puffy eyes of a regular and long-time drinker. The hands that gestured from behind the reading stand were soft and white, with manicured nails.

Norman Mote's voice was calm and friendly, warm and welcoming. Ryan immediately disliked and mistrusted the man.

"Mah dear, dear friends," he began, smiling broadly around the packed building. "Welcome to our little morning get-together. Blessed is the worm!"

"And blessed are the scales thereof," responded the congregation.

Jak was sitting to Ryan's right. He put his face closer and whispered, "Fucked if find chilled their double-best god, huh?"

Ryan nodded. There hadn't been any choice in chilling the giant mutie rattler, but that might not go down well if anyone in Snakefish found out about it.

Mote continued to smile around, rubbing his hands together in an odd washing motion. Ryan heard Doc whispering something about the perfumes of Arabia, but he didn't get the reference.

"We have new brothers and sisters to welcome to our humble gathering," Mote continued. "I will ask them to introduce themselves to us, one by one. Perhaps, Mr. Cawdor, you would care to begin to do the honors for us?"

"Sure, Reverend. Name's Ryan Cawdor and I'd like to thank the kindly ville of Snakefish for helping me and my friends."

"I'm Krysty Wroth and I'd like to back up what Ryan said. Thanks."

Norman Mote held up an imperious hand. "Such thanks do credit. But there are those in the ville who think that generosity begins at home. Too much kindness to those from outside means less wealth for those within Snakefish."

"Wealth isn't all," someone countered from the front of the congregation. Ryan was sure it was Baron Edgar Brennan or his brother, Rufus.

"Some say, some say," Marianne Mote called from her golden throne.

It was the first time she'd spoken, but the co-guardian of the temple made a big impression, just by sitting there.

She was short, struggling to make four-ten. Marianne was also struggling, by the look of her, to keep her waist down under forty inches. She wore very heavy makeup, which made her look like an aging gaudy queen. She was dressed in a loose, rustling gown of what was either snakeskin or a very clever imitation of it. And her belt was silver, like the collar that Ryan remembered all too clearly from around the throat of Azrael. She wore shoes with totteringly high heels. The piled-up hair was of a shimmering blond color—obviously a wig. Marianne Mote was one of the finest bits of mutton dressed as lamb that Ryan had ever seen.

Her eyes had the flat, incurious dullness of a killer shark.

Norman turned to her and gave a slight bow, moving to face the congregation once more. "I must apologize to everyone here in the name of the Great Worm for the interruptions. Pray carry on introducing yourselves, outlanders."

"John Dix. Good t'be here."

"Jak Lauren. Same."

"Richard Neal Ginsberg. I'd like to say that I appreciate the kindness shown to me personally. Good to see strangers treated so well. Thank you."

"Lori Quint."

"Theophilus Algernon Tanner." Doc bowed deeply to everyone around him and glanced up at the people in the balconies. "I've been to a lot of places and have seen a lot of things, which is better than seeing a lot of places and being a lot of things. I guess." The old man shook his head disappointedly. "Not tuned in for my kind of humor. Well, let it pass. So it goes. I'll simply add my own gratitude to those of you who've been kind to us."

He sat down and Norman Mote clapped his hands together, very softly and gently. "We thank you all, brothers and sisters. We trust that in the days to come you'll all find some way of putting back into Snake-fish what you're taking out."

"Most generous little ville in the west," Krysty whispered sarcastically.

The service was complex and long. There were innumerable readings and prayers, not all of them centering on snakes. But most of them did. Some of the religious elements were more traditional, with hymns that were more recognizable. But again and again either Norman or Marianne Mote returned to the reptilian theme—coiling, striking and crushing.

Their son, Joshua, preached a short sermon, which he read with stumbling difficulty from a series of large cue cards. He was in his early twenties, had sagging, unhealthy skin and puffy eyes, and wore a shirt of pale blue silk and a neck thong holding a large, polished nugget of turquoise. He was barefooted. Blond curls peeked out from under the brim of a black Stetson-style hat. His voice was faltering and high-pitched.

His reading was a supposed parable about a family who owned a lot of wheat but gave so much away that they began to run short and suffer themselves for their generosity.

"For wheat, read 'oil,' I guess," Ryan whispered to Krysty.

Swiftly becoming obvious was the extent to which the ville was divided. Baron Brennan had seemed a friendly and generous old man, but the roots of a long-buried bitterness were becoming exposed. And it was also becoming clear that the baron's hold on the power in Snakefish was as nebulous as the dew upon a summer pasture.

Joshua finished his reading and sat down again on his chair.

"Before our final prayer for the morning," Norman Mote announced, "I shall give out one or two important notices."

Ryan saw that there was a strip of wooden carving above the stage. The lettering, deeply incised and in shadow, was difficult to read. By putting his head on one side he was able to decipher it: The Ophidian Way Is the True Way.

"What's ophidian, Doc?" he muttered.

"Means to do with snakes. That's all," came the reply. "From 'ophis,' a snake in Greek."

"Please shut down on the talking during services, Brother Ryan," Norman Mote called with the sweetest and most conciliatory smile, a smile that fell a good few miles short of reaching his eyes.

"Sorry, Brother Norman," Ryan replied.

"The notices. Sister Laurentia is holding a clambake on Thursday next. Three in the afternoon, is it not, Sister? I see her nodding in the balcony there. Praise the Worm, Sister."

A faint "Amen" filtered down from the gallery above them.

"Some bad news. Zombie has reported to me that the base on the fringes of Death Valley has been raided twice more by stickies. I shall be talking to Baron Edgar to find out what he intends to do about this further incursion to our gas supply." There was a buzz of chatter. Ryan was able to see that Edgar Brennan was talking animatedly to Carla Petersen and to his nephew, Layton.

"Go chill the coil-bound mutie bastards!" someone yelled from the back. Ryan would have laid jack that it was the gun dealer, John Dern.

"Amen, amen to that, brother," Mote called, lifting his hands for quiet. "One more thing. At feeding last night, there was no sign of our beloved Azrael. Belial and the others came to the call, but not Prince Azrael himself."

"Could be shedding, Pa," Joshua Mote hissed from the rear of the platform.

"No, Apostolic Apprentice Joshua, no. It is the wrong time for Azrael to shed. No. It has happened before that he has missed a feeding."

"Maybe caught him a juicy stickie," Marianne Mote suggested.

"Maybe, my dearest. Maybe that. Anyway, I'd like eyes and ears kept open for any news of Azrael Twelve. That's all. We'll end on our usual prayer, brothers and sisters. Let us pray."

There was a series of pattered responses, similar to those that had opened the service. A final, swelling "Amen," and it was time to leave.

As they filed out, there was a double line of the Last Heroes, standing *so* casually out in the bright morning sunshine. Zombie caught Ryan's eye.

"Reverend Mote'd like a word, brother. His room at the back."

"I'd like to go and see him." He turned to the others. "Be out soon. Wait for me."

Zombie walked through the empty church, escorted by Riddler and Dick the Hat. Ryan strolled at his elbow, deliberately taking his time.

"Come on in," Norman Mote invited. "Zombie, you wait in here. Other two outside the door. Don't want to be interrupted till I say so."

The Mote family was relaxing in a suite of elegant rooms behind the temple. Norman was smoking a large cigar, feet resting on a table. Joshua was picking his nose and thumbing through a crudely colored porn mag. Marianne had changed into a loose gown of chem-cloud-pink chiffon that swirled loosely about her as she moved. Ryan couldn't help noticing that she hadn't been very careful about the fastening and it kept swinging open to show the top of her thighs. The reverend mother looked like she didn't believe in wearing panties.

"Nice church," Ryan said. "Good number of the folk of Snakefish there."

"Break their piss-ant knees if they didn't come," Joshua mumbled.

"Now, now." Norman smiled. "Boy will have his joke, Ryan. You understand that? You got any children of your own?"

He was taken off guard by the question. It had been such a long time since anyone had asked him that. Oddly Krysty had never asked him. She'd talked about their future together. Even kind of hinted that maybe one day she'd like kids. But she'd never asked him...

"No. I don't think...."

"You don't think, Ryan?" Marianne Mote laughed. Close up the resemblances he'd noticed were stronger. The gaudy queen with the dead eyes. And she was years older than he'd even guessed.

"That's right."

"Mean you don't know? Lots of little Ryans running around Deathlands looking for their long-lost daddy? I declare!"

Norman resumed control of the conversation. "Just wanted a word, Ryan. One or two folks say you and your...party look mighty like a load of mercies. What d'you say to that?"

"I say that I don't like answering the same question more than once."

There was a shocked silence in the room and, for the first time, Ryan realized that he was dealing with real power.

"Daddy asks a question, folks answer it," Joshua hissed.

"That's right," Zombie added. "Reverend Mote says 'jump' and you just say 'how high?' and do it."

But Norman wasn't thrown by Ryan's attitude. "Now this is the core and kernel of why I wanted a quiet word. I see that you seven outlanders have the look of... of folks that can handle themselves if there was any trouble. I just wanted to satisfy myself that you hadn't been hired by..." He paused then carried on. "By anyone in the ville to take their side if there was to be some sort of difficulty."

"Or firefight," Joshua said loudly.

"Yeah. A scale-blasted firefight," Zombie enthused, clenching his fists.

Marianne swept closer to Ryan, so that he could smell a cloying scent, overlaying the stale odor of her body.

"We don't believe it will come to that, Ryan. But you have arrived, no doubt by coincidence, at a key time for the ville. There is change in the air. Most of us believe that what comes from the ville belongs to the ville. All of it."

"The gas," Ryan said.

Norman nodded. "Indeed. Man of perception, Ryan Cawdor. I saw that right away. Now, if... let's imagine you might have been hired by someone." He raised up a hasty hand. "I know what you say about happening by. First time's happenstance. Second time it's pure luck. Third time and you're on your back staring up at the sky. We'd double whatever you'd been paid. Double it, clear and free."

"Bear it in mind," Ryan said.

Mote moved closer. "I'm not a man to fuck around with."

"Yeah," Ryan agreed, his voice flat and steady.

"Stick your prick into my business, and you'll get it cut off."

"Yeah, Reverend."

"Go and have a nice day now. Zombie, see Brother Cawdor here off these premises. Good day."

"Well?" Krysty pressed when Ryan joined his friends.

Ryan took a deep breath of the morning air, tasting the sickly taint of gasoline. He grinned. "Like you said, lover. Friendliest little ville in the whole fire-blasted west."

Chapter Twenty

"SAW AN OLD MOVIE, back when I was . . . you know. It was Japanese, and about a sort of ace swordsman coming to a ville like this. He found two warring groups there, and they both wanted him to help them against the other. In the end, they kind of wiped each other out and he moved on. Seems a bit like that, here in Snakefish."

Ryan nodded. "Sure is. Looks like this place is a pan fit to boil. Baron's lost his hold. The Motes got the power. Folks in the middle go along with the power."

Doc was sitting on the bed, cleaning his nails with one of Jak's throwing knives. "Go with the power. Always have and always will. Show them a whip and they'll fall down to kiss it."

Rick stood and walked to the window, stooping to peer out across the street. Ryan noticed that he was less steady on his feet than he'd been on the way to the service, when he'd had the help of the stick.

The freezie turned back to face the others in the room. "Meant to ask you, though I have the feeling I'm not going to like the answer very much. Just what is a stickie?"

J.B. told him. "After the long winters Deathlands was full of hot spots."

"Centers of high radiation?"

"Right. Seems that the nuking did some strange things to animals and plants."

"And people," Lori added with a dramatic shudder.

"And people," the Armorer agreed. "You saw the snakes. There's plenty of mutie creatures of all kinds. Some grossed out. Some you have to look real hard to see what's wrong. Stickies are kind of obvious."

"What do stickies do? Stick to you, I guess. Is that it?"

The smile faded at the expression on J.B.'s face. "Right, Rick. They have kind of suckered hands. Some have feet the same. They can hang on smooth surfaces, like the side of a wag."

"Terrific. And there's a gang of them around here someplace?"

Ryan nodded. "So they say. Oh, there's a couple of other facts you should know about stickies. First is that they generally love all kinds of fires and explosions. Sometimes get themselves killed going too close to grens or flames."

"What's the other thing this twentieth-century boy should know about stickies, Ryan? I can hardly wait."

"Stickies all have a homicidally vicious hatred of all other living things."

Rick whistled. "Hell's bells! Like I said, I can hardly wait."

THEY WERE halfway through lunch when Carla Petersen arrived at the Rentaroom Hotel. Ruby Rainer was bringing in a tureen of stew with sweet potatoes and okra, sniffing with audible disapproval at Baron Brennan's assistant.

"Good noon to you, Mrs. Rainer. I'm not here to help myself to your food, though that *does* smell so good! I just want a word with our outlander brothers and sisters, if you don't mind."

"Sure. Go ahead." The woman flounced out of the room, muttering something that sounded amazingly like "mercies" as she went.

"Hollow tooth! That dried-up old bitch would sell her own kin to the feedings. If she had any kin to sell."

"What's a feeding?" J.B. asked quickly.

Carla picked at a small gravy stain on the cloth in front of her, hesitating briefly before she answered him. "A feeding's when... Only about one a year. Less some years. More in... Gas doesn't run so free or there's a sickness in the cattle or the crops fail or the rains don't come."

"And the creeks don't rise," Rick muttered absently to himself.

"Then the Motes have a big service...lasts for hours on end. They go into the brush and consult the oracles. How the big snakes are moving. Trails. Shedskin. All kinds of things. Then they proclaim a need for a feeding."

Doc coughed, laying down his knife and fork. "I have lived long enough, Miss Petersen, to hear the words behind the words."

"How's that, Doctor Tanner?"

"A feeding. To my ears it sounds as though you really mean a killing."

She didn't answer, remaining preoccupied with the mark on the cloth.

J.B. took up the question. "That right, Carla? What Doc says? You mean someone gets chilled and offered to those slimy mutie bastards?"

"John!" Carla looked quickly at the closed door of the dining room with something very close to panic in her eyes.

"What?"

"Words like that will bring you all into the coils, John Dix. Ruby Rainer's one of the best informers in the ville. A breath here becomes a hurricane by the time it reaches the ears of the Motes. You *must* take care with your talk!"

Ryan leaned across the table, the congealing stew on his plate forgotten. "We're talking sacrifice, Carla? Is that it?"

"Edgar tries to stop it. Maybe he holds it in check. Marianne and her kin, they got the blood taste, Ryan. If the baron falls, then the ville will slide into butchery. If you could only help him. You got blasters and you look like you know how to use them. Couldn't you ... ?"

Ryan caught J.B.'s eyes across the table, but was unable to read them behind the blank glass of his spectacles.

"We keep telling everyone that we aren't mercenaries, Carla. Means we won't hire out. There's enough men around Deathlands who'll chill for a pocketful of jack."

"Women, too," Krysty added thoughtfully.

"Yeah. Women as well. But not us. We saw the problem—old baron weakening, generous with the ville's main wealth. The Motes, scenting power for themselves. It's not a new story, Carla. We've seen it all before. But that doesn't mean we'll get involved in it. I'm sorry."

"They'll kill him and use the bikers to shut down anyone who tries to stand up. Doesn't that matter?"

The words were aimed at Ryan, but her eyes focused on J.B., who answered her. "It matters, Carla. In Deathlands you just can't step aside for every problem, every difficulty. There's always been killing in Deathlands, since the smoke settled after dark day. Rad-blast it! We just can't help everyone."

It was an unusually strong outburst from the taciturn Armorer. His normally sallow face was flushed, and his fingers tapped nervously on the edge of the long table.

"Edgar said you wouldn't help."

"Norman Mote offered to double whatever you were paying us. Told him the truth." Ryan remembered his food and stirred it with his fork, sniffing. "Guess I'll pass on this. No, Carla. Couple of days and we'll be gone."

"A lot can happen in two days," she said, standing slowly, looking around at the seven faces. "Sorry to have interrupted the eating."

After she'd left the dining room, bumping into Ruby Rainer in the hallway, the silence lasted a long time.

THE ROAR of the two-wheel wags told everyone in the rooming house that the Hell's Angels had come calling.

The engines were cut, and Ryan, sitting on his bed, heard a voice shouting. Krysty tugged the window open and leaned out, seeing Jak's head at the next window along. She turned back to the room and warned Ryan.

"They come for the kid," she said.

"How many?"

"Four. Not Zombie. What d'you think, lover? Gonna stop him?"

Ryan swung his legs to the floor and cat-footed across the creaking boards. He pulled the edge of the curtain back and peered out, letting one hand gently caress Krysty's nape. She eased her body against his, the dazzling crimson hair brushing over his fingers.

There was Priest, with his beard trimmed, on his Triumph twin; Ruin, wearing sunglasses with one lens missing, on a flame-streak BMW; the huge bulk of Riddler, oozing off both sides of the saddle of his enormous motorbike, which had been chopped together from a variety of different machines; and the bare-headed Dick the Hat.

"Wanna come for a run, Jak?" Ruin bellowed, staring up at the albino boy.

"Mebbe."

They saw Ryan behind the curtain. "Hey, Cawdor. Wanna come for a run?"

He wrestled with the stubborn window, finally managing to lever it upward. "Where?"

"Death Valley Road. See if we can find us some stickies."

"Don't go, Ryan. Could be a trap. Got a bad feeling about it." Krysty's fingers tightened on his hand, squeezing hard enough to make him wince in surprise.

"Sure? I can't see those double-stupe rednecks ever getting a stickie."

"How about the stickies getting themselves some double-stupe rednecks, Ryan?"

"Got a point. I'll go along with Jak. Kind of keep an eye on things."

Krysty smiled and kissed him on the cheek. "Since you've only got one eye, lover, that's about all you *can* keep on him."

"You coming?" Dick the Hat shouted.

"Can go?" Jak called eagerly to Ryan.

"Sure," the one-eyed man replied. "Bring your blaster."

Jak rode pillion behind Ruin on the big BMW bike. Ryan clung on to the rear seat of the Triumph, balancing to the bends and bumps in the road, seeing ahead over Priest's shoulders. The light blue ribbons in the long, greasy hair fluttered in the wind of their passing.

Ryan hadn't ridden on a two-wheel wag for years, but the breathtaking rush of exhilaration came speeding back. His own hair was ruffled, and he could feel the warm desert air plucking at the patch covering his left eye. He'd left the caseless G-12 checked at the Rentaroom, contenting himself with his handgun and the long steel panga.

"You ever seen stickies?" Priest shouted, his words almost whipped away by their speed.

Ryan leaned forward to reply, suddenly catching the stench of the rider's stained blue denims. "Seen a few," he said.

"We never catch 'em. I seen some, in the distance like. But they all fucked off when they heard us coming. Got no balls for a mix with the Last Heroes."

"They giving you trouble?"

Priest didn't reply immediately, concentrating on swerving the heavy chopper around a massive hole in the road. It looked like a landie had gone off, by the size of the crater.

"Yeah," he finally grunted. "You know we got a lotta gas. Ground's full of it out near where we have our base. By the old park. But there's some outlying wells. That's where we're going now, the one toward Death Valley."

The knowledge that none of his companions had ever actually faced stickies gave Ryan pause for thought. Of all the muties that roamed the Deathlands, stickies were among the worst—ferocious and inexorable in their desire to attack normies. He wished that he could have warned Jak about what they might be riding into. But the noise of the hogs and the speed at which they were traveling made that impossible. A glance at the speedo told Ryan they were racing along the shifting surface of the old highway at something close to seventy miles an hour, which was about as fast as he'd ever been. Because of the poor quality of processed gas, few wags could manage much more than forty. A tuned-up war wag with all its armor was lucky to reach fifty.

Jak was leaning perilously on the BMW, hands locked in the small of his back, his keen-edged reflexes allowing him to roll with every movement of the powerful two-wheeler. His long hair blew behind him like a streamlined helmet of purest white and his eyes, as he turned to grin across at Ryan, flamed like living embers.

The boy gave a piercing banshee scream of unbridled pleasure, punching the air with his right fist, making the rider wobble and yell a curse over his shoulder at the teenager.

The land was a monotonous reddish orange, with occasional relieving areas of gray or pale yellow. The road unrolled itself, mainly straight, with an occasional dip and swoop. On one side the ruins of an old post-and-wire fence leaned drunkenly toward the distant hills. They saw no signs of life. Twice they passed abandoned drilling rigs, twisted and rusting.

"Any snakes around here?" Ryan shouted.

"Not this way. All in the brush between the ville and the mountains. Nobody goes far that way. Azrael and his brothers and sisters see to that."

The sky was a rich pink, streaked with blue, stippled with fragments of high, scudding chem clouds. Once Ryan spotted a circling hawk, riding a thermal far above them. It was so high that he couldn't judge its size, but the wingspan seemed unusually wide.

They stopped after a half hour for Riddler to relieve himself, standing by the side of the highway, legs spread, whistling loudly to himself.

Dick the Hat was waiting, close by Ryan. "When you get to join the Last Heroes, you get your colors initiated like that."

"Like what?"

"Put on the denims and lie down and all the brothers stand around and piss all over you."

"Fireblast!" Ryan said. "Sounds a whole wag of laughs."

The Angel looked at him suspiciously, but said nothing.

"MUCH FARTHER?"

"Five miles. Road gets worse. Gotta slow some. Beyond that bunch of hills."

Eye watering from the dusty wind, Ryan squinted around the bikers back and saw that the highway was rising slowly, leading toward a group of mesas. As they drew nearer he could make out that there had been some major earth movements and rocks had slipped down across the blacktop.

Ruin was in the lead, and he held up a hand as a warning to the others that they were swinging off the pavement onto a dirt trail with deep ruts that coiled to the left. Speed dropped to a little more than walking pace; dust billowed around them, choking and blinding. The three other Last Heroes dropped back, spacing themselves to avoid the orange clouds.

"Nearly there!" the biker shrieked, his face a mask of sand-covered sweat.

The rocking and bouncing was almost unbearable as the bike jolted over the bumps, its century-old suspension creaking and rattling. Ryan had to hang on to

Priest's back to keep himself on the bike, trying to breathe through his mouth to avoid choking.

Dimly, on either side of the Triumph, Ryan could make out walls of tumbled, frost-riven boulders, rising forty feet or more above them.

Concentrating hard on breathing and staying in the saddle, Ryan had neglected his fighting senses. The hair at his nape had begun to prickle, warning him that this was a dangerous place to be.

He was taken completely by surprise when a semi-naked, mewing creature launched itself at him from out of nowhere, hurling him from the bike. He landed flat on his back in the dirt, with needle-sharp teeth questing toward his neck and a suckered hand reaching for his good eye.

Chapter Twenty-One

RYAN HAD FOUGHT MUTIES before, all kinds, shapes and sizes. But there was nothing on God's nuked earth to compare to close combat against a stickie.

Part of Ryan's brain told him that the stickies must have been attracted by the powerful roaring of the engines of the two-wheel wags. Another part of his brain wondered how many of them there were in the ambush.

But most of his mind locked instantly into the fundamental problem of staying alive.

The skin of a stickie always seemed slippery, like moist rubber, but sand was clinging to this one, enabling Ryan to grip its arm and prevent the hand with its greedy suckers from fastening on his face. Years ago he'd seen one of the drivers off Warwag Two, Harpo, go down in a skirmish against stickies.

The screeching creature had slapped its hand over Harpo's forehead and eyes. The grip was unbelievably powerful. As the mutie pulled its hand away, half of the man's face came with it, including both eyes, ripped from their sockets by the appalling suction of the fingers and palm. All of Harpo's skin and much of the flesh beneath also came away at the same time.

It hadn't been a good ending.

Ryan could hear shouts and screams all around him, as well as the engines revving and choking, wheels spinning and thickening the whirling bank of sullen sand.

The face of the stickie was only inches away from Ryan's as he struggled against its great muscular power and almost reptilian agility. The creature was breathing hard, hissing between a triple row of pointed, edged teeth, spewing foul, rancid breath—a soughing eructation from a rotting, age-old swamp. Its tiny eyes, with pupils that divided vertically, gazed straight into Ryan's eye, blankly hostile. The mutie wore only a pair of torn shorts, and like all stickies it was weaponless. Even the skillful use of a knife was beyond its mental powers.

With a great effort Ryan managed to raise a foot between the creature's legs and push it away from him, sending it staggering backward, until it completely disappeared into the dust storm. As it went, its fingers brushed against Ryan's arm and he felt and heard his shirt tear as the suckers dragged at the material.

He could still hear yelling and squeals of pain, and the snuffling, grunting sound that a stickie makes when it has its jaws clamped on flesh and is gnawing inexorably through to the delicious marrow of the bone.

One by one the engines faltered and died, choked in the dirt. As they stopped, the veil of orange sand began to clear and Ryan was able to see what was going on.

Without even realizing he'd made the move, Ryan found that the SIG-Sauer filled his left hand, the warm hilt of the panga in his right.

Seven stickies.

Dick the Hat down and dead, his neck ripped apart. Suckers had peeled skin and flesh away, showing the whiteness of bone beneath the welter of blood. One of the stickies was on its knees, face buried in the pulsing wreckage of the biker's throat.

Jak was standing, half-crouched, a small knife in his right hand, facing two gibbering stickies that danced and capered in front of him.

Ruin had lost his sunglasses and was wrestling with another of the muties, screaming as the suckers tore strips of bloodied skin off his right arm.

Priest ran up a steep slope, pursued by one of the stickies. It chased him in an odd, skipping, shambling run, like a child. He tried to draw his .32 as he ran, but the fall from his bike had dislodged his holster.

Riddler was the only one who looked like he was making any progress. He'd felled his opponent with a roundhouse swing of his huge fist. As the stickie scrabbled in the dirt, shaking its bald head, thick blood oozing from the corner of its lipless mouth, the Angel was drawing a short-hafted ax from the back of his belt. It looked to Ryan as if Riddler might be doing all right.

Ryan's own stickie was crouched behind the fallen Triumph, clenching its fingers and chattering in a tiny, high-pitched voice. Gas was leaking from the tank of the chopper, close by its feet, and the creature put its round head on one side and sniffed the air, dipping a hand into the liquid and licking it.

"Know what that is, you double-chilled bastard?" Ryan said conversationally. "That's gas. One pyro-tab and you'd be dead meat."

But the gas soaked instantly into the dry sand.

The mutie stood only fifteen feet from Ryan, who took careful aim with the powerful pistol then pressed the trigger once. With the integral silencer the explosion was muffled and soft, no louder than the snap of fingers.

The 9 mm bullet smacked home right between the little eyes, drilling a neat, blackened hole that immediately began to drip dark blood. The exit hole wasn't much bigger than the one going in, and didn't take out a fist-size chunk of bone—as it would have done with a normie—due to the gristly, cartilaginous skull of the stickie.

But it was still a killing shot that punched the mutated monstrosity back, away from the tumbled two-wheel wag. Its hands went up, as though exploring its own wound. The suckers were activated in its death throes, tearing out one of its own eyes as it toppled down in the dirt, dead.

Meanwhile, Riddler had successfully defended himself, swinging the ax in a short, brutally effective blow to the side of the stickie's neck, very nearly severing its head from its repulsive body.

"Two down and five to go," Ryan muttered to himself.

But all the successes weren't on the side of the humans.

Finding that Jak's speed and aggression were too much for them, the two stickies that had been threatening him decided to go for easier game.

One went after Priest, the other joining the creature that was rolling around in the dry earth with Ruin. The mutie that had butchered Dick the Hat was still busily occupied with its feasting. Ryan thought for a moment about putting a bullet through the top of its soft skull, but there were more important things to take care of.

Ruin was screaming and cursing, a stream of noise pouring from his open mouth. He'd managed to break one of the stickie's arms. A jagged end of bone protruded through the creature's torn flesh. But his own injuries were severe. Blood gushed from his gashed arm, and the stickie had succeeded in getting a grip with its good hand on the inside of the bikers left thigh, near the groin. The suckers shredded the denim of his jeans and began to strip skin and flesh from the long femur.

Priest had finally managed to draw his rebuilt .32 and leveled it at the nearest of his attackers, pulling the trigger. Ryan actually saw the bullet pass clear through the body of the stickie, in a gout of blood, just above the waistband of the tattered pants. The mutie staggered but didn't go down. Priest fired again and again. Each round found its mark in the body of the advancing stickie, but the creature wasn't even knocked off its feet.

"In the head!" Ryan yelled. "Only way to chill them!"

Priest was too locked into his own panic to register Ryan's advice, and repeatedly fired his weapon, riddling the chest and stomach of the stickie. By now it was only a few paces away from him, hands reaching out to draw him into its lethal embrace.

Jak tried to help, throwing two of his elegant knives. Each found its target with pinpoint accuracy, thudding into the neck of the mutie, making it falter for a moment.

"Why not fucking down?" the albino yelled turning to look at Ryan.

"Told you. Stickies aren't like anything else. You can rip their guts open and it hardly slows them. Gotta hit their fireblasted heads."

Ruin had kicked his way clear of the one stickie, but it clutched a dripping haunch of meat in its hand. Blood was pouring from a gaping wound in the leg of the Last Hero. Ryan had seen enough fatal wounds in his time to know that the odds were effectively down to five against four. Three if you counted Priest as doomed.

At last Ryan could get in some clean shooting.

Standing with his feet a few inches apart, blaster firmly held in his hand, he fired three carefully placed shots.

One stickie had already closed on Priest, who'd turned at the last second to try to run from his slobbering, gnawing nemesis.

But the other mutie was halfway up the slope and the 9 mm bullet smashed into its head, exiting close to its left eye, sending it crashing down the face of the slope, legs and arms thrashing and twitching.

The second bullet hit the stickie that was chewing at the hunk of Ruin's upper leg—precisely where Ryan had aimed, near the mucous-rimmed pits of its pig-like nostrils. Angling sideways and splintering teeth, the round exploded through the side of the head, above the residual knobs of gristle that were the creature's ears.

The third round struck the stickie that had been moving toward the dying Ruin, chattering excitedly to itself in its own guttural tongue.

It was half turned toward Riddler, who'd screamed at it to try to distract it. The stickie had raised a hand when it had seen Ryan's raised blaster, and the bullet smashed through the nest of suckers in the middle of its palm, carrying on, entering the right cheek. The slug tore out the inside of the face, leaving the palate in tatters of mangled skin and flesh.

"Two of them and three of us," Ryan said.

"Five." Jak pointed to the kneeling figure of Ruin and to where the small, bearded Priest had vanished over the top of the rise.

"Three," Ryan repeated.

Ruin made a last desperate effort to get up, half falling, clawing his way toward his beloved chopper. But the blood loss from the torn femoral artery closed him down and he finally lay still in the dirt, his outstretched fingers inches from the dusty metal of the BMW.

"Come on," Ryan ordered, leading the way up the slope, followed by Jak. Riddler, clutching his bloodslick ax, waddled along at their heels.

The three of them paused at the top of the ridge, looking down into a shallow dip on the far side.

"Yeah," Jak finally agreed. "Three."

Priest hadn't made it far. He lay facedown in the sand, naked, the ragged remains of his clothes scattered around him. The stickie was crouched over the corpse, dabbing its hand at the bare flesh, each time bringing away a dozen tiny circles of crimson, raggedy skin. A maze of red rivulets trickled down its chin, testifying it was already relishing the feast. The creature became aware that it was being watched and looked up, snarling its venom.

"Me," Riddler demanded, hefting his sawed-off scattergun. "Me."

"Not at that range," Ryan replied. He'd been reloading his blaster as they stood there. Trader had always drummed into anyone who rode with him that a man had to keep his blasters fully charged whenever he could. Because you might not get another chance.

"Me," Jak said, pulling out his .357 Magnum.

"Head," Ryan reminded him.

The stickie was up and moving, leaving the ragged body of Priest behind. Its eyes were blinking, hands reaching out.

Only minutes had slipped by since Ryan had ridden into the ambush.

The noise of the handgun was deafening. After the mild popping of the .32 and the muffled sound of Ryan's silenced blaster, the air sang with the violence of its explosion.

The Magnum was so much bigger than Jak that the boy had to clutch it in both hands to fire it.

The white-haired boy was quite brilliant at close combat and knife fighting, but Ryan didn't rate him very highly when it came to blasters.

Jak was aware of his own limitations and cautiously aimed to score a hit, not taking the chance of missing with a more risky head shot. He put the bullet smack through the middle of the stickie's naked chest. The power of the Magnum made the advancing mutie totter on its heels, mouth dropping open in a squeak of shock and pain.

"Again," Ryan shouted. "Come on, Jak, hit it again. Now!"

The boy fired two more rounds, one going clean through the left shoulder, spinning the stickie around. The third one, better aimed, caught it at the angle of the jaw, destroying teeth into splintered fragments of razored bone, shredding the creature's tongue, almost removing the lower jaw. The distorted bullet exited in the center of the right cheek, flaying a hole the size of a baseball.

And it still didn't go down.

It lurched and stumbled, waving its hands with the tiny sucking disks. Blood sprayed down its body, coursing over the rubbery flesh, pattering into the thirsty earth.

"Let me chill the fucker with me ax," Riddler roared. "Or the ten-gauge."

"No. Mine," Jak insisted, steadying the gun and squeezing the trigger a fourth time, the sound booming out across the desert.

The bullet smashed into the side of the head of the staggering, blood-sodden monster, an inch from the corner of its left eye. The slug pulped its diminutive, malevolent brain, turning its lights out forever.

"Ace on the line," Ryan said. "Noise like that could attract every stickie from the Sierras to the Lantic. Let's go."

Something nagged at his memory, something that he'd forgotten in the rush and the excitement of the fight and the chilling.

He turned on his heel to lead the way down the slope to where the four choppers lay abandoned in the sand—and walked straight into the seventh and last of the attacking stickies, the one that had been cowering behind the spilled corpse of Dick the Hat, its mouth crusted with congealing human blood. Overlooked and forgotten.

Ryan's needle reflexes saved his life. Instinctively he punched out at the creature, feeling the impact jar clear to his shoulder. He brushed aside the lunging, clawing hands, hitting the stickie twice more with short stabbing punches to its maniac face and soft belly.

"Roll away!" someone bellowed behind him. Riddler, he realized.

Unhesitatingly Ryan pulled away, hearing the other sleeve of his shirt tear beneath the questing suckers. He rolled on his shoulder and came up in a fighting crouch, wincing at the nearness of the heat and blast from the Last Hero's shotgun.

"Fuck a dead armadillo!" Jak gasped.

It was an amazing sight.

The nervous system of a stickie was sometimes rudimentary. The burst of shot from the shotgun had torn the thing's head clear away from its narrow shoulders, leaving its skull to dangle, held only by frayed strands of ligament and ragged muscle. But it still walked!

The impact sent the creature several drunken steps down the flank of the hill, but it miraculously maintained its balance, wobbling several more uneven strides before it finally tripped and fell, rolling to the bottom of the slope. During the fall its head had become detached and bounced off, coming to a stop against the rear wheel of Priest's Triumph.

"Owe you one, Riddler." Ryan examined himself to make sure none of the suckers had actually broken his skin. Sometimes they carried a virulent infection that could possibly kill.

"Yeah, man. You said something about these ugly mothers liking fire and noise. Seems we've been doing enough blasting to bring 'em running for fucking miles around."

"Right. Don't forget to collect your throwing knives, Jak, and reload that little Magnum of yours."

Riddler's bike was the only machine in working order. It spluttered and protested at having to carry three on the road back to Snakefish. They left the other two-wheel wags and the bodies where they'd fallen.

As they pulled out onto the highway, Ryan glanced behind him and was sure that he saw signs of movement toward Death Valley, as if other stickies had been attracted by the noise and were coming to investigate.

A lot of stickies.

Chapter Twenty-Two

THE LOSS OF THREE sec men brought Norman Mote running to see Ryan. His breath smelled of whisky and his clothing was disheveled. It was late afternoon and Ryan had just finished telling his colleagues about the attack of the stickies. Jak was upstairs in his room washing away the dirt and sweat of the encounter.

Riddler had dropped them off at the Rentaroom and gone to report to Zombie at their headquarters in the old Sierra Sunrise Park.

"What the scale-blasted rad shit is all this, Cawdor?" Mote bellowed.

Ryan didn't move from the chair in the lobby. "What's all what, Reverend?" he asked calmly.

"Coil-bound stickies! Chilling the Last Heroes! What do you know about it?"

Mote's suit was crumpled and there was a stain on the lapel of his jacket. He stood so close to Ryan that spittle was landing unpleasantly near him.

The one-eyed man stood so suddenly that Mote stumbled backward, catching his heel on a worn place in the carpet and nearly falling. Ruby Rainer had been listening in to Ryan's story, and she rushed forward to help him.

"Take care, Reverend Mote. Could have taken a nasty tumble there."

"Hollow tooth, woman! I'm all right. Leave me be!"

"You were asking me what I knew about it," Ryan said quietly. "I'll tell you. Me and Jak were invited to go on a run to one of the drilling rigs, toward Death Valley. We went along. They said they'd heard of stickies. They took us off the highway and we got ambushed. Seven of them. Three of your boys got downed."

"And the stickies?"

"All chilled. But I'd swear I saw more coming out of the hills. Noise and gunfire brings them running, Reverend."

"And that's it?"

"Yeah. Good of you to call by. Jak's fine and so am I. Had my torn shirt sewed up by Mrs. Rainer there. That's it."

"This is awful. First Azrael goes missing on us and now this massacre of the innocents."

Ryan considered questioning the use of the word "innocents" to describe the two-wheel wag riders, but thought better of it.

"It's a visitation," Ruby Rainer proclaimed, hands clasped piously together.

"That's just what it is," Norman Mote agreed, nodding furiously. "And we must do something about it. I must speak with Zombie about recruiting some more young men to the colors. And then... perhaps it's time for another feeding. It has been many months since we... Yes, indeed." His whole manner brightened at the thought. "A feeding! I shall go and consult with my consort and with the apostolic apprentice on the matter."

Without even a farewell, he was gone, leaving the front door open so that a gust of warm, dusty air blew into the rooming house.

Ruby rubbed her bony hands together, beaming at her visitors. "A feeding! Well, now, isn't that lucky for you? Outlanders coming into the ville at the time of a feeding. Still, I mustn't stop here chitchattering with you. Got me some supper to go and cook for you."

After she'd gone Rick Ginsberg broke the silence. "You guys can't appreciate how weird this is for me. I'm in a house built around 1890. My head tells me it's around the year 2000. My body tells me that the period of remission of the ALS is perhaps ending. I feel tired and sort of off balance. Then I see Hell's Angels and I meet the biggest snake in the ever-loving world. But I'm still hanging on in there. Then this bullshit— the stickies show up! I don't feel ready to cope with whatever comes next. A feeding! And you figure this is a fancy word to hide a human sacrifice. Hell's bloody bells, Ryan! I'm going to bed. I'll take a rain check on the supper. Maybe I'll wake up tomorrow and find this is all some twisted nightmare. Good night."

Jak passed him in the doorway. The boy's hair was once again bleach clean, swimming around his lean shoulders.

"Freezie tired?" he asked when he'd joined the others in the lobby.

"Yeah," J.B. replied.

"What now, lover?" Krysty asked.

Ryan sighed, rubbing at torn skin on the knuckles of his right hand. "I don't know. We go or stay. If we go, then now's the time. First light tomorrow. Before this feeding. Before they find the dead snake. And before the big in-fight starts."

"Could help," J.B. said unexpectedly.

"You said that—" Ryan began, but the Armorer checked him.

"Yeah. But now the odds have come down some. They lost three from eleven. We get in first, preempt them?"

Ryan's tongue probed the small hole in his back tooth. "Chill them . . ."

"Before they chill us," J.B. finished. "Take out the bikers and the Motes fall with them. You can see that, Ryan."

"Sure. Seven of us."

"Six. Sorry, folks, but I was a peacenik then and I have to be a peacenik now. Make it six of us in the killing bits. But this is crazy. We just got to this town. Sure, they're a touch mad about snakes, but it doesn't mean there's going to be civil war. You can't kill people just because of something that might or might not happen."

"Thought you'd gone to bed." Ryan looked around and saw Rick leaning in the doorway.

"I had, but I got a feeling that something like this was going to happen."

Ryan nodded. "You travel with us and you got a voice. Same as we all have. But in the end this sure as fireblast isn't a democracy, Rick. Best you realize that."

"I have," Doc offered, "lived long enough in the Deathlands to know that there is often a mortal imperative and, indeed, a moral imperative, in chilling some people. Baron Teague and Cort Strasser are instances that leap readily to my mind. But the putting down of a beast you know to be rabid or a mindless creature or some... I fear that I have somewhat lost the thread of my argument."

"You're saying don't jump before you've been looking good," Lori explained.

"More or less, my bunch of happiness," Doc replied, smiling toothfully. "More or less what I meant to say."

"Two votes against interfering," Ryan said.

"Last Heroes not fucked us," Jak said. "And baron's not done nothing neither."

"Sounds like a third hand against. Krysty? Do we run, fight or just stay?"

She sat back in the overstuffed chair, booted feet crossed in front of her. "Nobody ever threw me a blaster and told me to run. Don't like running. But Mother Sonja always taught me you don't waste someone for no good reason. Motes might be the slime pits of the universe, but we haven't really seen much that earns them a nine mill through the back of the neck. I say we stay a couple more days and keep the old glims open."

Lori stood, her blond hair tied back in a bunch with a blue ribbon. "How about me? I say we should leave all alone of them. Not nothing to be doing for us."

Ryan shook his head, looking across the lobby at the Armorer. "Five says either go or hang on here and watch."

"What d'you say, Ryan?"

There was an edge to J.B.'s voice, and flecks of color gleamed high on his pale cheekbones. It wasn't like him to become emotionally involved in any situation.

"I say that Krysty summed it up for me."

"Yeah. She would, wouldn't she? Krysty's your woman, Ryan. Speaks like you speak."

"Watch it, J.B." Krysty warned, green eyes glowing with anger. "You just better take some care. I go with Ryan because I want to and because he wants me to. You try and make me out like some fucking echo of his and . . . !"

Krysty Wroth very rarely swore. The fact that she did now was proof of her rage at what J.B. had said.

"All right, all right. Blackdust!" J.B. took off his spectacles and began to polish the lenses. "I didn't mean that, Krysty. Sorry. But you feel that way, Ryan?"

"I guess so. Baron seems friendly enough. Motes don't. I say we'll stay around Snakefish for a couple more days. Watch and wait."

SUPPER WAS a subdued affair.

Rick finally went up to bed without eating. J.B. didn't speak a single word during the entire meal, concentrating on finishing fast. He left the table as soon as he'd eaten his fill, muttering that he wanted to field strip his blasters.

Lori and Doc were having one of their increasingly frequent bickering rows, the girl sniping at the old man, badgering him, trying to elicit a response. But Doc kept his cool, smiling at Lori, managing to eventually shame her into being nice. Before the coffee arrived she'd dragged him off to their room.

"Make it up for being real bitching," she told him.

The main course had been ham, smoked over a slow fire, served with fat-dipped bread and roasted beans with chilies. Ruby served them watered milk as an accompaniment. Some small, sour peaches were dessert, with a small jug of molasses to pour over them.

Jak leaned back in his chair and loosened his belt. He opened his mouth and belched loudly.

"Your manners are terrible, Jak," Krysty protested.

The boy grinned. "No. Really wanted to fart, Krysty. Should be grateful self-control."

"Get out, you red-eyed brat. When I was your age I'd have gotten sent to my room if I'd behaved like that."

"Lady," he said, rising from his seat with unusual dignity. "You *never* my age. Never. Going bed now. Tired. G'night."

Ryan and Krysty were left alone at the table, sitting with a steaming jug of the landlady's coffee in front of them.

"Want to go upstairs, lover?" she asked. "Could give you a healing massage after the fight with the stickies."

"Thanks. You know what always happens when you start those healing massages of yours."

"Sure, I know. You complaining?"

"No. But it's kind of early. How about a walk around the ville?"

"And then the massage?"

"And then the massage."

IT WAS A WARM, gentle evening.

The sun was sinking to its rest, far over the snow-tipped peaks that lined the western horizon. Stars were appearing, diamond bright, scattered across the soft velvet of the sky.

The ville was settling down for the night. Lamps glowed in downstairs windows, between undrawn draperies. Here and there they passed folks sitting on their porches. One old-timer was plucking at a banjo, quietly singing a song that neither of them recognized, words about a candy-colored clown who came and scattered sleep over everyone's eyes.

They'd only gone a hundred yards before they spotted Carla Petersen walking quickly on the other side of the street, boot heels clicking on the sidewalk. For a moment it seemed as though she were going to ignore them, but at the last second she crossed over to where they waited.

"Evening, Ryan. Krysty."

"Hi, Carla."

"Taking in the sights of Snakefish?"

"Yeah," Krysty said. "You out on pleasure or business?"

"A bit of each, I guess. Do you know if John's in the hotel?"

"J.B., you mean? Can't get used to hearing him called 'John.' Not after all the years we've ridden together. Sure. He was staying in his room, cleaning his blasters."

"Thanks, Ryan. I might just walk by and see how things are." The setting sun gave a pink glow to everything—including the woman's cheeks.

"I'm sure that he'd be real glad to see you, Carla," Krysty told her.

"Sure," Ryan agreed, the penny finally dropping as he realized what was going on, realizing at the same time how slow he'd been at picking up on the clues. It was just that he'd never, ever thought of the Armorer having any interest in ladies.

"Heard about the deaths. You and Jak weren't hurt?"

Ryan shook his head. "Could've been worse. If there'd been another four or five stickies we'd have struggled. Mote was pissed about it, losing three of his boys."

Carla Petersen looked solemn. "I heard he blamed you for it. Thought it was part of a plot. Riddler spoke for you. He said it couldn't have been arranged, that you didn't even know about the run. Mote was all for taking action."

"Action?" Krysty asked.

"Lining you up for a feeding."

Ryan nodded. "You got a good weapon, you'd be a stupe not to use it. One thing puzzles me, Carla. How did Mote get this snake cult started?"

"Nobody really knows. Or remembers. There'd always been big snakes out in the brush, toward the foothills, but nothing the size of Azrael and the rest. The Motes came out of the desert in a couple of wags. One of the wags was enormous, and some folks say it held straw and was like a kind of cage inside.''

''You mean the Motes brought those rattlers with them?'' Krysty's voice betrayed her shock and disbelief.

''That's what people say. But these days they say it quiet behind closed doors and shuttered windows. Edgar's brother was one who said it aloud. Never found even a bone of him.''

''Nice,'' Ryan muttered. ''Real nice.''

''And they brought this worshiping and chilling with them as well?''

Carla glanced around, as though she thought she'd heard a sound in one of the dimly lit alleys behind her. ''That's about the breadth of it, Krysty. Like I said before, step careful.'' With that advice Carla left them to visit with J.B.

The sun had vanished, and night came across the land in a shifting, sideways, skulking run, dragging its black cloak in the dust behind it.

Ryan and Krysty decided that they'd leave a recce of the Sierra Sunrise Park to some other time.

Chapter Twenty-Three

J.B. HAD BEGGED some clean, dry rags from Ruby Rainer, explaining that he wanted to do some cleaning. She'd also supplied him with a white enamel bowl that was half-filled with steaming water. He'd carefully drawn the curtains shut across his second-floor back room, sliding the bolt in the center of the heavy oak door.

The Armorer always made it a policy to try to fieldstrip and clean all of his weapons at least once a day. In the Deathlands that wasn't always possible. But here in Snakefish he had everything that he needed to perform the task.

He was whistling quietly to himself as he began—an old hymn tune that dated right back to the shadowed days of his childhood. "The Day Thou Gavest, Lord, Is Ended." If asked, J.B. probably wouldn't even have realized he was whistling any tune at all.

This evening he decided to check out the contents of his voluminous pockets: the plas-ex, detonators and wires; the sextant and the garotte; and the grens—the scarlet-and-blue implode and the slightly smaller frag-gren with the flip-top firing.

He fisted the Tekna knife, feeling the dark metal hilt with the holes cut for lightness and grip, admiring the

honed steel blade with the jagged sawing part, nearest
the grip. J.B. held the blade to the lamp, turning it to
catch the reflection, rubbing with one of the pieces of
cotton waste to remove a barely visible smear.

As he concentrated harder, the whistling ceased and
the room was quiet. He caught the noise of one of the
Last Heroes thundering past the Rentaroom, but he
ignored it.

Once the knife was cleansed, and a fine film of oil
applied to it from a small screw-top container in one
of his pockets, J.B. began to work on his blasters.

Time slipped by. Outside his room the sun dipped
below the horizon and the streetlights came on. With
a sigh the small man stood, stretching his arms above
his head. He moved aside the corner of the flowered
curtain and watched his two friends, close together,
strolling through the dusk.

The ritual went on.

All the parts clicked, one from another, and were
laid on the bed, on the cloths, in their ordered positions. Springs, catches and gleaming muzzles. J.B.
started to whistle once again. Happiness wasn't a
concept that preyed much on the mind of John Barrymore Dix from Cripple Creek, but if he'd thought
about it, times like this would have been equated with
happiness.

His strong, capable fingers rubbed, oiled and
cleaned, sliding the various machined parts of the
Heckler & Koch MP-7 SD-8 together. It was warm in
the room, and the steam from the bowl of water began to condense on his spectacles, fogging them. J.B.

took the glasses off and began to wipe at them with a corner of one of Mrs. Rainer's old bed sheets.

The knock on the door of his room was soft and hesitant.

J.B. didn't reply. He drew the knife and stuck it into his belt. Hefting the automatic rifle from the bed, he moved, light-footed, to flatten himself against the wall by the door.

The knock was repeated.

He still kept silent.

"John? John Dix? You in there? It's me. It's Carla."

His expression unchanged, almost, the Armorer threw the blaster on the bed and slid back the bolt on the door.

"Come in."

"You're a careful man, John Dix," she said as she walked across the threshold. He closed the door behind her and locked it again.

"I try to be."

"And you succeed. I saw Ryan and Krysty out walking a few minutes ago."

"Yeah."

There was an awkward silence.

The room wasn't large—around ten feet by ten feet. A small pie-crust table with a broken leg was at the head of the bed; a bureau with three drawers stood alongside the window, next to another small chest with a water jug and bowl on top of it. The carpet was faded and worn near the door. The only attempt at any kind of decoration was an attractive watercolor painting on the side wall, showing some trees and an expanse of grass.

There was also an armchair in a patched, loose cover. J.B.'s jacket was flung over the back of the chair; his stripped handblaster covered the bedspread.

He looked at the woman. Carla was dressed much as she'd been at the morning service in the snake temple: polished boots, trim skirt, crisp white blouse fastened at the neck with a sapphire clip. A jacket of dark brown corduroy had been draped over her shoulders against the night air.

"Well," she said, trying to defuse the sudden tension that she felt between them. "Looks like you're busy."

"Busy?"

"The blaster." She gestured toward the bed.

"Oh, yeah. Cleaning it . . . them. Cleaning them while I got the chance."

He was aware that Carla was still standing uncomfortably by the locked door, her arms folded defensively across her chest.

"You want to sit down? I mean, I'll clear off some space for you. The chair or the bed? Which would you . . . ?"

"Sure. Bed'd be fine, John. Can I give you a hand to move anything?"

"No!" he answered sharply. "Sorry, Carla. Just that I don't like . . ."

"Anyone to touch your blasters," she finished, smiling at him. "I should have guessed, John. You go ahead."

His hands were almost a blur of movement as he reassembled the Steyr pistol, slotting the parts together in a series of soft, greased clicks, whipping away the stained rags with the flourish of a magician performing his greatest trick.

"There," he said, patting the bed. "Sit down, Carla. Can I ask Mrs. Rainer to bring you up anything?"

She sat down primly, crossing her legs with a whisper of rustling sound. "Thanks, John. If Ruby brought me anything it'd probably be cyanide."

J.B. laughed and sat down at the far end of the bed, licking his lips and blinking behind his glasses. It seemed odd to him how the room had become so very much smaller in the past few minutes, and how the bowl of hot water had made the bedroom feel uncomfortably humid. He ran his finger around the inside of his shirt collar.

"Want me to open a window, Carla?" he asked. "Seems kind of stuffy."

"That would be nice, John."

He stood and slipped the catch across, levering the top half of the casement upward a few inches, which brought a breath of cool evening air into the room. Before he could turn around, J.B. felt the woman's hand touch his shoulder, her breath against his neck. Suddenly she was in his arms, and the soft caress of her lips was against his. After a split second's shock, he found himself responding to her warmth.

A moment later she broke away from him, carefully adjusting the curtains across the window. "Don't want the whole ville to see us, do we, John?"

"Guess not," he replied hoarsely.

Her hand still rested on his shoulder, fingers teasing at the short hairs curling onto his neck. She was smiling into his eyes. "I really wouldn't want you thinking I did this all the time, John," she whispered.

"Me neither."

"Truth is, I haven't actually done this, anything like this, for a very long time."

"Ne neither, Carla."

"Would you like to . . . you know, John?

J.B. kissed her on the mouth. "Yeah, Carla. I would."

Doc HAD BEEN DOZING, fully clothed, his battered knee boots standing crookedly by the side of the bed. He'd been dreaming, but he couldn't remember what about. There had been a horse and a river, flowing fast and clean over white stones. He thought that his long-dead wife, Emily, had been in the dream, but he couldn't be certain. All he knew was that he'd been crying in his sleep.

He couldn't be certain, either, what it was that had woken him. A door closing or a shutter banging loose?

"What was it, Lori?" he whispered into the darkness of the room. Ruby Rainer had given them two single beds, pushed side by side.

There was no answer. He sat up, grunting at stiffness in the small of his back. Peering across, he saw that the other bed was empty.

"Lori?" Where in thunderation had the girl gone off to?

With a weary groan Doc swung his legs over the edge of the bed and tugged on his boots. He glanced at the small silver chron on his left wrist and saw that it was just past ten o'clock. Through the window he could see that the main street of the ville was quiet and deserted.

Not quite deserted.

A tall figure was striding along on the far side of the road, in a general direction of the Motes' temple. The ghostly illumination of the streetlights danced off the long blond hair. In his imagination Doc could almost hear the tinkling sound of Lori's spurs.

Doc was about to leave the room when an afterthought struck him. He went back and buckled on the heavy Le Mat pistol and picked up his swordstick. He made his way quietly down the stairs, through the sleeping building and out onto the porch that ran the length of the frontage. An elderly swing-seat creaked as the night wind moved it gently to and fro. Doc stood a moment, wrinkling his nostrils at the pungent odor of gasoline that permeated the ville.

Lori had vanished and the old man set off after her, keeping to the shadows. Doc found it difficult to maintain a grip on his memory and his sanity. Walking through the slumbering ville brought back a tumbling flood of images from his long-gone past. Most of the buildings on that end of Main Street dated from the late 1890s, the period during which he had last seen his wife and his two young children. Before the white-coated, faceless men and women of Project Cerberus had trawled him into the future.

With a great effort of will he succeeded in suppressing the memories, concentrating instead on trying to work out where Lori would have gone. Since she knew nobody in Snakefish, it seemed logical that she had walked out into the night.

But why?

Doc very nearly went on by the temple, heading into the wilderness of desert beyond. But a flicker of pale light caught his eye, somewhere around the back of the building—a narrow vertical strip of gold, as though a door had been left open.

Looking around him cautiously, praying that his knee joints wouldn't creak, Doc made his way around the path at the side. Very slowly and carefully he eased his way inside, catching the odd smell of stale sweat and makeup, which dredged up memories of the vaudeville theaters of New York, back when... Once again a black curtain descended, cutting off the trickling memories.

He could hear voices talking quietly and a sudden giggle.

"Lori," he said.

On an impulse he drew the Le Mat from its ornate Mexican holster, thumbing back the hammer on the antique piece as he walked past a table and some shelves. The voices came louder. Another muffled, sniggering laugh made him grip the butt of the pistol more tightly.

Doc could see them now, together near the front row of pews. There was a sailing moon outside, and it cast enough light in through the windows of the reptilian temple for the old man to be able to see them quite clearly.

"I am most dreadfully sorry to interrupt," he called, marveling inwardly at how calm he'd kept his voice. "But I don't think Lori should be out this late on her own."

"What the skin-shedding fuck is that?" The male voice was high and reedy. His blond curls glinted in the moonlight. Doc could see a black Stetson near the altar.

"It's Doc Tanner. And you are Joshua Mote. Do your parents know that you profane the tabernacle with your lusts?"

Lori broke away, nervously smoothing down the front of her coveralls. "Hi, Doc," she greeted. "Josh said to come see this place at night and I thought it be no harms."

"I should kill you! You interfering old fuck-pig!" Joshua Mote shouted, facing Doc across the aisle.

"If you attempt to draw out whatever blaster you have concealed about your person, I shall pull this trigger and blow a hole in you big enough to drive a horse and buggy through."

Mote let his hands drop to his side. "Sure. This time you get your way, Doc. But there's things happening in this ville soon and you'll be on the wrong scaling side of 'em."

"Very possibly. Come on, Lori, my dear. Time to go home."

The girl didn't argue at all. She took Doc's arm and walked quietly with him back to their hotel. Neither said a word.

JUST AFTER SUNUP everyone was awakened by the throbbing roar of the powerful engines of the two-wheel wags. All eight of the Last Heroes rode past in formation, heading down Main Street toward the Motes' temple. Zombie, at the head, shouted something to Ruby Rainer, who was busily sweeping dust off the front porch, but Ryan couldn't hear what was said.

"Going down to find out," he said tersely to Krysty, pulling on his pants and knotting the laces of his combat boots.

The landlady was in the lobby, adjusting a scarf around her throat. She turned as she heard Ryan's feet on the stairs.

"Oh, Mr. Cawdor!" she exclaimed. "Such dreadful, dreadful news!"

Ryan felt the short hairs at the nape prickle in anticipation. Keeping his voice calm, he asked, "What? What's the news?"

Chapter Twenty-Four

"SLAUGHTERED, MY FRIENDS. That very deity that has watched over the fortunes of this ville for so many, many years! Butchered out there among the sagebrush and the prickly cactus. Food only for the rending beaks of the hawk and the buzzard. Oh, now shall we share our lamentations for poor, poor Azrael Twelve."

Norman Mote was well into his harangue. As he lifted his arms to exhort the packed church to greater heights of emotion, he revealed great patches of dark perspiration. His silver-gray hair was matted and disheveled. Marianne sat next to him, hands folded in her lap. There was a silver ring on the little finger of her right hand, designed like a cobra, coiled and hooded and ready to strike. While her husband was ranting at the good folk of Snakefish, Marianne nodded her agreement and rolled the ring around with the fingers of her other hand.

"Our brothers, the Angels, were out before dawn, at my orders, to search for Azrael. I knew that something was grievously wrong. And I was right, brothers and sisters! Oh, was I ever right!"

There was a muffled chorus of "Amens" from the benches.

Ryan sat cramped in next to Krysty. Then came Jak, J.B., Lori and Doc. Rick had found himself squeezed out, into the row behind. The news of the discovery of the giant mutie rattler hadn't been much of a shock. It had been bound to happen quite soon. The best of it was that Zombie had told everyone that the eternal wind had wiped away any tracks from near the carcass.

"What shall we do?"

It was a rhetorical question and Norman Mote was obviously angered when someone near the back called out, "Try and find out who done it, Brother Mote. That's my idea."

"Yes, yes, of course we'll try and find out who did it, Brother Thaxted. But there's more. Much more. How about the stickies suddenly appearing in our beloved ville? Taking away those three good, good boys from our hearts. And now Azrael! Something is rotten, my friends. Rotten and bad and wicked. The demons are abroad in Snakefish!"

"Let me go and drop some gas bombs on them stickies from my plane," Layton Brennan shouted. "I could burn them out."

"We aren't sure where they come from, nephew," Baron Edgar said testily.

John Dern, the dealer in blasters, raised his voice. "Then let's all go after them. Do it 'fore the stickies come into the ville!"

This time the chorus of agreement was much louder and more positive.

Mote held his hands up for silence. "Peace be among us, my friends. What we must ask ourselves is who could have done this bloody thing? Who would have shot Azrael to pieces? Who would have blasters capable of that?''

The words were addressed to the balcony, and to the people ranged around the three walls of the temple. But Mote's eyes raked the pew where Ryan sat with the others. It couldn't have been more obvious where his suspicions lay if he'd thrown a bucket all over them.

The muttering and whispering that filled the sudden stillness confirmed that Mote was simply saying what others thought.

It wasn't time for a sitting on your hands and waiting for the stones to begin flying in your direction. Ryan stood.

''Hope you don't mind an outlander like me speaking out in your service, Reverend Mote.'' The man, looking surprised, nodded. ''Thanks. I've been around plenty of frontier villes in my life. I know that trouble always gets laid at the doors of any outlanders. Way of the world. That's what could happen here if you aren't kind of careful about being fair. Know what I mean? Accusations sometimes bounce right on back against . . . well, the person who made them. We just heard about the death of your snake. Anyone got any proof we had something to do with it, Reverend? Nobody? I'm glad to hear it.''

And he sat down again.

The whispering swelled for a moment, then faded away. Mote looked around at his wife, who waved her hand at him, as if to tell him to get on with the service.

"We're all pleased to hear from Ryan Cawdor that any suspicions . . . uh, what he said. But none of that changes anything. Three of the Last Heroes and Azrael. Only one thing to be done, brothers and sisters. Only one thing!"

Once again the preacher flashed his sweat-soaked armpits at the faithful.

"A feeding!" he shouted at the top of his voice.

In the bedlam that followed, the congregation was on its feet, yelling and clapping in a crazed fervor.

Right at the front, Ryan could make out the diminutive baron, facing the congregation-turned-mob, trying to shout something. Carla Petersen stood at his side, face pale and anguished. J.B. had pushed his way through the crowd, to take Carla by the arm, pulling her with him and towing Edgar Brennan in his wake, heading toward the main doors of the temple.

Ryan saw something else—the anger and hatred that was etched deep on the face of Marianne Mote.

BY THE TIME Ryan had led the others to their rooms, J.B. had calmed down the baron, who sat in the armchair, his legs not quite reaching the floor. Carla was perched on the bed, long legs folded under her, leaning back against the pillow.

Rick had become tired, and it had been a struggle to help him along the street, through the throng of Snakefish citizens that had poured out of the temple, their eyes alight as if they'd witnessed the coming of some great miracle. And the word that was on everyone's lips was "feeding."

"Want to go lie down, Rick?" Krysty asked, concerned.

"Yeah, but I'll stay if you don't mind. Looks like this could be some sort of council. I wouldn't want to miss out on that. But couldn't we move to a bigger room? Then I could lie on the bed and rest."

After a brief discussion they adjourned one door along the corridor to Doc and Lori's light and airy room.

Rick, forehead beaded with perspiration, lay back, unable to stifle a groan. He glanced around at the worried faces and managed a half smile. "Don't worry. I'm not going to invest in six feet of earth yet. It's just that my muscles ache and get real tired. But I'm fine now. Really."

The other friends ranged themselves around the room, finding somewhere to sit or lean. Jak squatted cross-legged with his back against the door, an ear listening for eavesdroppers. Carla stood with J.B., close by the open front window. Edgar Brennan had the wicker chair alongside the bed.

"So," Doc began. "They got their way. As easily as winking. One dead snake and they can swing most of the ville behind them."

Carla shook her head. "You don't understand. Outlanders often don't understand. If you argue against the Motes when it comes to a feeding, then it somehow seems that the fingers point at you. And it's you out there in the brush waiting for the forked tongue and the hollow tooth."

"It's true, my friends." Edgar Brennan sighed. "And I call you 'friends' because I see that you are not the hired mercies that we feared. The appearance of the stickies and that big pet of Norman and Marianne's being chilled ... It's all rushed events too fast. I'd hoped that I could, somehow, persuade some of the decent folk of my ville to follow my lead and stand up against the Motes.''

"It was impossible," Carla said ruefully. "I explained to John how the Motes rule through fear and through their backing of the bikers. Edgar was too kind for too long."

"So kind so long will ne'er rule long, 'tis said. Now you don't have a lot of choice," the freezie said, leaning up on one elbow.

"Nicely put, Richard," Doc observed, smiling appreciatively at Ginsberg. "By the three Kennedys! What is that towering inferno out back?"

Thick gray smoke had begun to billow around the back window, and they could all hear the crackling of flames.

Jak peered out. "Rainer burning garden shit. Big flames."

"And lots of smoke," Lori added, pushing the boy out of the way so that she could look out the open window.

"How does this feeding work, Baron?" J.B. asked. "How do they pick who gets ... chilled?"

"The Motes do it. She throws a trance. Thrashes around and screams. Wriggles like a snake." Carla laughed bitterly. "Be double-funny if it wasn't all a way of removing opposition. Fat hag like her, pretending to be a snake! The one she picks gets driven out into the brush. Nowhere to go. No food or drink.

Zombie and his brothers wait to make sure the chosen never comes back. Doesn't take those rattlers long to know when there's food to be had.''

"Like stickies to an explosion or a fire," Ryan growled.

"When will the feeding be?" J.B. asked.

Carla answered him. "Probably around dusk tomorrow. It's a big production. They all shout and scream, and they light gas fires. See it for miles, lighting up the sky."

Edgar Brennan buried his head in his hands. "Perhaps if I was to leave Snakefish? I'm no use to anyone. I can't order anyone to do anything. Nobody listens to me anymore. They just want us to stop selling our gas so cheap. Everyone wants more jack. More power. It'll turn this little settlement into one of those villes with a gaudy house every block and a murder every night."

"You triple-feeb!" the Armorer exploded. "All you gotta do is borrow a blaster. Walk down the street and blow them away. We'll handle the Angels for you. But it's got to be *you*, Baron."

"John! Edgar can't—" Carla began, but J.B. turned on her.

"No, I *know* he can't. Course I know. I know the world, Carla. He's lost it. If Ryan and I walk down the street and chill the Motes it won't help him, because we'll move on. We always move on. And then the baron here might have a few good days. But there'll be another Mote. And another. Carla, there'll always be another Mote. It has to come from inside!"

Ryan could hardly remember J.B. ever making a more emotional speech. Carla Petersen was looking at him, questioning.

"He's right, lady. Ace on the line all the way. You don't like it. You want some handsome hero with flashing teeth and a blaster that kills sec men with every round. You want someone to come in and open all the doors.

"It's not us you want, Carla," Ryan continued. "That's not the way. Now, I've had it right up to here with you and the baron. I'm getting out with my friends before any of us get to buy the farm. I'm sorry, but that's the way it is."

There was an uncomfortable hush in the bedroom, with nobody prepared to meet anyone else's eyes. Lori broke the quiet.

"Someone outside," she said.

"Where?"

"Heard someone. But I can't seeing because of all the heavy smoking."

Ruby Rainer's bonfire was roaring away, sending a great pillar of roiling gray smoke into the calm morning air.

"Can't see anyone," Krysty said, coughing and spluttering as some of the smoke became sucked into the crowded room. The main window of Doc and Lori's bedroom opened onto the street, but the fire was at the rear of the large house, overlooking a rough garden with a dual privy. Beyond that was a deep draw that ran parallel with Main Street, vanishing into the thick brush of the desert.

"Close the window," Doc demanded. "Smoke's bad for my asthma and I don't desire another of my nasal eructations."

"What?" Carla said.

"Nosebleeds," Doc replied.

The conversation flagged and faded away. After another ten minutes or so Carla Petersen suggested to Baron Edgar that they should be going.

"Lots to do," she said. "Day's still young. Norman wants us both to go out and check where they found their snake dead. His idea is to keep on putting pressure on Edgar as baron until the string stretches too far and snaps."

"Guess I'm not ready to snap yet," the little man protested, sliding back onto his feet from the chair.

"Do well to visit Dern and lay out some jack on a blaster," J.B. suggested.

"No."

"Edgar," Carla begged, "please. Why not take John's advice? He and Ryan and the others know what they're talking about."

The chubby face managed a smile. And a strange kind of dignity. "Guess not. Thanks for the thought, Mr. Dix. But the day I need to pull out a blaster to defend what I believe in, then that's the day I've lost it all. You can't convince folks to goodness with a loaded gun."

With that he bowed to the others and left the room, followed by Carla Petersen. The door closed quietly behind them.

J.B. punched his right fist into his left hand. "Dark night! You might not be able to convince folks with a blaster, but you can sure as rad blast save your skin with one!''

''I can see his point,'' Rick said. ''Remember that I believe in peace, as well. Back in my time there was a lot of folks who figured it was better to live on your knees than die on your feet.''

''You believed that?'' Ryan asked, unable to conceal his surprise.

''No, of course not. But I always thought that any problem could eventually be sorted out by talking. Rather than a finger on a red button somewhere beneath the prairies of Kansas.''

The view from the rear window was still obscured by the turmoil of smoke from the garden bonfire.

Krysty, standing by Ryan, glanced toward the window. The one-eyed man felt her start, but her voice, when she spoke, was calm and measured.

''Don't anybody turn and stare, but we got us a stickie hanging on the glass, looking in at us.''

Lori immediately turned and stared.

And screamed.

Chapter Twenty-Five

ONE HAND WAS HOLDING the wooden wall of the house, the other flattened against the central pane of glass in the window, showing the white circles of the suckers on fingers and palm. The face was pressed flat, glowering at the seven companions.

The tiny insensate eyes, blank and lacking any spark of humanity, gazed unblinkingly in, and the mouth sagged open, revealing the lines of saw-edged teeth and the small, leathery tongue. Smoke from outside wreathed around the mutated monstrosity, making it appear, truly, like some creature from the depths of hell.

At Lori's shriek, the creature opened its mouth still farther and rattled the casement with its fist. A thick, bloody drool hung from the lips, dripping onto its naked chest.

"Mine." Ryan drew his SIG-Sauer and squeezed the trigger in a single, lethal movement.

The 9 mm bullet exploded through the glass, driving dozens of keen-edged splinters into the rubbery flesh of the stickie's face and neck. The full-metal-jacket round hit precisely where Ryan had aimed it—into the cavern of the gaping jaws, chipping teeth as it went, slicing the tongue into ribbons of oozing flesh, carrying on through the back of the throat. The slug angled off the spine and exited through the second cervical vertebra in a burst of pink spray.

The stickie went over backward, its one hand contracting, sucking out the pane of glass it had been holding. Everyone heard the crash as it landed near the back door of the house—followed by a shrill scream from Ruby Rainer, who'd just walked out of the house and had nearly been struck by the flailing corpse.

"Attracted by the smoke," Ryan guessed, holstering his warm gun. "Should do something. Bad news when stickies start coming into a ville like that in the middle of the morning. Should do something."

ZOMBIE ARRIVED an hour or so later, with Riddler and Harlekin.

"Reverend sent us t'ask you 'bout stickies," Zombie informed Ryan.

"Yeah?"

"You know all 'bout them," Riddler continued. "We seen that from the way you chilled them out in the desert."

"Told you. I've fought them before. But stickies aren't all the same. Just got some patterns in common. Like the way they get attracted by flames and by big explosions."

"Yeah. Reverend Mote said to come and ask if you figured they might attack Snakefish. Gang of 'em in the ville?"

"Mebbe."

"Worth going out t'look for their nest, Ryan?" Riddler queried.

Ryan grinned at the fat biker, amused by his enthusiasm to go out after the murderous muties.

"Mebbe. Can't you get the Baron's nephew to go up in his plane and look for them for you? Be great for a recce."

The three Last Heroes looked uncomfortably at one another. Harlekin answered. He'd had a bad accident some time in his past that had left him with a mess of scars around his mouth, and most of his upper lip was completely missing. His speech was blurred and sibilant.

"Fat boy wouldn't help Mote. He'd help the fugging ville and his dwarf uncle, but not the reverend. We could find the stickies' nest if we had someone along to tell us what to do."

"No."

Riddler looked around the room. "Could be better if you was to help, Ryan."

"No."

Zombie hissed between his teeth. "Reverend Mote said he wouldn't come. Said to tell you that the stickie in the ville has changed things. Said to tell you the feeding wouldn't be tomorrow dusk. Said to tell you it'd be today dusk."

"Answer's still the same," Ryan replied.

"What?"

"No."

THE BOTTOM TIP of the sun had fallen out of sight over the western horizon. The whole of the ville was gathered on the edge of the desert, near where the highway ran out into oblivion. Men, women and children stood huddled together, an air of expectant tension almost visible in the atmosphere. There was very little conversation.

It was cool and most folks wore jackets or shawls. Ryan and all of his party were warmly wrapped against the evening chill. Rick leaned heavily on his cane, shivering, his face pale and sweating.

On the way there, Ryan had found himself jostled in the back. Whirling around he'd been surprised to see the huge bulk of Riddler. But the Angel was wearing a long wool sweater over his colors, trying to make himself insignificant.

"Wanted a word, Ryan."

"Yeah?"

"I owe you. That's why. But I could be in deep shit if Zombie or the Motes knew I'd spoken to you 'bout it."

"About what?"

Riddler had looked cautiously around. But in the throng, with everyone moving quickly toward the site of the feeding, nobody seemed to be taking any notice of him.

"The feeding."

Ryan was becoming exasperated. "Fireblast! Tell it. It'll be night before you finish telling me what it is."

"Sure. Yeah. You're right, Ryan. Course y'are. It's that I heard talk 'bout who's gonna get picked for the feeding."

"Me?"

"No."

"One of us?"

"No. Mote's scared 'bout the blasters you carry. Won't cross you face-on, but if he had the chance to back-shoot, well, could be different. You know what I'm saying?"

"Sure, Riddler. But if it's not one of us, then who is it?"

"Reverend Mother Marianne likes to settle up scores, pay debts. That's what'll happen here. It don't pay to—"

"Who?" Ryan muttered.

"Can't tell you."

"Then why, for . . . ?"

"Warn you, Ryan. You did good with me."

"But *you* saved *my* life, Riddler," Ryan insisted. "How come you figure you owe me?"

"No. You chilled most of the stickies. I'd have been dead meat in a muties' pot if you hadn't been there. So, I'll pay some."

"Quickly!"

"Sure. Keep out of it. That's my word and that's my fucking warning. Who she picks . . . stand away. Or there'll be some serious blooding. Most of the Heroes got sawed-offs. They'll be watching close."

"So it's the baron?"

"No, not him. Not yet. Not open. But can't say anything more, Ryan. They'll have my balls if they . . . Just don't interfere!"

"Okay, I got you," Ryan said quietly. "Thanks, Riddler. I still owe you."

There had been a quick squeeze of the hand and then the big man had contrived to vanish into the crowd, reappearing a couple of minutes later with his brothers—and with a cut-down 12-gauge scattergun in his arms.

Baron Brennan arrived several minutes later, driving from the ville in a small passenger wag, with Carla Petersen in the front seat with him. His brother, Rufus, was in the rear seat with Layton, who was still in the leather flying suit. None of them spoke to anyone in the crowd, but Carla and the baron nodded to Ryan and his friends.

There was an almost tangible withdrawing of the other people from the baron, as if everyone knew that he carried the taint of some nameless disease and would contaminate them by even the slightest touch.

At last, signaled by Zombie firing his shotgun into the dark sky, the Motes themselves appeared among their congregation.

Both Norman and Joshua were carrying small drums—slung across their shoulders—which they immediately began to beat in a slow, driving rhythm that duplicated the beating of a heart.

Marianne Mote was dressed completely in scarlet. A long gown of silk, flowed down to her chubby ankles, and she was shod in a pair of high-heeled shoes that she could barely control on the rough ground. She was heavily made-up, like an aged doll, and she carried a long whip of silver leather in her right hand. The dress was cut so low in front that her breasts swelled against the thin material and seemed about to break for freedom.

At a sign from Norman, a pair of the Last Heroes strode in a half circle in front of the gathering, setting light to a series of gasoline fires. They immediately flared and roared, surrounding everyone in a ring of flame, giving the illusion that their only line of escape would be the dark desert behind them.

Where the snakes dwelled.

ONE THING that the Motes were extremely good at was whipping up the frenzy of a mob, repeating their exhortations to worship the worms of the desert, crying out in unison for divine intervention to point the finger at the guilty person in the ville who was responsible for the spate of bad luck.

"Use me as the oracle of Thy vengeance!" Marianne screamed, arms waving, the thin material of her dress dancing about her.

Ryan and the others huddled in a tight group, halfway back through the crowd. The Brennans and Carla Petersen, as befitted their nominal status in Snakefish, stood near the front.

The Last Heroes stayed ranged in a semicircle, eyes raking the congregation.

The yelling and praying grew louder and louder. And the fires, topped up from jerricans of gas, flamed and roared. Deep shadows skipped over the watching, wide-eyed faces. Standing with his back to the blackness of the desert, Ryan felt himself becoming nervous, feeling his spine tighten at the thought of the giant reptiles he knew were stirring in the wilderness behind him.

"Got a real bad feel about this one, lover," Krysty whispered.

"Me too." He'd brought the G-12 caseless, holding it casually under his arm, finger close to the trigger of the sophisticated blaster.

"The Spirit of the Worm comes upon me!" Marianne screamed, closing her eyes, pirouetting around in the orange light of the fires, smoke swirling about her, giving her a demonic look.

"Here we go," J.B. muttered.

The middle-aged woman faked her fit of religious frenzy quite skillfully. Ryan doubted it would have worked so well in the cold light of morning. But here, in the manipulated, drum-beating atmosphere of fervor, in the bizarre light of the bonfires, it was clearly working well enough.

Cries erupted from the crowd, calling on the snakes to witness and help. Amens, hallelujahs and hosannas rose from all, throughout the expectant congregation.

Marianne didn't stint herself in her performance. She thrashed around in the dust, dropping her whip, scooping up handfuls of pale sand and throwing them over herself. Her hair became disarrayed, her makeup covered in a mask of dirt, her rolling eyes winking dementedly out at the world. Her dress rucked up as she fell and kicked, revealing once again that she wore no panties.

Ryan turned to the Armorer, but J.B. had slipped away from his side. It was just possible to see the jaunty fedora, perched on top of his head, moving purposefully toward the front of the crowd.

"Krysty, Jak. Follow me. Don't do anything until I give the word."

Ryan's gut feeling told him that J.B. had guessed who had been chosen for the feeding.

"Show us the evil, show us! The Worm protects us all. The Worm is the power. The Worm is the way and the light!" Marianne's voice was straining ever louder. "Yes, oh yes! I can feel the spirit moving in me! Hallelujah, brothers and sisters! The word is coming to me!"

Marianne rolled over and over, legs kicking, her body caked in dust.

Ryan started after J.B., but the Armorer was nearly at the front, close by the Brennans and Carla.

Helped by her husband and son, Marianne staggered to her feet, beginning to spin around, arm outstretched, finger pointing at the congregation, her body a black shape against the brightness of the ring of fires. She spun faster and faster, the skirt of the dress flying out around her, like a child's top. Her face blank, her eyes staring wildly. Her finger accusing.

And the chanting began, led by Norman Mote, picked up by his son, Joshua, carried by the group of eight Last Heroes, racing through the crowd like a flash fire in a dry summer, swelling all around Ryan and the others.

"A feeding! A feeding! A feeding! A feeding!" Louder and louder, like the pulse of a raging and insensate heart.

Fists were punching the air, in unison, pounding the beat of the cry: "the feeding." A thousand voices raised together. The piping tones of little children and the trembling sound of the aged. It rose around Ryan, deafening him.

Marianne Mote stopped.

Immediately the yells began to fade away, until there was only the stillness of the night and a gasping intake of breath as everyone realized that the woman's finger pointed, rock steady, straight at the figure of Carla Petersen.

"Gaia!"

The Heroes began to move forward, stopping when a slight figure stepped from the front row and stood between them and Carla.

"First person moves, man or woman," J.B. said coldly, "and they're on their back looking up at the stars. With a bullet through their skull."

Nobody moved.

Chapter Twenty-Six

"HE'S ONE MAN, alone. Chill him! Feed him to Belial!"

Marianne's voice broke the silence like the shattering of a crystal goblet.

"He's not alone." Ryan leveled his G-12. "Someone makes a mistake and there'll be a lot of death come to this ville."

"Two or three or four! What does it matter? We are a thousand strong," Norman shouted, coming to his wife's support.

"Six!" came Doc's melodious voice from the middle of the crowd. "I urge discretion upon everyone here. You may o'crwhclm us, but the cost will be most appallingly high. Who would wish to die?"

"Looks like a hot-spot standoff," J.B. called. "You don't get at us without taking a high body count."

"You can't get away, scum!" Zombie shouted, looking across at Norman Mote for his orders.

"Mebbe not," Ryan agreed. "But it's triple-sure you won't live to find out."

A little girl with freckles and plaits, in a patched gingham dress, broke the stand-off, calling out in a clear, ringing voice, "Look, Mommy! See the funny mans!"

"Holy shit!" someone said hoarsely.

"Stickies!" Riddler bellowed, immediately blasting away with his shotgun.

To encounter stickies three times in two days was kind of unusual. Ryan's first reaction was to glance around, trying to place the members of his group, and trying to gauge the opposition.

J.B. stood at his elbow, one arm around the shoulders of Carla Petersen, Krysty was just behind with Jak. And somewhere in the center of the panicking mob were Doc, Lori and Rick.

Out front, cavorting around the fires, were a dozen stickies, bodies glistening in the light. Some held the cans of gasoline and others had seized blazing branches, waving them in the night like medieval torches.

Ryan was just able to grab Krysty by the arm when the mob swept by them, a shrill, hysterical gaggle charging aimlessly toward what they hoped might be some sort of freedom and escape from the threat.

"Keep close, lover!" he shouted.

Chaos.

Fire and explosions and screams and bodies, jostling, pushing. Ryan had the caseless rifle in his hands, but it was useless. The press of frightened men, woman and children was too great.

Ryan fought to maintain the ground where they stood, knowing that those who drove and pushed toward the road would fall among the stickies and the rolling wall of flames.

Suddenly Doc Tanner was with them, supporting Rick with an arm around his waist. The freezie was pale, gripping his walking stick with white knuckles, eyes wide with terror.

"Get ... me out ... of here, Ryan," he stammered. "I can't take it!"

"Where's Lori?" Krysty asked, striking out with the butt of her pistol at a fat man who lumbered into her, who grinned with the dreadful tension. Blood gushed from his face, but his expression didn't alter and he staggered on, toward the line of gasoline fires, toward where the flames bloomed and danced.

"What?" Doc bellowed.

"Lori? Where is she?"

"Don't know! We got separated. She's a big girl now. Hope she can look after herself."

Ryan heard a shotgun boom and decided that it wasn't his imagination. He *had* felt the wind of the charge, close by his face. He caught Zombie's eye and saw that the president of the Last Heroes motorcycle club was holding a smoking shotgun.

But now wasn't the time to do anything about it.

"One thing," Krysty pointed out.

"What?"

"Noise and flames and shooting should keep those bastard snakes away from here. With one of those up our asses we could find ourselves in some real heavy trouble."

"Plenty trouble anyway," Jak said, pointing to where one of the stickies had grabbed a woman who had tried to run past it. She clutched a small baby in a white lace shawl.

Before Ryan could fire he saw J.B.—only a few yards away—put two rounds through the middle of the mutie's face, showering the shrieking woman and her child with its stinking ichor.

The Armorer glanced around, seeing Ryan between the running people, and shouted to him at the top of his voice.

"Get out of this!"

Ryan nodded vigorously and pointed to the right of the fires, indicating that they should cut through the desert for a couple of hundred yards, hitting the blacktop on the Snakefish side.

"Why not stop and chill the stickies?" Krysty asked as Ryan began to move.

"Not our fight, lover. Going to be some dead here. Stickies got fire and gas. We could pick off a few, but they might get close to us in the dark. They got good night-seeing. No. Main thing is to get us all back to the ville safe."

SURPRISINGLY the missing Lori was at the Rentaroom before any of them, and was sitting on her bed, washing sand from between her toes.

Doc was helping to half carry the exhausted Rick and was near the limit of fatigue himself. But he cheered up at the sight of the girl.

"My angel of the brightest dawning! I was worried when I couldn't find you. How did you get back here so fast?"

"In a wag."

"With the baron?" J.B. asked. He'd seen the Brennans and Carla safely into their own vehicle before rejoining the others.

"No."

"With the Motes?" Ryan asked.

"Yeah. Josh asked me and I say yes I'll go with them. What other can I do? Stickies everyplace and smoke and I didn't see all of you! They safed my life."

"Main thing is that Lori's alive," Krysty said quickly, defusing a potential argument between Doc and the blond teenager.

"Best get something for Rick," Ryan said, leaning his G-12 against the wall. "He's spent."

"Shot my load, friends." The freezie sighed.

"Want drink?" Jak asked.

"Strawberry daiquiri and make it a large one, barman."

"I'll get water," the albino replied, leaving the room.

Ryan lifted the corner of the curtains, peering out at the front. The street was a hubbub of men and women, running everywhere, gathering in small knots, talking animatedly. One of the Heroes went by on his chopper, revving the engine, kicking up clouds of dirt in the glow of the streetlights.

J.B. checked the rear window. "Nothing out here. If the stickies had come into the ville and started a fire, the whole place would have gone up like tinder. Wooden houses, close together. Unless they're cleaned out, Ryan, they'll do that. Only way you stop a stickie is by chilling it. No other way to do it."

"I'm dying," Rick moaned. "Have kaddish sung over me. And put my baby shoes away, Mama."

"Shut up and drink," Jak said, returning with a tumbler.

Ryan whistled through his teeth. "I reckon this is coming up to a good time to shake the shit of Snake-fish off of our boots, friends. Stickies that close in those numbers mean serious bad news. Like I've already said, I'm sorry for that fat little baron. No doubt in my mind that the Motes'll run him out of the ville. Probably in the next few weeks, the way it's shaping. But that isn't our fight. Never was. Never will be."

J.B. looked as if we were going to argue, but they were interrupted by a knock on the door. It was Ruby Rainer, her face smeared with soot and dirt, her "feeding" clothes stained and torn, the hem of her skirt sodden with what looked to be congealing blood.

"Shedskin!" she panted. "You outlanders all made it back safe? There's a hollow-tooth miracle. Azrael himself must have been looking after you. In all that death..."

"You all right, Mrs. Rainer?" Krysty asked.

"I'm delivered, mercy be to the coil and the scale," she replied, leaning against the wall to recover her breath. "But there's many a dozen good folk of this ville who won't see the sunrise tomorrow."

"How many chilled?" Ryan asked.

The elderly woman shook her head, the electric lamp casting deep shadows across the stark bones of her face. "I'd count on two dozen or more. There was the whole Locke family burned when one of those mutie spawn poured gas over them all. Dancing in the flames they was, and all their flesh was melting and dripping away from them. Danced until they fell, they did. Every one. And there was Miriam—"

"How many stickies done for?" J.B. interrupted.

"I don't know. There seemed to be hundreds. One gripped my dress and pulled me down. May the hollow tooth feed John Dern for saving me. He blasted the monster back to the pit, but its blood went all over me and... Forgive me," she said, on the edge of tears.

"Most escaped?"

"Yes, Mr. Cawdor. I think—" She stopped and blew her nose noisily on a kerchief she pulled from her sleeve. "So many hurt and chilled. I saw poor Mr. Vareson, his whole face scorched black, eyes bubbling holes in... Oh, dear, dear. I must go and lie down. I don't think I can prepare any food tonight, if you don't..."

Krysty patted her on the arm. "We can raid the larder if we feel hungry, Mrs. Rainer. You go and take a rest. I don't think any of us are going to feel much like eating tonight."

As the door closed behind her, Jak turned to Krysty. "Speak for self. I'm real hungry."

NOBODY ELSE WAS STAYING at the hotel, and Ruby Rainer kept a well-stocked pantry. It was an indication of the wealth of the ville, with all its processed gas, that she was able to store so much. And so little of it grown locally.

A rare sight in the Deathlands was a freezer, yet Ruby had one, humming away to itself in a room off of the kitchen. It was filled with beef, pork and chicken, several different sorts of fruit and steaks of some large and unidentified fish.

Jak and Lori set to, frying some of the fish in oil and serving it with potatoes and tender green peas. They dished out some large raspberries, but they hadn't thawed properly so most of the group chose to leave them.

"Not bad," Rick said. "Not quite as good as Mom used to make, but it comes close. Best thing I've eaten since I've been in these Deathlands."

"You should appreciate, my dear young friend, that this is also one of the best meals that I have eaten in Deathlands. And I have been here a great deal longer than you."

Doc's comment cast a pall over the freezie, and he refused a second helping of the bulletlike fruit. "Maybe I should have stayed frozen," he said. "Or never gotten frozen at all. The cryo business isn't all they say."

"You said there were other cryo centers, Rick?" Ryan said.

"That's right. One up on the Lakes and one some place in south Texas. It'll come back to me, I guess."

"Could be this is a good time to tell us just what you know about jumps and gateways," J.B. suggested.

Rick put down his coffee mug. "If I could remember what it is I know about gateways, J.B., then I'd be happy to tell you."

"How 'bout how to control where you go?" Jak asked.

"No. Sorry, guys. That wasn't my scene. I can perhaps help out in ways of detecting faulty gateways and how to return. I know I knew all that stuff. Knew it. Once."

It was a disappointment. Ryan had, at the back of his mind, the hope that some day, somewhere, they might come across some piece of information that would reveal how to master the gateways. And the freezies had been one of his hopes.

Time had drifted by.

It was around ten o'clock and the bedlam out on Main Street had died down. Just as the seven were beginning to think about bed they heard the noise of several of the Last Heroes' two-wheel wags rumbling through the night from the old funfair.

"Company," Rick said unnecessarily as the motorbikes came to a halt immediately outside.

"Or trouble," J.B. said grimly.

Finally they heard the front door crash open and booted feet drum along the hallway. Except for the freezie, all were wearing blasters—and all went for them.

"In here!" Ryan shouted, taking the initiative away from the bikers. "If you're coming to assassinate someone, you don't make so much noise about it."

Zombie stomped in, backed by Riddler, Harlekin and Freewheeler.

"You in here?" Zombie said.

"Looks like it," Ryan replied calmly.

"Nobody chilled or injured?"

"No."

"Come from the ville's council."

"Who's that?" J.B. asked, standing near the table.

"Your friend Carla and the baron. And the Reverend Mote and his lady and Josh Mote."

"Since when?" J.B. said.

"Since long enough," Riddler replied defensively. "Keep free, bro. This isn't your fight. Remember that, huh?"

"So everyone tells me. Bro."

"What did the council decide?" Ryan asked, easing the tension.

"That at dawn we all go out and blow the shit out of those fucking stickies."

"Who's this 'we' you mentioned?" Krysty asked.

"Baron Edgar, his nephew and his brother. And a few others. And us. And Josh Mote. Oh, and you outlanders, of course."

"Why us?"

Riddler answered. "You took the jack from the ville and food and beds. Now the council says you gotta ride with us after the stickies. Sort of pay the debt, Ryan." He shrugged his shoulders as if to explain that it wasn't his idea.

"How did the council vote on this?" Ryan asked. "No, let me guess. Wouldn't be three to two in favor, would it?"

"No." Harlekin laughed.

"No?"

"No, Ryan, you too-smart fucker. It was three to nothing. Carla and the old baron didn't bother to vote at all!"

"If..." J.B. began, hand blatantly on the butt of his Steyr blaster.

"Forget it." The wolfish smile disappeared from Zombie's face. "Your gaudy's fine. Nobody hurt her or Edgar. They're fine as sunshine, Mr. Dix!"

"Dawn, you said?" Ryan asked. "We'll leave the woman and the free . . . and Rick here in the ville."

"Please yourself. Don't matter. Just so long as we waste the stickies."

"Ryan. I don't—" Krysty began, stopping as he turned and looked coldly at her. She knew better than to push it. For the time being.

"So be there," Riddler said.

"Or be square," Rick concluded.

"Not you, feeb," Zombie sneered. "The others. Be there or be fucking dead!"

Chapter Twenty-Seven

LAYTON BRENNAN FLEW so low over their heads that
they could see his amiable face, grinning at them over
the edge of the cockpit of the Sopwith 1½-Strutter, his
goggles glinting in the dawn sunlight. He waved a
cheery hand, then angled the plane away, heading
across the dusty desert toward Death Valley.

The search was on for the stickies.

The inbred muties didn't have anything that resem-
bled an organized camp. They burrowed into the sides
of hills, or took over old, abandoned houses and
buildings, staying sometimes for only a few days.
Sometimes for months. It all depended on how long
it would take for them to strip the region around their
nests of anything edible or useful. Then they would
move on.

Ryan had been pressed by Zombie and by Norman
Mote about how many stickies he thought might be in
the area. In the panic during the feeding ceremony
only three of the muties had been chilled.

"I've seen them alone, and often seen them hunting in packs around ten to a dozen. Biggest nest I saw
was probably forty or fifty. Trader once told me of a
kind of ville of stickies he'd come across. Said there
could easily have been two hundred or more. If I was

a guessing man I'd say that we'd probably find us around fifty. Good-size pack.''

As the airplane shrank to a tiny dot in the pink, cloud-dappled sky, Norman Mote called his hunting posse to order.

"Quiet, brothers. You all know why we're here. You've seen the sad corpses lying there in the temple. We don't want any stickies left alive. Not a single one.''

Ryan made a quick count: eight of the Last Heroes; himself, with J.B., Jak and Doc; Edgar Brennan with his brother and his nephew, off in his plane; and twenty-seven other men from the ville. The only one Ryan recognized was the gun dealer, John Dern.

Everyone was armed, many carrying a variety of patched and repaired scatterguns. Ryan's warning that the only way to be sure of downing a stickie was to blow its head apart had been passed all around the group.

Ryan had faced a bitter argument from Krysty during the night and on into the early hours of the morning.

"Why?"

"You know.''

"Tell me, lover. Tell me why you four get to go and I'm left here holding the baby. No. Check that. Holding both the babies. Lori and the freezie. Why is it me?''

"Because there's no women going on the cull. That's why.''

"Gaia! It makes me sick, Ryan. I tell you that for jack in the dirt.''

"I know. But I wouldn't want to leave Rick on his own. His health's worse again today."

"If he was a man he'd have picked a blaster and be out on the hunt."

"Not fair, lover. You know the poor bastard's gut-sick."

In the end Krysty had reluctantly agreed to drop the quarrel.

THEY TRAVELED in a fleet of battered wags, mostly open-bed market wags. Norman Mote and his son rode in the half-armored wag that had brought them to the feeding. Edgar Brennan and his brother had chosen to ride with Ryan and his three friends.

"For safety," Rufus had whispered.

J.B. had taken off his fedora to avoid losing it in the wind. As he rubbed his fingers through the cropped stubble of his hair he heard the baron saying to Ryan, "Carla said to watch out for a back-chilling out on the hunt."

"Least we can do is watch for it," Ryan agreed. He turned to J.B. "Pass the message to Jak and Doc."

Doc Tanner was enjoying the ride. The wag bumped over the rutted highway, enveloped in a cloud of gray dust. "On the road," he shouted to Ryan, baring his perfect teeth in a wide smile. "I was a great reader, you know. During the days after they trawled me I read all of Jack's books. The beat romances. Traveling and searching for...what was it they called it? Satori. That was it. I searched for it, but never found it."

Most of the time that the old man began to ramble, he left Ryan way behind. Or way ahead. It was never clear which.

THEY WERE ONLY a few miles out of the ville when they heard the crackling sound of the airplane returning.

"Flywag!" shouted the lookout man who was on the front of their truck.

Trader had once explained to Ryan that the quality of fuel needed for jet-powered air wags was beyond anything that the Deathlands could produce. He'd found a cache of it north of where Boston had been, but they didn't have a plane to use it. Nor anyone living who had the least idea of how to pilot one of the fighter jets. But the old biplane flown by Layton Brennan used a much more basic type of fuel. The engine sounded rough, but it worked.

"Get yourself six of those and some good machine guns and you could take damned near any ville you wanted," J.B. said.

"Yeah, but you and me found us some missiles around the redoubts that could pluck that out the sky. Easy as spitting."

"This MP-7 could do the job," the Armorer replied, patting the H&K blaster on his lap. "But air wags got so much surprise. Look at the way he's gotten back here so quick."

The Sopwith 1½-Strutter lurched and the engine faltered as it came swooping low over the convoy. Zombie, leading the way on his Electra Glide, held up his fist and stopped the wags. As the dust cleared, everyone could see the hand over the edge of the plane, dropping something near them, something with a hank of rag attached to it so they could find it easily.

Ryan swung over the bed of the truck and walked to the rounded stone, three or four of the Last Heroes following him. He bent and picked it up, peeling away the sheet of handmade paper from around the small rock, flattening it out.

The writing was crude and childish, the letters of uneven shapes and sizes.

Fifteen miles. Northeast. Leave road at old school. Dirt—the next word was illegible—over hill. Caves. Counted thirty. They saw me and gotten jumping good around.

"What's it say?" Riddler asked. Ryan handed him the note, but the fat biker passed it to Kruger.

"Don't read good, Ryan. Frankie here got the spelling and figuring."

Kruger was old with a badly scarred face, as if he'd been in a devastating fire some years earlier. He followed the lines with a painful concentration, tracing them with the knife blades he'd sewn into the fingers of an ancient pair of gauntlets.

"Take us a half hour," he said, looking across at Zombie.

"Read it again," Zombie ordered, listening while Kruger stumbled through it. "Yeah. They could be ready for an attack. Best we leave the wags by the old school. Go for 'em on foot. You reckon, Ryan?"

"Yeah. I reckon."

THE SCHOOL WAS an adobe building that looked as if it had been abandoned long before dark day. The windows were gaping sockets and there was no trace of a door. The structure stood at the junction of the highway and a dirt track that wound away into some low hills.

The leadership of the group was peculiar. Norman Mote proclaimed himself in charge, yet he left all the major decisions up to Zombie, who, in his turn, deferred to Ryan. Baron Edgar, who should have been at their head, waited patiently with the rest of the men.

Ryan agreed that it would make sense to split into two groups, to circle around the nest of the stickies and attack from the rear, making sure that none of the creatures escaped the trap.

But the division of the two sections led to querulous squabbling.

Ryan didn't want to split his own group, nor did Zombie want to split up the Heroes. The Brennans insisted that they should go with Ryan's group. Norman Mote pressed that the baron ought to be with them "for his own safety."

In the end everyone settled on a reluctant compromise. Ryan and Jak were grouped with four of the bikers, including Riddler, as well as Joshua Mote, Edgar Brennan and a dozen of the men of the ville, including John Dern, who was carrying a customized M-16 carbine.

Zombie and Norman Mote led the other group, with J.B. and Doc there to keep an eye on Edgar's brother, the partially blind Rufus.

"We go left," Ryan said. "You got a chron?"

Riddler shook his head and grinned, showing a mouthful of broken and stained teeth. "Told yer. Don't go for all that figuring shit."

"My timepiece will suffice, will it not, Ryan?" Doc asked, displaying the trim silver watch on his left wrist.

"Sure. Say forty-five minutes from...now. Unless you get attacked. Find a way, close as you can and get ready. I'll lead our squad in. You come in straight after, Zombie."

"Sure. Be there, Ryan."

Ryan glanced around his group, seeing the nerves and ragged tension.

"Most muties run from blaster fire. Stickies run, but they run straight at you. Explosions and fires bring them. We all know that. Just keep in mind that they're triple-stupes. Body wounds hardly slow them at all. Lot of you got pump actions. Best thing for a stickie. Wait for them to get close, then take their heads off. Any questions?"

A skinny, middle-aged man raised a tentative hand.

"Yeah?"

"I have a question, Mr. Cawdor."

"Fire it."

"What do we do if we get grabbed by one of them stickies?"

"Pray. No more questions? Then let's go and do it."

"TEN MINUTES to go. Could do with Layton and his plane, Baron."

"Might it not warn them?"

Ryan nodded. "Could be. From the note, we should be virtually on top of them by now."

Edgar Brennan looked exhausted. He wasn't dressed for a cross-country trek. His shoes had lost their polish and his pants their crease. The laundered shirt was stained around the back and chest, the collar ragged and limp. He'd torn off the paisley cravat and held it in his hand, using it to mop at his brow.

"Want me to go ahead and scout with one of the brothers?" Riddler asked eagerly.

"Word is there's a lot of stickies there. Couple of scouts'd whet their appetite for the rest of us. No."

The Last Hero didn't argue, grinning cheerfully at Ryan.

John Dern sidled up to the front, clutching his carbine. "Could find a good spot and pick off the evil devils from safety with this?" he suggested. "Be happy to do it."

"Good combat blaster. Not the best for wiping out a triple-dozen stickies. They'd walk over you. We go in together, fast and blasting."

"LOOKS LIKE IT. Sounds like it."

Ryan held up his hand to stop the straggling file of men. He'd heard the familiar, guttural grunting noise that the suckered muties usually made, coming from just over the next ridge. He dropped to hands and knees and crawled swiftly forward, followed by Jak.

Cautiously Ryan eased himself to the crest of the hill. Squinting over the top, he saw a steep-sided valley that was honeycombed with shallow caves. Gathered together in the middle were a group of stickies. It looked as though Layton Brennan's rough count had been about right.

"Thirty-five or so," he whispered

The boy was licking his pale lips, his scarlet eyes glittering with the anticipation of the firefight to come. "How long?" he asked.

Ryan glanced at his chron. "Three minutes. Wonder if the others got here yet. Can't see any sign of them on the far... Yeah. There."

He spotted the flash of sunlight off metal. A line of heads appeared on the far ridge, all looking down at the stickies. Ryan knew that J.B. wasn't in command of the other raiding party. The Armorer would never have been stupid enough to risk being spotted before the attack began.

"Fireblast! Best go now, or they'll see us and we'll lose the surprise."

He turned and beckoned to Riddler. The fat biker crouched and waddled to join them. "What the fuck's up?"

"We gotta go now. Stupes there are going to blow the whole attack."

He suddenly heard an outburst of shrill squealing from the far side of the ridge.

"Too late." Ryan shouted the command. "Come on! Now! Let's go!"

Chapter Twenty-Eight

THE STICKIES HAD initiated the attack, taking the impetus from the men of Snakefish. Most of the muties rushed toward Zombie's group, ululating and waving their suckered fingers. Some turned back as they saw Ryan leading his twenty or so men over the rim of the hill and down into the valley.

"Let 'em get close!" Ryan yelled.

The muties had a slight numerical disadvantage, but they made up for that by their unbridled ferocity. Other than the night assault at the feeding, few of the men from the ville had ever seen a stickie and many were almost paralyzed with terror at the hideous sight of gibbering death running at them.

Some turned and fled in panic.

Almost all of them died early.

The skinny man who'd asked the question about what to do if he got grabbed by a stickie got his answer with horrific speed.

He stumbled blindly into the embrace of two of the scuttling muties. One was a female, with pendulous breasts, who used her suckered hand to tear away the man's clothes, leaving bleeding weals on his pale flesh. Her other hand clutched at his groin, the tiny disks clamping to his shrunken genitals. With a slobbering whoop of delight, the creature exerted all her power, emasculating the screaming man and flourishing the severed flesh and sinew above her head before lifting them greedily to her mouth. Her companion had already buried its face in the side of the man's neck, near the throbbing temptation of the carotid artery.

Death was mercifully rapid.

Scatterguns boomed all around, interspersed with the lighter, thinner sound of the .32 which were the common handblasters of the ville.

If Ryan's original plan had been followed by the group containing Zombie and Norman Mote, the initial wave of the assault could have hoped to chill sixty to seventy percent of the hostiles. Now it was a bloody battle for the upper hand.

Ryan had his rifle set on triple burst, knocking over any mutie that came within easy range. He made sure that the caseless rounds were head shots, exploding the blank-eyed skulls like eggs under a mallet.

Ryan nearly tripped over a human corpse on the far side of the valley, near the opening of one of the caves, recognizing who it was only from the pair of dark blue spectacles that lay near the headless body. Layton Brennan, in his air wag, would soon learn that his grandfather was dead.

The sand was rapidly becoming a quagmire of trampled mud, with the stench of death hovering above.

The biker called Freewheeler was facing a stickie who'd snatched his scattergun, but couldn't work out how to fire it. The Hero had drawn a long-bladed knife and was cutting away at the mutie's chest and stomach, opening up gaping wounds in the rubbery flesh, but hardly harming the creature.

Ryan was about to blast it when he heard the crack of Doc's Le Mat pistol. A section of the creature's face and jaw became detached, dangling loose like a broken storm shutter. The stickie staggered then reached up and pulled away the chunk of bone and flesh, peering at it bemusedly until Doc shot it once more at close range between the eyes.

"This appears to be easier than stealing candy from a little baby," Doc shouted.

Ryan leveled his G-12 and fired a trio of bullets, missing Doc by less than a yard. The old man stumbled sideways, his jaw dropping in shock. He glanced behind him and saw a stickie falling over backward, half its face blown away by Ryan's shots.

"Some little child!" Ryan yelled. "Watch your bastard back, Doc!"

Riddler was nearly pulled down by two young female stickies as he fumbled in the pockets of his denim vest for more ammunition. They mewed at him as their hands reached out, their bloodied teeth exposed behind leathery lips.

He swung the butt of his shotgun in two clubbing blows, knocking both muties to the crimsoned earth. He thumbed the twin hammers and leveled the twin barrels at the semiconscious females. "Eat lead," he snarled, firing first one round and then the other. Both the heads disappeared in a spray of bone, skin and blood.

Riddler grinned at Ryan. "Best advice anyone ever gave me," he bellowed. "Shoot 'em in the head and they fucking die! Right on, bro!"

The combined firepower of the attackers finally tipped the balance firmly in their favor. The initial charge by the stickies left, at Ryan's swift count, around eight or nine of the norms dead. But the shotguns were taking their toll, aided by the blasters of Ryan, J.B., Doc and Jak. Well over half of the stickies were already dead meat.

The remaining creatures had begun to retreat, heading away in a clumsy run over the ridges, while others backed off into the shallow caves where they were easily trapped and butchered. This part of the day's hunting, Ryan noticed, was particularly relished by Norman Mote and his whooping, jeering son.

J.B. joined Ryan, carefully reloading his blaster. "Looks close to done," he said quietly.

"Yeah. Looks that way. Could have gone worse, I guess."

"Least none of us got caught by any stray lead. There was plenty flying for a while."

"Where's the baron?"

J.B. turned and pointed. "There. Near where his brother bought the farm."

"Best go see to him. Wouldn't want any accidents to happen. Not now."

They were almost too late.

The air was filled with the rumbling explosions of the scatterguns, and the thinner cracks of the small-caliber pistols. The valley was brimming with the stench of powder smoke, hazy and blue.

"There he is," the Armorer said.

Edgar Brennan, a kerchief pressed to his red-rimmed, weeping eyes, was moving unsteadily down the far side of the valley.

"Let's go help him. Looks flattened by his brother's chilling."

He and J.B. walked quickly across, feeling the stickiness of the dirt on the soles and heels of their combat boots. The sounds of gunfire were dying down.

When they were only a few yards from the stumbling little man, he looked up and saw them, still rubbing at his eyes. "Rufus has..." he began. But his feet slipped from under him and he fell, full length, rolling toward them.

Simultaneously the earth behind the baron exploded in great bursts of mud. Both J.B. and Ryan, their ears tuned to the sounds of a firefight, picked out the sharper noise of the shooting. Each man immediately recognized the distinctive sound of the blaster that was being used.

"M-16," J.B. shouted, rolling for cover.

"Yeah. Dern. There he is."

The owner of the gun shop stood on the ridge, about a hundred paces behind them. When he saw them looking his way he hesitated, then stood and waved to them.

"Chill him?" J.B. asked.

"He's one of Mote's boys," Ryan replied. "Could push things over the brim and get the pot boiling on the fire."

Dern began to approach them, rifle at his side. "Hollow tooth, brothers!" he called. "That was close. I was aiming at a stickie behind you, but there's something wrong with the sights on my blaster."

Brennan had stood and brushed himself clean, his hands trembling with shock at the near miss. "He tried to chill me."

"Yeah, Baron, but I'd keep my lips zipped," J.B. suggested. "This isn't the time or place, with all Mote's men round us."

"For sure, John, but . . ."

Dern reached them. "Never known this blaster to let me down. That was terrible. Could have gunned down the baron."

Ryan looked him in the eye. "You could have, but you didn't. Now, that's either lucky or unlucky. Depends on how you look at it."

"I don't understand, Mr. Cawdor."

"Yeah, you do. If you'd killed the baron, some would say that was lucky. Some might say it wasn't. You missed him. Some'll say the same."

Dern swallowed hard and looked away. "I sure don't know—" he began.

But J.B. interrupted him. "One thing to keep in mind, gunsmith. Anything happens to the baron now, we'll know who to come looking for. Won't we?"

Zombie joined them with six of his chapter. Ryan had seen one of them—Vinny, he thought—go down under an unusually tall stickie, his body a welter of blood.

The gunfire had faded away. The fight was over and won.

"That's it," the Last Hero said. "We got 'em all. Don't think a single one escaped. We found us some tinies in one cave. Blowed them away. Can't let the fuckers breed."

"Sure," Ryan agreed. "We going back to Snakefish now?"

He looked at Baron Brennan, but the little man was still too shaken by his narrow escape and the death of his brother to make any sense. It was Norman Mote, arriving with his arm around his son's shoulders, who answered.

"Surely will. And thanks to everyone here. Y'all played your parts. We'll have a service of thanks this night."

"And you got some burying to do, Reverend," Ryan said.

"And I have to see to the obsequies for poor Azrael Twelve, Brother Cawdor. And pursue the quest to find out who butchered him. Perhaps it could have been the stickies. Then again . . . perhaps not."

Ryan looked around the place of blood and death, resolving that he and his friends had to leave Snakefish as soon as possible. Before it was too late.

Chapter Twenty-Nine

THOUGH NORMAN MOTE tried to make those in the ville believe that the raid on the stickies had been an unqualified success, there were too many corpses from Snakefish to convince everyone.

By the time the excitement and the grief had died away and become more private and seemly, it was early afternoon and the sun rode high in the nuke-polluted sky.

Ryan and his friends dined in their hotel, with three guests. Carla Petersen sat next to J.B. Beside her was Baron Edgar Brennan, stricken by his bereavement, only picking at his plate of stew and rice. His nephew, Layton, sat next to him.

Once Ryan and the others had given an account of the morning's firefight, conversation flagged and faltered. Eventually it faded into an almost complete silence.

Krysty leaned nearer to Ryan, lowering her voice. "Rick's been ill. Couple of times during the morning his mind sort of slipped and he was talking like he was back to being a kid, out on a summer picnic with his folks. Place called Bear Mountain. He was dozing and mumbling to himself, like Doc does every now and then."

"We always knew that these freezies were only frozen 'cause they were close to dying. I'd still like to try to find the other two cryo centers that he mentioned."

Krysty smiled. "I've already asked him about that, while you and the rest of the good old boys were out playing with your blasters."

He ignored the gibe. "And? What'd he say about them?"

"I took notes in case I forgot it. And he also talked about gateways."

Ryan whistled softly. "Been real busy, lover. Tell me more about gateways."

The news wasn't good. Rick had told Krysty, while he lay resting on his bed, that he could recall that his special area of expertise had been the gateway controls. But like many technical specialities his had been contained within a narrow band. All he knew was how to make sure the controls weren't set for a gateway that didn't exist or had suffered a major malfunction. It was an easy number and letter code, which Krysty had written down.

"Better than nothing" was Ryan's comment. "Always been worried that we might materialize inside an earthslide or under five hundred feet of water. Anything else useful?"

Krysty nodded. "One thing. But this time he's not so sure. There might be an automatic reset if you want to come back within thirty minutes to the last redoubt you left from. He thinks it was universal and applies to all gateways. Just use a gateway less than thirty minutes after you've arrived and you'll be sent back to the redoubt where you started from. But remember that Rick wasn't a hundred percent positive."

"What percent was he positive?" Ryan asked, taking the note from Krysty's extended hand.

"Bit more than fifty. Not enough to stake your life on."

"No. Not to stake lives on. Then again, if we ever needed to try it out, it'd probably be because we were one foot in the grave."

Layton Brennan leaned across the table to interrupt their conversation.

"Ryan, Uncle Edgar says you'd like to come up for some bird sky."

"In your air wag?"

The fat face creased with pleasure. "Wanna try it?"

"Yeah. Always wondered what it felt like from some old vids I've seen."

Layton beamed. "You got some steel, outlander. Most folks in the ville here'd put their pants in for the gravy-chute treatment rather than come up in the Sopwith."

"When?"

The young man looked across at the baron, who was closeted away in his own thoughts and didn't even glance up. Carla Petersen had been listening, and she answered.

"Best make it soon, Layton. Trouble's simmering in Snakefish."

"I'd really like to try the air wag, as well," J.B. said.

Carla put her hand on his sleeve. "John, it's very dangerous."

"It's not," Layton protested petulantly. "Hardly had a scrape. Well, hardly any *real* bad scrapes."

"When can we go?" Ryan pressed.

"Could get her gassed up in an hour. Take off a half hour after that."

Ryan glanced at J.B., trying to judge his reaction to the idea. But the Armorer's head was turned toward Carla and he didn't look up.

"Yeah. That'd be fine. Where d'you take off from? Down by the gas plant?"

"Sure thing. Sierra Sunrise Park had a big parking lot for wags. I use that. She only needs a short space to get up, up and away."

"It's a deal." Ryan felt an unusual frisson of excitement at the knowledge that he was about to do something that very few people had done in Death-lands in the past hundred years.

He was going to fly.

"CHOCKS AWAY."

"Chocks away."

"Contact!"

Mealy, the Hell's Angel with three fingers missing from his left hand, swung the propeller of the Sopwith 1½-Strutter, bellowing, "Contact!" as he did so.

Several of the other Last Heroes stood around the biplane, watching intently. Ryan was in the observer's cockpit of the old air wag, wearing a pair of blurred goggles, peering out through the dust. He saw Riddler standing next to Zombie, the two men talking animatedly about something.

The leader of the bikers had stayed close to his lieutenant during the preflight preparations. A couple of times it seemed as though the fat brother was going to say something to Ryan, but Zombie was always there at his shoulder. And whatever it was remained unsaid.

"Swing it again!" Layton shouted as the engine coughed and spluttered. A cloud of blue-gray smoke jetted from the side of the engine, but the propeller refused to move.

"Contact!" Mealy yelled, pulling down on the polished and varnished wooden blade. This time the engine fired, hesitantly, then with a full-throated roar. A great jet of wind blew back, and Ryan was grateful for the goggles.

Krysty and J.B. stood watching at one side of the makeshift runway. Lori had chosen to stay back in the hotel to rest. Jak had decided to go scavenging around the ville. Doc and Rick had just arrived, walking slowly together, their walking sticks tapping in unison.

Most of the instruments on the panel in front of Ryan had been adapted and altered from their original condition, and Layton had pointed out to Ryan that very few of them actually worked.

"I read they used to call this flying by the seat of your pants," he had said, giggling. "Well, if that's right, then I sure should be a great pilot. I reckon I got the biggest seat of the pants in the whole of the Deathlands!"

He turned in his seat and gave Ryan the thumbs-up sign. The plane began to roll forward slowly, ready to turn into the wind for takeoff. Ryan relaxed, check-ing that the straps were safely buckled across his chest.

For the first time he was able to look over at the tumbledown remnants of the theme park. It was in a worse condition than he'd imagined. Ryan knew about these places and their so-called "white-knuckle rides," that people had gone with their children and paid good jack to go on spiraling rides in miniature wags with the main purpose of being frightened.

To someone born and reared in the Deathlands, where every waking moment was tight with potential danger, it seemed a bizarre way of spending jack and passing the time.

"Here we go!" the baron's nephew yelled.

Ryan found that his mouth had gone dry with nerves. Flying was something that he'd always wanted to do, never imagining for a moment that he'd be able to do it. Now, here he was, racing along, faster and faster, the ruined buildings of the Sierra Sunrise Park smearing into one another.

"Fireblast!" he shouted, suddenly feeling the ex-ultation of lifting off the earth.

He was flying.

It was one of the truly wonderful moments of Ryan Cawdor's life.

The wind raced by and the earth opened up under them, the sky tilting at a crazy angle as Layton banked the ancient air wag first right then left. Beneath the Sopwith biplane Ryan could see the ville of Snakefish unfolding like a living map—the houses along Main Street and the neat gardens at their backs.

They were flying along only a hundred feet above the ground, enabling him to pick out the individual shops and homes. There was Ruby Rainer's rooming house, with her diminutive figure hanging some washing on the line. He saw her shade her eyes as they soared by.

Ryan stared at the shadow of the plane, trailing beneath them across the dry earth. He glimpsed someone walking hurriedly from the front of the Rentaroom, but he couldn't make out who it was. There'd been the glint of startling blond hair, but that was all.

The engine coughed then picked up again.

The air wag dipped and climbed, soaring skyward.

Ryan wasn't a great lover of poetry, but he recalled a line that Doc had once quoted. Something about a bird.

"Morning's minion, dapple-dawn-drawn falcon."

That was it. The lightness of spirit was utterly wonderful.

The engine coughed, cleared, spluttered. Revived again. Coughed once more.

Died.

In the startling quiet, Ryan was aware of the wind as it whistled through the frail struts and bracing wires. Then he heard Layton Brennan's voice, loud and clear.

"Oh, fuck!"

"Can't you start her again?" Ryan shouted, glancing over the side and seeing that they were out over the rough landscape of the desert, around five miles from the nearest edge of the ville. And descending fast.

"No chance. Sorry 'bout this. We're going' down, Ryan. Could be hard and bumpy. You'd better hang on real tight."

It still didn't seem to Ryan that there was any real danger to either of them. The air still floated around the plane, and the ground looked safe enough from that height. And they didn't seem to be moving very fast.

Two hundred feet.

Layton was struggling to turn the plane around and head toward the ville, where there was level ground for an emergency landing. But they were losing altitude fast.

The round, jowled face looked back at Ryan, the eyes invisible behind the goggles. The creaking of the leather flying suit was audible in the unreal silence.

"Fuel's run out. Can't have been more than a couple of gallons put in. That bastard Mealy was in charge. He's sabotaged us, Ryan!"

Less than a hundred feet.

It was now obvious that they couldn't hope to reach Snakefish. They were going to have to put down among the dips and hollows of the mesquite desert.

Ryan guessed they were down to twenty or thirty feet. As they dropped lower, their speed seemed somehow faster. And for the first time he realized that they were in serious danger. The lightly built plane, with its frail fuselage, would crumple like paper when they hit. Unless Layton was good enough or lucky enough to put them down easy.

The fat young man could have been good enough, but he wasn't lucky.

"Here we go!" he shouted.

The wind had died away, and there was a faint crackling as the undercarriage brushed through the low scrub. Ryan readied himself, one hand on the release buckle of his harness, knowing that death in any crash could often come from being trapped and burned.

They were moving appallingly fast. Quicker than he'd ever been. Or so it seemed in those last blinking seconds before the impact.

Layton managed to get one of the wheels down, but it dug immediately into the soft sand, making the air wag slew around. The tip of the propeller snagged a boulder and the whole craft lurched sickeningly forward onto its nose.

Ryan's head was filled with the noise of splitting wood and snapping wires. He thought he heard a scream, but it could have come from him.

He was enveloped in darkness.

Chapter Thirty

RYAN HADN'T SLIPPED completely into the stygian depths of unconsciousness.

Despite the crushing force of the impact, he'd managed to brace himself. The straps across his chest held him tightly, making his ribs creak. He found himself dangling, upside down, with something warm and sticky running down his forehead, over his face, behind the broken glass of the goggles and into his good eye, blinding him.

His nostrils were filled with the overpowering stench of spilled gasoline, and he could feel the chill of it, soaking through his pant leg. His right ankle was twisted and held in place by some part of the plane that had been rammed backward in the crash. And he could hear someone moaning.

Apart from that sound, there was a deathly stillness. His ears had been battered and deafened by the racketing of the engine, and only now was his hearing slowly returning to normal.

He became aware of the pit-pat of dripping liquid. With an effort he lifted his right hand and pulled off the goggles, wiping cautiously at his good eye and wondering where all the blood had come from. If it was his, he wasn't surprised that he felt no pain. He knew from experience that the body had some strange and effective defense mechanisms when inflicted with a major injury.

His vision cleared. "Oil," he said quietly. Thick oil had oozed from a ruptured part of the air wag's engine.

"Time to be moving," he muttered.

Now that he could see, Ryan realized that the middle of a tangle of broken wood and varnished fabric wasn't the best place to be if the oil ignited and fired the gas that had splashed around. Even in that dire emergency, Ryan's logical fighting brain told him that there couldn't be that much fuel, since the plane had crashed because of a lack of gas.

He couldn't see anything of Layton, but he could hear the man groaning.

"I'll get you out," he called, but there was no response.

The buckle opened easily, and Ryan clung to what had been the front of he cockpit, swinging himself carefully around and down, dangling for a few moments with his feet scraping the air. The drop was only a short one and he let go, landing and rolling onto his knees. His ankle was cut just above the top of his boot, but he'd been able to pull free without difficulty.

Ryan stretched and straightened, automatically checking himself for any injury. Apart from some stiffness in his neck and a little blood from a cut lip, he'd gotten away almost scot-free.

The plane was tipped on its nose, the propeller splintered and snapped into several pieces. Strips of wire hung to the ground, black against the sun. They reminded Ryan of the clusters of crepe paper that had been pinned to so many front doors of Snakefish, to cry out the homes of the recently dead. The wings on the starboard side of the air wag had been sheared off and lay a few yards from the rest of the fuselage.

Then he saw the pilot.

Layton's immense weight had thrown him forward in the crash, snapping the seat belt like rotted canvas. He'd then pitched sideways, his hips gripped by the collapsing walls of the cockpit. He was pinned upside down, his head only a few inches from the dirt. Blood darkened the front of his flying suit and flowed over his face in a steady, gurgling trickle, crimsoning the earth beneath him.

Cautiously Ryan stepped closer, ready to throw himself clear at the first flicker of golden fire among the wreckage.

Now he could catch words, muttered in a low monotone.

"Sorry 'bout this, Dad. Going down. Hold on tight. Mom, we're going in."

Ryan reached out a hand and pulled away a jagged section of one of the wing struts. Then he could see the injury. The cockpit glass had shattered when Layton's bulk was crushed against it, and some of the shards had buried themselves deep in the rippling walls of the young man's stomach.

Ryan had seen enough abdominal injuries in his thirty-five years or so of living to be able to tell major from minor, serious from terminal.

Layton Brennan wasn't going to be seeing another sunset. Even if Ryan had been able to get him out of the wreckage without worsening the wound, it would take a skilled doctor to patch up the gashes.

Ryan looked around. They had come down in a dip in the ground, and he couldn't see how far they were from the ville, but he could hear the noise of some sort of wag and one of the Heroes' hogs moving his way. Obviously the watchers in Snakefish would have seen them losing altitude, swooping lower and never rising again. But rescue wasn't needed for him, and it would come way too late for Layton.

The muttering faded, and the baron's nephew quivered once and died. The blood continued to drip from his forehead for several more seconds and then that, too, stopped.

"EDGAR'S NEAR a breakdown," Carla said angrily. "All this at once. Too much for him. You've got to do something, John!"

J.B. scratched the side of his nose. "Not that easy. Seems like the Motes have damned near the whole town on their side. We got the firepower. Sure, we could probably chill those bikers, mebbe even take over the ville. Then what?"

"We're moving on, Carla," Ryan said with a quiet finality.

"They murdered Layton and tried to kill you, as well. Nearly made it."

Ryan nodded. "I hear what you say, Carla. But you have to realize that this isn't a game. Not some idle story in an old vid. There's no half measures in real life, Carla."

"How d'you mean?"

"I mean that if I kill Mealy I have to kill Zombie. And the rest of the chapter. And the Motes. And Dern. And any of the ville's folk who back them. It'll be full-out bloody war."

The woman sat slumped in a chair in the bedroom shared by Krysty and Ryan. The others were there, except for Lori, who'd gone out an hour earlier.

"So, you're just going to walk away."

"He who doesn't fight but walks away lives to walk away another day," Doc said.

"Just like that," Carla muttered bitterly, standing up and walking to the door. She turned to look at J.B. "I was wrong, John. Wrong about you. And I'm real sorry for it."

"Yeah. Me too, Carla. But there's some things a man just has to ride around."

His last words were overlapped by the sound of the closing door.

LORI STILL HADN'T reappeared by late afternoon. When Ruby brought up a tray of her coffee with some pecan cookies, Doc asked her if she'd seen the blond teenager.

"Mebbe I have and then again, mebbe I haven't, Doctor Tanner." There was a curl to her lips and a leer in her eyes as she spoke.

"I would be most obliged if you could see your way clear to elaborating that statement, my good woman."

"How's that?"

"I mean that I'd like you to cease your petty-minded prevarication and tell me where the girl is!" Doc roared.

"Oh, land o'reptiles! I just heard someone say how she heard someone else talking 'bout how they seen the young lady walking out with Apostle Joshua Mote, down by the temple of the Lord's own anointed ones. But it might just be..."

The words trailed away as Doc stared at her balefully. Without another word she turned and left the room. Doc took his Le Mat from the top of the dresser and spun the chamber thoughtfully. "I believe I'll take a short walk."

"Guess I'll come with you," Ryan offered. "Let's go."

"YOU KNOW what we could find?" Ryan asked as they walked down Main Street.

Doc stopped midstride, digging the ferrule of his swordstick into the trampled dirt at the edge of the road. "We've known each other for some time, my dear Ryan, have we not?"

"Sure."

Doc stared into Ryan's face, the old man's eyes steady and unblinking. "There are times when I confess that my brain wanders a bit and slips a notch sideways. Or backward. But in general, would you say that you concluded that I was a cretin?"

"No."

"Then kindly give me credit for anticipating what we might find. I am not a fool, Ryan. I'm an old man in many ways. Too many ways. Lori Quint is a young and lively girl. I always knew that the day would surely come when she and I would no longer be... I think you understand me. So, if she and Joshua Mote are busily making the beast with two backs, then I believe that I shall be able to cope with it." He hesitated. "That does not mean, my dear Ryan, that I relish the idea! But I think I shall cope. However, I would rather she chose better than the vile young Master Mote."

They resumed their walk.

FOUR OF THE LAST HEROES lounged outside the temple, leaning on their two-wheel wags, watching as Ryan and Doc approached them.

"Going far, outlanders?" Kruger croaked, tapping on the polished gas tank of his hog with the tips of the knives in his glove.

"Just collecting a friend," Ryan replied, moving easily into the stance of a gunfighter prepared to draw.

"Straw hair?" Rat giggled. "She's sort of busy right now."

"We're going in anyway."

Riddler moved to block the entrance to the temple. "Could be better if you went back to Ma Rainer's and waited, Ryan. She'll be along later."

"No. Going in now. You and the brothers aiming to stop us?"

Riddler looked at his companions, seeing no signs of support against the ice-eyed outlander. He shook his head. "Guess not. But it's a wrong move, Ryan. Believe me."

"I believe you. Come on, Doc."

"Right with you."

They walked together up the path toward the side door of the large building. "Sure you want to do this, Doc?"

"No, Ryan. But I'll do it anyway. J.B. had it right about there being things a man can 'easy ride around.' Conversely there are also things that a man can't ride around. This is one of them."

The door was on the latch and Ryan pushed it open, his right hand dropping naturally to the butt of his SIG-Sauer. He glanced behind him to make sure that the Heroes weren't following, but all four had remained by the gate, leaning against their bikes. One or two townspeople had also appeared and were watching the temple.

As soon as they were properly inside the gloomy building, Ryan knew that his suspicions—and those of Doc—were about to be justified. He could hear the rhythmic jingling of small silver spurs, the heavy panting of a man's breath and a woman gasping and moaning.

"Lori," Ryan whispered.

They crept closer.

The soft-bodied young man lay flat on his back, in front of the snake altar, his pants hooked around his ankles. His head was turned away from them, his arms stretched out wide.

Lori was riding him, her own legs spread apart, the bells of her high red boots clicking on the polished wooden floor. Her head was thrown back and her long blond hair almost reached the thrusting cleft of her buttocks. Her hands were on Joshua Mote's chest, nails digging crimson furrows in his skin.

She was naked apart from her boots. Even in the dim light inside the temple, Ryan could clearly see that the girl's nipples were hard with her own driving passion.

"Bit longer, Josh . . . One time more . . . Don't stop now . . . don't . . . Come on, baby, come on . . ."

"Now," Ryan shouted his loud voice bursting into the coupling.

"Who the fuck . . . !" Joshua exclaimed, trying to sit up and see around the girl's body.

Lori ceased her pleasuring but didn't bother to turn around.

"Got the old dribbling fucker with you, Ryan?" she asked. "Guess you have had. Now he can see how many a real man could get on fucking. Can't you, Doc? Can't you, Doc?"

"Come with us, child," Doc urged, his voice quiet and controlled. "You deserve better than this imbecile, Lori."

Joshua pushed her off, fumbling as he tried to pull his pants up over his suddenly limp penis. His face was flushed with anger. "Who're you calling names? You're dead, old man. Dead. Nobody does this to Joshua Mote and lives."

"Shut up, boy," Ryan ordered. "Talk's cheap. Action costs. Get dressed, Lori."

"Why?"

"Just do it. I'm not here to argue. Get your clothes on, or I'll drag you naked down Main Street. Come on, girl."

There was an icy tautness in Ryan's voice that convinced Lori to do as she was told. She stood, deliberately not bothering to hide herself from either man.

"Quickly," Ryan snapped.

"I'll wait outside," Doc said quietly. "I need some fresh air. It's stuffy in here."

For a moment it seemed as though Lori were going to make some smart-ass crack at the old man, but she caught Ryan's eye and kept silent.

"I'm going to my father," Joshua spit, feeling more confident now that he had his pants on. "He'll see to you, outlander."

"I'm shaking in my boots, boy. Just go on home, now."

The door slammed and Ryan was left alone with Lori. She'd nearly finished dressing, and her mouth was set in a stubborn, angry line.

"You don't understand, Ryan." Her voice was pitched so low that it scarcely reached him.

"You're wrong, Lori. I understand. We all do. Even Doc does."

"It's just that . . . I don't want to be hurt him. He's being very kind to me, Ryan."

"Hell, I know that. But he's got a lot of goodness in him, Lori. He's generous and brave. Braver than you could ever know. You shouldn't have treated him like that."

"Guess not. Maybe he and me can pick some times to speak with it. After. When we leave the ville."

"You won't stay with Joshua Mote?"

She smiled, and Ryan saw how very beautiful the girl was. And how young she still seemed. "No. Double-big cock. Double-small brain."

"Often the way, so I hear," he replied as they walked out.

Joshua Mote yelled a parting shot as the three friends walked toward the Rentaroom.

"Going back to grandpa, you gaudy slut?" he bellowed. "You fucking wait! We got the power in this ville, you useless, dry bitch. We'll give you to the snakes."

"*Your* snakes!" Lori screamed, wildly provoked. "We'll chill them all like we chilled your fucking big Azrael!"

There was a brief moment of utter stillness after the revelation.

Chapter Thirty-One

"NONE OF THEM tried to draw on you?" Krysty asked.

Ryan shook his head in remembered disbelief. "No. Thought that was going to be it. Had my blaster half out its holster."

"I believe that they were too surprised to do anything," Doc offered. "There was a great dropping of jaws."

"I'm real sorry, people," Lori said from where she sat on the bed. "But he didn't should have called me them names. The dirty hot-cocked bastard pig!"

Ryan laughed. "Yeah. That's telling them, Lori. What you did is done. Can't take it back. Like a bullet on its way out the barrel."

"What we gonna do?" Jak asked, standing by the window and peering out from behind the curtains at the street. Since the hasty return of Ryan, Doc and Lori, the ville had appeared to be suddenly and peculiarly deserted.

"Lines are drawn now," J.B. answered. "Like it or not, there won't be any running now. They know we did for their pet idol. Just the excuse they wanted to come at us. Could be best we go at them first. Ryan?"

"Could be. We're too few. There won't be anyone in the ville we could look to for help. They'll either back the Motes as the power or they'll stand off and wait and watch."

"Why can't we leave?" Rick asked. "Would they try and stop us?"

"Course," Krysty said. "What J.B. says is right. Running time's gone."

"I saw an old movie the day before they froze me. Can't remember much, but there was a line about how dying time had come. Is it like that now, Ryan?"

"Don't be a stupe, Rick. We've got the blasters. More important, some of us know a lot about chilling. People don't realize that killing is an art like any other. You have to learn it."

"Not me. Sorry and all that, guys. I'll help and do what I can. But I won't kill another human being. Sorry." Rick was adamant.

IT WAS DUSK before the first move was made.

"Mote's son an' Zombie," Jak called to Ryan from his place by the window.

J.B. was covering the rear of the building, but with darkness falling it would be easy for the enemy to approach undetected and hit the Rentaroom from any side. Ryan's plan was to move outside as quickly as possible, once the last shreds of light were gone.

"Tell J.B.," Ryan said. "Could be a feint out front here."

"Chill 'em?" asked the albino teenager, his snowy hair tinted crimson by the bloody light of the tumbling sun.

It was tempting to try to get rid of Zombie, possibly the biggest threat on the other side. But Ryan preferred to wait.

"No. Keep back. See if they got something to say to us."

They had.

Joshua Mote stopped about fifty yards away, half hidden by a dusty sycamore on the far side of the street. Zombie stood at his shoulder, carrying a large piece of ragged white cloth that was tied to a broom handle. Nervously he waved it at the watchers in the room.

"You gonna let us near?" Joshua shouted, his voice cracking with nerves.

Ryan eased the window open a few inches. "Could've chilled you by now if I'd wanted to!" he yelled. "Come closer. Say what you got to say. We won't open fire."

"Don't trust them!" Rick whispered, leaning on his stick at the other side of the window. "They'll try to trick you."

"No. They got no reason to. We're here. They know we aren't going anywhere. Not yet. They can wait us out. I figure there's a ring of armed men all around us right now. How can they trick us?"

"I don't know. Wouldn't trust them, Ryan."

It was such a stupid and naive thing to say that Ryan ignored it, concentrating instead on the two men in the street. Joshua Mote flourished a sheet of paper.

"Message from Pa and Ma. They say someone's gotta pay the blood price for Azrael. That's the law here. They say it's time for a new baron."

"Wouldn't be Baron Norman Mote, would it, son?" asked Ryan.

"You shut your..." Zombie said something Ryan couldn't hear, and Joshua spit in the dirt. "You give us the two women and leave, and you forfeit your blasters to the ville. You get an escort to the limits."

"And a bullet through the back of the skull," Krysty whispered.

"Yeah. I know it." Ryan raised his voice. "What happens if we don't accept?"

"Y'all get chilled and handed over to the snakes. They like a lotta fresh food."

"Wc got long to think this over?"

"One hour, starting now."

Zombie advanced a couple of paces. "We got the place ringed, One-Eye."

"Figured you would have."

"You got no chance."

"No."

"It's a good deal. Best you got. The women won't suffer none. Be over quick. Rest of you ride off without a care."

"We'll think on it."

"One hour, outlander!" Joshua yelled. "Then we come in after you."

Ryan had an almost overwhelming temptation to send the arrogant young man off to buy the farm. His finger actually itched to squeeze the trigger of his G-12. But that would mean having to play the hand out on their terms. It wasn't worth it for the passing satisfaction.

The two men vanished into the flourishing darkness and the street was quiet again.

"We got an hour to move," Ryan said.

CARLA AND BARON EDGAR arrived at the rooming house a half hour later. Ruby had made a hasty departure even before Joshua delivered the ultimatum.

By now Ryan's group was spread out in defensive positions: J.B. was outside the back door; Jak stood just inside the windows of the first-floor rear; Doc and Lori were covering the two sides of the building; Ryan and Krysty watched for a main frontal attack up the street. The streetlights on Main Street had been switched off, but the companions could hear the throbbing of the ville's generator. The sweet smell of gasoline told them that the processing plant was still working full out, beyond the ruins of the old theme park.

Carla was wearing her riding breeches and a dark maroon shirt. She carried an unidentifiable .32 pistol with polished walnut grips in her belt. Baron Edgar had aged ten years in the past twenty-four hours. His clothes were stained and creased, and he hardly seemed to know where he was.

"We had to come, Ryan. I know they plan to chill us both. We had no choice. Where's John?"

"Out back. Keep away from the window. Let Edgar sit a spell on the bed, by Rick. You're welcome. Things have changed some."

"They know we killed their pet rattler," Krysty told her.

"I heard. I also heard that they say they want you and the blond girl as sacrifices. Josh'll want her for his own use first. And they said they'd let the rest of you go."

"That's what they say. We know what they mean."

"What are you going to do, Ryan?"

When it came down to it, there were only two choices: stay and fight defensively or go out into the night and fight offensively.

The gateway wasn't all that far away, but with the freezie in tow, the journey wouldn't be easy and it wouldn't be fast. But if Mote and his army were attacked, there was a chance that enough of them would be chilled to allow the companions to break free. And to discourage pursuit.

They had discussed it as soon as Ryan, Lori and Doc had returned to the Rentaroom. It had been J.B. who had made the vitally important point.

"Saw them at the feeding, and when the stickies made their move out in the desert. Take out the bikers and one or two others, and you got a pack of white-bellied runners. Most men in the ville can stand behind a wall and pull a trigger. Put them against someone who knows what he's doing and half'll run scared."

It was true, Ryan reflected. Despite overwhelming numbers, Mote didn't have many fighters. The Trader used to say that he'd rather have five men with firefight experience than a hundred without.

"Ryan," Carla repeated. "What can you do now?"

"Do?"

"Yes. Can you explain your plan to me?"

"Lady," he said, "I don't have the time."

"But..."

"All right. We go out. Attack the bikers and the Motes where they're set up. Hit anyone hard who gets in our way. Try and burn out the old theme park there, then move out. How's that sound?"

Carla looked across at the baron. The old man was sitting hunched over, hands to his face, weeping quietly.

"Can we come with you? I can use this blaster, and I'll look out for Edgar."

"Why take so much trouble over a defeated baron? It happens all the time in the Deathlands. Barons come and go. You don't have to carry on being loyal to him now."

Her voice was very quiet. "He's my father. Is that reason enough?"

"Yeah. Guess so. Sorry that... Fireblast! You know?"

She half smiled and patted his arm. "Course I know. And now you do, too. You still didn't say if we could come with you."

Ryan nodded. "Whatever happens, I figure it'll be better than staying around for the snakes."

"TEN MINUTES of the hour left, lover," Krysty said. She sat cross-legged, her back against the wall of the room, resting. Her fiery hair was coiled tightly around her head, ready for the combat to come. She looked amazingly relaxed.

"Jak!"

"Yeah?" The boy's voice floated up the shadowed staircase.

"Get J.B. up here. You come up, as well."

"Sure."

"You decided what to do, lover?"

"Yeah. I decided fifty minutes ago. Been examining the plan since then, looking for holes. Looking for anything better. Can't think of anything. So this'll be it."

When everyone had gathered in the room, he outlined his idea.

"Throw them off balance. We go down to the first floor and gather near the rear door. We wait and keep silent. They won't be totally sure if we've sneaked out or not. They'll be uncertain. Won't know whether to come in at us or not. Then, as soon as they finally make a move to attack, we go out like the hounds of hell. Make for the draw that runs parallel to Main Street and outflank them. We try to fire the Heroes' base, then double back along the far side of the street and into the brush. And away. How's that?"

The Armorer took off his fedora and scratched at the light brown stubble of hair. "Can't see anything wrong with it. Experienced sec men . . . they'd see it coming and cut us apart. Not those no-hopers and blankers. Yeah. Let's do it that way."

The passing of the hour was announced by a shout coming from one of the buildings across Main Street.

For the next twenty-eight minutes, nothing happened at all.

Then everything started to happen at once.

Chapter Thirty-Two

"WAG ON THE WAY," Krysty announced.

"Can't hear an engine. You sure, lover?"

She nodded. "Being pushed. I can hear men's feet and the sound of wheels on sand. They're aiming to get in the front under cover."

"Then it's time to move. Keep an eye on Edgar. Rick?"

"What? Sorry, Ryan. I was miles away. What is it? Are the black hats coming?"

"Yeah. They're on the way. Take charge of the baron, will you? Just keep him close. And keep your eyes open. It'll likely be kind of busy for the next few minutes."

His eye accustomed to the darkness, Ryan was able to see the armored truck that Krysty had picked up with her mutie hearing, the rectangular bulk blacker against the blackness. The pale faces behind it were heaving it ponderously forward. It was about eighty yards from the rooming house. Ryan could pick out men strung along the far side of Main Street, on roofs and peering from behind curtains.

"This is it," he said. "Let's go."

He led the way, followed by Rick and Baron Edgar. Krysty brought up the rear and quietly closed the bedroom door behind her.

Jak was at the top of the stairs and he turned, cat-like, his red eyes seeming to glow with a smoldering fire.

"Now?" he asked, responding to Ryan's nod and taking the lead down to the first floor.

Doc and Lori waited there, one at the front of the long hallway, the other in the entrance to the kitchen, watching the rear of the house.

"Are the redcoats coming?" Doc asked in a hoarse whisper.

Ryan didn't try to guess at the strange allusion. The meaning of the question was plain enough. "Yeah. Out front. Hiding behind a big wag. Be at the front door in four or five minutes."

"Can't we blast some and stop them down?" Lori asked eagerly.

"No. Best plan is to keep them guessing. If it's dark and quiet and there's no sign of any of us, they'll be uncertain. That means frightened. Nobody wants to be first up the ladder or number one through a closed door. It'll slow them."

They padded through the kitchen in single file, past the antique pots of copper and brass and the scrubbed tables. Jak looked at the rack of old knives with bone handles. Ryan caught the glance.

"Leave them be."

Ryan eased the back door open a couple of inches and saw the stocky figure of J.B. standing close to Carla.

"They're coming out front, pushing a wag ahead of them. Still don't figure they're likely to rush at us out of the darkness."

The Armorer grinned, his teeth showing white in the night. "Guess not. I haven't heard a gnat fart out back. If they got it covered, then they're either very good or they're keeping themselves way, way off there."

During their whispered conversation, Ryan had been peering down Ruby's trim garden, past the neat rows of okra and beyond the outhouse to where the brush began. And where the steep-sided draw ran behind Main Street.

"We go now?" Krysty asked.

Ryan hesitated. "What can you hear?

Krysty shook her head. "Wind's blowing this way. All I can hear's the gas plant. Drowns anything else out."

"Jak, you got the best night seeing of any of us. You make anyone that way?" He pointed toward the desert.

Jak stood silent for a long moment. "Think there's one or two about fifteen feet left of outhouse. Crouched behind heap of cut wood."

Ryan strained his eye to try to see what the albino had spotted. But it was all a dark, swimming blue to him.

There wasn't time for any more doubts. Behind them, at the front of the hotel, the night exploded with the dull, heavy sound of scatterguns and the busy crackling of pistols. And the distinctive chatter of John Dern's M-16.

Glass broke and wood splintered, and above the noise they heard the angry screech of Ruby Rainer's voice protesting the ruination of her property.

"Let's go," Ryan hissed, leading the way with his pistol in his left hand and the eighteen-inch steel blade of the panga in his right.

JAK HAD BEEN partly correct.

Zombie had placed Mealy in charge of the rear guard. Six men were sitting down, talking quietly, behind the cords of kindling. Two more were crouched at the side, keeping watch for signs of movement in the building.

They had been warned to look out for anyone sneaking quietly out of the darkness, but they weren't prepared for the utterly ruthless speed and violence as Ryan and the others hit them.

"Fastest and hardest," had been another of the Trader's endless number of homilies—most of which concerned better ways of chilling.

Mealy had time to set his finger onto the trigger of his shotgun but he didn't have time to pull it. The long cutting edge of the panga opened his throat in a screaming, red-lipped cry, nearly slicing his head from his broad shoulders. As the biker fell in a welter of blood, Ryan was already among the circle of relaxing men, his steel blade hissing and singing, jarring on bone, ripping through flesh.

J.B. took out one of the men who had been watching the rooming house, his Tekna knife driving forcefully into a soft stomach. The Armorer twisted his wrist brutally hard, letting the saw edge spill the sentry's intestines into steaming coils about his feet.

Doc's swordstick flashed and stabbed the other sentry neatly through the center of the chest, between the upper ribs and clean through the heart. As he withdrew the delicate rapier, the man slithered to the dirt, eyes wide in shock.

"Touché," Doc said.

Any cries of fear or pain were totally drowned by the bedlam from the front of the small hotel. By now every window in the Rentaroom had been smashed by lead.

Nobody out front heard the muffled sounds of eight of their fellows departing from this life.

It all took well below a minute.

"Anyone hurt?" Ryan asked, panting from the exultant burst of adrenaline energy. He stooped and wiped the blood from the panga blade on the long duster coat of one of the corpses. "No? Good. Then let's go down into the draw and get moving."

"Hell's bloody bells," Rick gasped. "I don't believe it. Seven, no, eight men. You just ran at them and killed every last one."

"The longer it takes before they realize we've gone, then the better chance we got."

J.B. agreed with Ryan. "And we've just brought the odds down some on our side. They find these good old chills, and they'll lose some balls for the fight. All helps."

Baron Edgar cleared his throat. "I'm not sure that I can lend the dignity of my office to this butchery. If it wasn't so dark I'd know all these men. Probably once called them my friends."

"Shut up, Baron," Ryan said, coldly dismissive of the old man.

"But this is my ville. I must insist that—"

Ryan grabbed him by the collar, lifting him up on the tips of his toes. "Shut up, Brennan. It's not your ville. Never will be again. And you don't *insist* anything. Not now and not ever. Just shut your mouth tight and do what you're told."

Carla took his arm. "Don't speak to him like that, Ryan. He's an old man."

"And he won't get any older if he doesn't stay buttoned."

"You got a cold heart, Ryan," she said quietly.

"Yeah. But I'm alive. Now, let's move."

THE MOON VANISHED behind a swooping bank of dark chem clouds, which brought with them a distant rumble of thunder and the threat of rain.

Visibility dropped from adequate to nil. Even Jak, with his heightened night sight, couldn't see more than a couple of paces ahead of them.

After Rick—and then Lori—had fallen on the rough ground of the valley bottom, Ryan called a halt. "Go on like this and we'll have a broken ankle. Best stop a while."

"They'll catch us," Carla protested.

They could still hear the crackle of small-arms fire behind them. By now Ryan guessed that someone in the attacking group would have figured that the birds had flown the coop. From what he'd seen of Zombie he didn't figure the bikers' leader was a great tactical fighter. But surely they would have moved in on the hotel when there was no sign of life.

"We go on we're in trouble," J.B. said, peering up at the sky.

"If we're making for the old park, I can lead us."

"What?" Ryan couldn't believe what he was hearing. "That you, Brennan?"

"Sure is. I'm as mad as fire day about all this. Sure I was kind of shocked for a while back there. Now I want to go and beat the living shit—pardon me, Carla—out of the Motes. I used to play in this draw when I was a kid. I know every rock. Let me go first, and you keep in tight."

"I don't know, Ryan," J.B. said doubtfully.

"Me too," Jak added.

"It's not that much of a risk," the baron insisted. "I mean it. I feel like someone who has been through a long, dark tunnel. Snakefish is my ville. I can get us there. I've sat it out for way, way too long, Ryan. Not anymore."

It was a difficult decision. Ryan didn't relish hanging around only a half mile from the hotel. He wanted to move along the draw and circle around to come up behind the headquarters of the bikers. But to let the diminutive, elderly man lead them? That was something else.

The wind was rising from the north. Ryan knew that the old park was near the gas-processing plant, on ground a little higher than the ville. But in the almost total blackness he wasn't that confident of leading the group there.

There wasn't much choice.

"All right, Baron. Go ahead. I'll follow. You tell me when there's any danger. Holes, ruts, slopes . . . any kind of deadfall. I'll pass the word down the line. It'll be slow, but it could be safe."

"Fine, fine. I'll be doing something useful. Hit a lick at those demons, the Motes."

The wind continued to rise, whipping up clouds of dust and sand, making everyone try to cover their mouths and noses. The baron led the way with surprising confidence, picking his way along the bottom of the draw, calling out occasional warnings that Ryan conveyed to J.B. and the others.

Ryan figured that by now they would have discovered, in the center of the ville, that the cage was empty. But he doubted many of the good people of Snakefish would be enthusiastic about following the gang of outlanders into the black heart of the chem storm.

"How far to the park, Baron?" he called out, having to repeat the question twice before Edgar heard him.

"I'd say about ten minutes. If this wind gets up more we could have trouble. Folks die in these parts when the twisters start."

Above the endless noise of the wind, Ryan had several times caught the sound of distant thunder. And there was lightning—not single stabbing forks, but vast explosions of smearing light that covered half the horizon and burned purple images into the retina, causing blindness for several seconds.

The sides of the ravine had begun to close in, giving more protection from the wind. Every now and then the lightning would illuminate the area immediately ahead. But the path was winding and treacherous, with no sign that they were anywhere near a road.

It was good news that they were nearly to their destination. The combination of blackness, the chem storm and the dazzling lightning was becoming impossible to overcome.

Edgar Brennan stopped and turned around, a few paces ahead of Ryan. The static electricity in the night air had made his fringe of white hair stand out like a halo. Behind him, around a turn in the trail, was open space.

"We're there!" he yelled. "We made it, Ryan! Made it!"

A deafening clap of thunder failed to drown out the explosion of the sawed-off shotgun.

The double-barreled charge hit Edgar Brennan in the center of his back, the impact driving him toward Ryan. He fell facedown, arms spread like a star.

Chapter Thirty-Three

"KNEW YOU'D TRY this way. Left the others. Came out here on my own and waited. Through the wind and the storm. Knew you'd come." The voice, a howl of delight and triumph, came from around the corner, just out of sight of Ryan and the others. "Get some good jack from the Motes for this!"

The voice was unmistakably Zombie's.

Baron Edgar Brennan had died instantly, almost at Ryan Cawdor's feet. The probability was that he never knew what had hit him, never had a split second's glimmering of the knowledge that eternity had claimed him.

"No, Pa!" Carla cried, seeing her father's slaughter in the almost continual sheets of violet lightning.

"Mine," J.B. growled, touching Ryan lightly on the arm.

Zombie, still yelping his delight, walked around the bend in the trail to examine his prize. The smoking scattergun was in his right hand. He was smiling behind the beribboned beard.

"Bastards," he said, spying Ryan and others. "Figured the baron'd done a runner alone."

"Mine," J.B. repeated.

The biker grinned at them through his jagged, broken teeth. "You're all dead. Every road's blocked. Only way out's past the snakes. You'll all die in the desert. Give up now."

"Chill him, John," Carla said quietly. "Do it to him. Now."

"Yeah," Zombie mocked. "Do it to me, you little prick. I wanna see you do it to me."

"Sure." J.B. shot him once in the throat and once in the lower stomach. The snap of the Steyr blaster was oddly muted in the eye of the storm. The big man dropped his shotgun, his face contorting with pain. He slumped to his knees, trying to cover the wounds with his hands.

"Feel fucking cold," Zombie said, sitting back on his heels, face puzzled. His fingers moved from the bullet holes and fell into his lap, resting there. "Oh, it's burning me. Like flames of ice."

"Again," Carla demanded.

"Waste of a bullet. Already wasted one on him."

"Then let me, John. He was my father. Give me your blaster."

"No need." Ryan walked to Zombie and pushed him with the flat of his hand. The biker fell limply to one side, rolling onto his back, eyes staring sightlessly at the chem storm that flared overhead.

TILTING HIS WRIST CHRON so that the numbers reflected the bursts of lightning, Ryan was able to make out the time. "Just after eleven," he said. It was later than he'd figured.

"Can we bury the baron?" Carla asked.

The wind had eased a little, and the center of the chem storm seemed to be passing. As the lightning became less frequent, the darkness was longer and deeper. Ryan had kept the others in the shelter of the draw, not wanting to risk leading them into the open. It looked as if Zombie had been on his own, but there wasn't any point in taking any chances.

"Mebbe later," he replied. "If there's time."

"It doesn't much matter. I guess it's not hurting him any. Not now. I'm glad you chilled Zombie for me. For him, John. I'll never forget you for that."

There was an awkward silence between them.

The others sat quietly, away from the corpses. Lori was picking dirt off the heels of her boots, wiping the little silver bells clean; Doc was at her side, whistling tunelessly to himself; Jak simply sat still; Rick was lying stretched out, clutching his walking cane. His face was ghostly pale, his breathing fast and shallow. Watching him, Ryan was beginning to wonder whether the freezie was going to make it—even if they did get past the rest of the ville and reached the gateway in safety.

Krysty leaned against a large, frost-scarred boulder, eyes closed. Sensing that Ryan was looking at her, she opened her green eyes.

"How d'you read it, lover?" she asked.

"Not good if they got the blacktop covered. We can't get any transport to move any distance. Desert'll chill us, like the biker said. What we have to do is find some way of bringing Mote and his buddies into a serious firefight. Distract them and hold them long enough for us to get through Snakefish and out past

the snakes. No way we can avoid them. Just step careful and light. But..." His voice trailed doubtfully
away.

Krysty smiled at him. "I don't see any better way.
They won't come at us until first light. We gotta be
ready. Either in the old park ruins or in the gas-
processing plant. Gaia! The smell from that place fills
my nostrils."

Ryan kissed her unexpectedly on the cheek. "Lover,
you've just given me the seed of an idea. It might
just..."

"What?"

"No. Let me think on it. Try and get some sleep.
Nobody's going anywhere until we get close to the
dawning."

RYAN, KRYSTY, J.B and Jak kept watch in turn
through the night. As soon as there was the faintest
pink lightening to the east, Ryan woke everyone in the
group.

Rick rubbed the sleep from his eyes. "Always feel
better first thing," he said. "Soon as the day starts it's
all downhill. Is that the sun I see?"

"False dawn," J.B. told him.

"How can you tell?"

The Armorer gave him a thin, humorless smile.
"Secrets of our trade, freezie. But since you're one of
us, I'll show you. Watch."

He stooped and picked up a white, smooth pebble,
tossing it from hand to hand. He looked at the walls
of rock that rose twenty or thirty feet above them.

Ryan grinned at Krysty. He'd seen J.B. pull this trick before, in a different place and at a very different time.

"Watch the stone," J.B. ordered.

He lobbed it as high as he could in the air. Everyone watched it rise then disappear into the darkness, before suddenly reappearing. J.B. put out a hand and caught it cleanly. "Now, you all lost sight of it, didn't you?" Everyone nodded dutifully. "I'll do it again, in five minutes or so. Then you'll all see the point of it."

The storm had drifted away to south toward the old looping Rio Grande and the barbaric wilderness that had once been the country of Mexico.

Ryan went around a bend in the draw and pissed against a rock, the urine steaming in the cool of the morning. Jak appeared at his side, on a similar mission.

"Ryan?"

"Yeah?"

"Me an' J.B. could circle and start diversion. Keep 'em off rest."

"No, Jak. Nice offer. We got Rick and we got Carla, and we got Lori and Doc. None of them are that strong in a firefight. We go down or we go through. But we do it together."

"Sure. Just thought—"

"Thanks, Jak. I mean it." He patted the slim boy on the shoulder.

When they rejoined the others, J.B. was holding the pebble again. "Come on, guys. Might learn something. I know you've seen it, Ryan. But the kid hasn't."

"Don't call—"

"Sorry," he said hastily. "Watch the stone now."

It spiraled way up, vanishing like before. Then, at its highest point, it reappeared, startlingly white, catching the first rays of the dawn from beyond the visible horizon. Krysty clapped her hands.

"Great, J.B., great."

"Nice," Jak nodded.

Doc beamed. "A fine example of the multifarious uses of physics, my dear Mr. Dix. If I was only back in my lecture room at... But I am not. And I never will be. So, let that pass."

The stone dropped into the dirt. Ryan rubbed at the stubble on his chin. "Tells us what we need to know. They'll likely be out here at full light. Best find some place to be ready for them."

A TWO-WHEEL WAG was parked in the entrance to the Sierra Sunrise Park, its chrome glittering, the flake finish bright. It was Zombie's beloved Harley-Davidson Electra Glide, propped on its stand, the sissy bars raked back. Carla walked over to it and tapped her thumb on the gas tank.

"Full." She hesitated, looking at the others. "Nobody objects if I take it, do they?"

J.B. answered for them all. "Nobody got a better right to it, Carla."

She swung her leg over it, straddling the soft leather of the narrow seat, hands on the grips. "The ville's done and I don't want to stay. I'm not running from the fight. It's just that it's not my fight anymore. I'll move on, away. Full tank'll take me a long ways off."

"Where will you go?" Krysty asked, seeing that J.B. wanted to ask, knowing that his pride would stop him.

"North. Have a sister in a ville called Chapmanston. I'll head there."

"Good luck," Lori said.

"Mebbe see you some day, Carla." J.B. took a half step toward the powerful motorcycle, then stopped.

Carla held out her hand to him. "If you're ever around Chapmanston, on the Missouri, come up and see me, John. I'd like that."

The Armorer took her hand and kissed her chastely on the cheek. Then he broke away and took off his spectacles, wiping them with an unusual vigor. "Go careful, Carla."

"And you, John. Bye, friends."

She fired the ignition and revved the engine a couple of times. Then she was gone, the rear wheel spinning in the loose dirt, fishtailing across the highway before gathering speed. They all watched the red glow of her rear light until it finally faded away into the distance.

"Time to get ready to meet Norman Mote and the others," Ryan said to his companions.

"Let's do it," J.B. agreed, his glasses finally polished to his satisfaction.

THEY FOUND that the main gas plant was completely unguarded. Krysty guessed that the Motes had called in every single available man for the attack on the rooming house, even bringing in his sec patrols. It seemed a likely theory.

By the industrial standards of the late twentieth century, the complex wasn't very large. But by the standards of Deathlands it was enormous. There were three large storage tanks, each holding what must have been thousands of gallons of processed gasoline. The actual processing was done inside a long warehouse-like building. To the north were at least a dozen rocking-donkey pumps, nodding away in the growing light.

"Good place to meet them," J.B. said approvingly, looking around thoughtfully.

"Sure is," Ryan agreed. "They aren't going to want to pour too much lead into a place like this. One spark and five miles around could go up."

"And us with it?" Doc asked.

"Worse ways of nailing down the lid," Ryan replied. "It'd be quick."

"Coming!" Jak shouted. "Lotta wags."

Ryan looked at his small group of friends. "Get ready. And good luck."

Chapter Thirty-Four

THE GAS PLANT proved to be an inspired defensive position against the overwhelming numbers of the opposing force. It had several low walls but only one possible entrance. So the Motes and their army had to come through the front door.

Riddler, bulging over both sides of his saddle, roared ahead of the others, doing a spectacular wheelie, bellowing to the hidden Ryan Cawdor.

"Where's Zombie? You seen him?"

J.B. answered. "Seen him and chilled him."

The fat biker throttled back his bike and stopped very close to the main gates, lowering his voice. "You got no chance, Ryan. Lemme talk to the Motes and try to work something out."

"Thanks, Riddler. But no thanks. Gotta be this way."

The rear wheel spit out a spray of dirt as the Hero rejoined the others.

Ryan and his companions waited.

IT WAS FULL LIGHT.

The wind had eased, but it had also veered and was now blowing briskly, parallel to the mountains where the redoubt was concealed.

Mote, taking charge of the operation himself, remained safely hidden behind his own sec wag. Ryan had glimpsed Marianne Mote, teetering on her high heels, holding the arm of her brutish son.

John Dern appeared to be in control of the main body of the attackers. Twice Ryan had a chance at a long shot at him with the G-12, but he elected to hold his fire, not wanting to reveal the effective range of his weapon.

Only five Last Heroes remained alive. As Ryan peered around the edge of the main gate, it seemed as though they were now without any sort of leadership.

Ryan knelt behind the wall, looking behind him at the thudding machinery and storage tanks of the gas plant and back down the hill to where the vehicles were grouped tightly together. Nobody wanted to make the first move. If Mote chose to play the softly-softly game he could probably drive them out of hiding with starvation. Or thirst. In another hour or so the desert would begin to heat up.

"Down the hill," Ryan muttered to himself.

"What?" Krysty said, just to his left.

"Down the hill! Fireblast! Why didn't I see that as the way?"

"You skull-flipped, lover?"

"No."

"Then...?" Krysty prompted, turning suddenly to look at the looming gas tanks behind them. "You're not...?"

"Yeah, lover. I am."

And he did, calling Jak over to quickly give him orders. The albino boy, hair gleaming in the new day's light, scampered off like an eager hound, keeping low to avoid being spotted by the attackers down the highway.

While Krysty kept watch at the front, Ryan moved to warn the others about what he was going to do.

Lori simply nodded and J.B. grinned.

Rick looked blankly up into Ryan's face, struggling to understand what he was saying. "It could..." The words trailed off.

"That's it, Rick. It could."

Doc considered the news for several long seconds. "It has a pleasantly Biblical ring to it, my dear Ryan. I believe that I approve of it."

Krysty called from the main gate. "Here they come, Ryan!"

Mote was encouraging the first wave of attackers with John Dern at their head. They were advancing in a skirmishing line, bunching on the road, filtering off into the light brush on either side. The Heroes were revving their two-wheel wags, all on the right. Ryan's guess was that they'd head for their base in the old park and come through into the adjacent gas plant.

It was time for the one big play.

"Now, Jak! Now!"

The assault party heard the shout and several hesitated, but Norman Mote, standing behind his own personalized wag, bellowed at them to keep moving.

"We got 'em outnumbered twenty to one. They'll give in, friends. By hollow tooth and black poison, I swear it!"

At Ryan's call, Doc, Lori, Rick and J.B. joined Lori by the main frontage to the processing unit, blasters at the ready. All except for Rick, who knelt behind the low stone wall, eyes closed and muttering to himself.

The sickly smell of gas grew stronger.

Much stronger.

Ryan, glancing over his shoulder, cautioned the others as he saw the glint of sunlight off a ribbon of liquid, the air above it shimmering like a desert mirage. Jak appeared around the side of one of the tanks, waving a clenched fist.

"Get out of the way," Ryan called. "It's spreading."

The stream of refined gasoline was gaining speed. Jak had opened the main valves on all the huge containers, and thousands of gallons of fuel were flooding through the complex, along the roadway, toward Mote and his people.

J.B. fished a burner gren from one of his pockets. "Best we get out 'fore I throw this," he suggested quietly.

"Wait till it reaches the first of them. Here come the bikers! It'll blow clear back to the tanks. Let's move."

There was a cheer from the attackers and a handful of ill-aimed, harmless shots as they saw the one-eyed man leading his ragged group away from the gas plant, apparently running in panic—running hopelessly, helplessly, toward the same draw that cut behind the ville.

"Go get 'em!" Marianne screeched, waving a red-nailed fist.

The stream of gas had become a torrent, bubbling its way down the slope. Some of it foamed off the sides into the thirsty earth, but most of it remained on the blacktop.

Ryan judged the moment, giving the nod to the Armorer. "Now, J.B., now!"

The gren was pitched into the air, catching the sun at its highest point, and dropped to the gasoline river. J.B.'s aim was perfect and the burner landed smack in the middle of the road, bouncing and rolling a couple of times.

And failing to ignite!

"Black dust!" J.B. cursed, watching as the bikers roared toward them.

There wasn't enough time to try another gren to fire the gasoline. Thanks to razor-gloved Kruger, it wasn't necessary.

Rat yelped a warning, waving his scarred arm to the right, managing to get the powerful hog off the blacktop before he splashed into the fuel. Freewheeler, Harlekin and Riddler saw the sign and followed him. But Kruger had his grizzled head down, concentrating on gunning his bike's engine for full power. He had a moment of extreme bewilderment as liquid sprayed all around his bike and over him.

"Rain?" he muttered.

The hot exhaust did the trick.

"Hell's bloody bells," Rick breathed, overcome with an almost religious awe.

The explosion was cataclysmic, beginning with a spark of infinitely bright white light that centered on Kruger's two-wheel wag. The flames engulfed the rider and his machine and spread with a breathless speed, racing along the surface of the gushing gasoline. The inferno barreled down the hill toward the paralyzed attackers, off the sides of the road and into the dry brush, quickly backtracking to the refinery and the spilling tanks.

"Get down!" Ryan shouted, grabbing Krysty and dragging her flat in the dirt behind a slight rise in the ground. He pressed his face to the earth, one arm around her shoulders.

The ground shook as the tanks blew, one after the other. The explosion was deafening. Chunks of metal erupted into the air, two hundred feet or more, then rained back to earth, deadly molten missiles of death.

Ryan leaped to his feet, blaster ready at the hip, eye raking the surrounding area, appraising what had happened.

Thick black smoke billowed everywhere, making it difficult for Ryan to see. His nostrils caught the familiar stench of roasting flesh. At the epicenter of the holocaust Kruger had fallen from his bike. He'd risen to his feet and then dropped to his knees like a monk at his morning devotions.

And so died. Flames continued to dance from his charred and blackened flesh, like the stump of a tree at the end of a forest fire.

The river of gas, as it caught, had devoured dozens of the men from the ville, swallowing them hungrily and moving on toward the center of Snakefish itself. The Motes' wag had gone, reversing in hasty panic, just avoiding the onrushing inferno of death and destruction.

Those who hadn't fallen to the flames were running into the brush in wide-eyed panic. Many were

screaming, and threw down their blasters as they ran.
But at the edges of the highway, the dust-dry mesquite and creosote bushes had ignited, crackling
brightly, passing the small flames from branch to
branch. The veering wind carried them as fast as a
man could hope to run.

"Any hurt?" Ryan called, watching as the members of his group got to their feet and brushed off sand
and dirt.

The sound of the gas plant blowing had almost
deafened Ryan, and only Jak's pointing finger reminded the one-eyed man that four of the bikers had
dodged the initial blaze.

Harlekin had fallen off his machine and was stumbling toward them, trying to cock his scattergun as he
ran. Ryan took careful aim with the G-12 and put a
round through the Hero's forehead, punching him
onto the ground.

Freewheeler had fought for control of his Indian
Chief, wrestling it in a sliding spin and aiming for
Lori. The tall blond teenager stood rock steady, her
pearl-handled PPK clutched in both hands.

The popping of the .22 was ridiculously flat and insignificant, but her aim was true. The rider threw his
arms wide, a bloody hole flowering in the center of his
bearded face. He crashed out of the saddle, the bike
rearing up like a frightened stallion and smashing on
top of him.

Only Rat and Riddler remained alive.

The smaller of the two men spied Rick Ginsberg,
standing stricken and helpless, empty-handed, to one
side of the group. Rat angled his hog in the freezie's

direction, flourishing his shotgun in his right fist. Rick whimpered and raised his hands to his face to hide his eyes.

"Mine," Krysty called, leveling her blaster and shooting Rat four times through the chest. The shotgun flew into the air and dropped almost at Ginsberg's feet. The bike swerved out of control, and Rat toppled from the saddle, his body bouncing twice. His head cracked against a boulder, rolled away then lay still.

His face twitching with shock, Rick picked up the scattergun and tucked it under his arm, as a stockbroker would do with his rolled umbrella.

Riddler had throttled down and stopped twenty yards from Ryan, amid the knee-high scrub. He still held his shotgun, cradled across his ample lap, but the hammers weren't cocked. He looked at the seven friends, his gaze returning to Ryan.

"Never seen a firefight better fucking named, Ryan," he said, grinning.

"Yeah. Time for us to move on," Ryan said, keeping the G-12 steady on the last of the Last Heroes.

"Time for me to move on, too." Riddler laughed. "Chance for you an' me to settle those fucking debts we spoke 'bout, Ryan?"

Ryan gestured with the barrel of the automatic rifle at his friends. "Lots of creditors here, Riddler," he said.

"I was thinking of moving...that way." The Last Hero pointed to the ribbon of blacktop that stretched out across the desert, behind the ruins of the gas plant. The remnants of the Sierra Sunrise Park had also caught fire, wood cracking and popping in the heat. Ryan considered for a moment. Trader had said that a dead enemy wouldn't ever come back to chill you. It would be simple to shoot the fat man, waste him with a single round. His finger tightened momentarily on the trigger, then relaxed.

"Get going."

"So long, brother." Riddler waved a fist to the others. "Brothers and sisters. Live righteous days. So long now."

Like Carla Petersen before him, Riddler revved up the powerful engine and roared away, beyond the pall of smoke.

Doc looked toward the ville. "The buildings are catching fire. I suggest that we might consider leaving."

"Best suggestion I heard all day." Ryan slung the blaster over his shoulder.

Chapter Thirty-Five

"VILLE'S DONE FOR," Jak observed, leading the way along the side of the scorched highway. Bodies lay everywhere, like blackened logs, one or two of them still moving. The smell of baked meat filled everyone's nostrils, and the smoke was whisked away by the changeable wind.

Snakefish was well ablaze. As the friends drew nearer they could see women and children scurrying frantically from the burning buildings, trying to save whatever possessions they could. Very few of the men had made it back, most of them having chosen to run into the brush on the wrong side of the blacktop, so that the rushing wave of flames pursued them to their doom.

"Look who's here." J.B. pointed with the toe of his boot to where one of the chunks of human charcoal was writhing in a slow-motion agony. The remnants of an M-16 near the clawed hand told them that this was what remained of John Dern, dealer in guns and failed assassin.

His eyes had been seared in their sockets, and his hair blasted from his wrinkled skull. Only the oddly gentle movements told them that life remained within the basted carcass.

"Chill him," Lori whispered. "I don't mind what he done. Nobody should—"

"Leave him be," Ryan ordered. "Man gets what he deserves."

They headed for the ville, the glowing heat of the burning buildings scorching their skin as they drew closer. Fire leaped from shingled roof to tarred porch. The whole of Snakefish, end to end, was blazing. Hardly anyone took any notice of the seven outlanders as they picked their way carefully around the streets of the ville.

At one point Ruby Rainer hobbled past them, eyes wide and crazed. Her blouse was smoldering across one shoulder and the hem of her shirt had been burned clear away. She held an empty bird cage in her right hand and a wooden spoon in the other.

"That's the Motes' wag," Krysty said, pointing down an alley near the temple.

Down the road a little way the whole storefront of Handmaid exploded out in a great blossoming of multicolored fire.

"Wind's veering," Krysty told her companions. "If it goes right around, it'll carry the flames into the brush where the rattlers are. Block us off from reaching the redoubt if we don't watch it."

Ryan coughed as the billowing smoke enveloped them. "Got me a triple-wish to see those three down and sky-staring."

J.B. shook his head. "Better we move on out fast, Ryan. Revenge won't buy you a good burying."

"We move through Deathlands. If we don't leave things a touch better after we're gone, then what's the point? I say we clear them out."

The Armorer hesitated a moment. "Guess you're right, Ryan. They must be along that dirt road, saving some jack from the temple."

"The doors at the back of the wag are open," Doc said, walking toward the parked vehicle with Lori at his side.

Joshua Mote suddenly appeared around the side of the armored truck, arms filled with a pile of papers. As soon as he saw Doc he dropped them, reaching for a blaster at his hip.

"Dead old fucker!" he snarled.

But Doc's Le Mat was already drawn and cocked and he fired first. The single .63-caliber shotgun shell hit the curly-headed young man low in the belly, doubling him over.

"Wrong again, Master Mote," Doc stated quietly. "The dead fucker is yourself."

Mote rolled on his back, clutching at his stomach, trying to staunch the massive blood flow from the gaping wound. Lori stepped forward quickly and lifted her foot in the air, stamping down hard on Joshua's open mouth. The heel of her boot smashed in his front teeth, the silver spur snagging the flesh of his lips. She leaned with all her weight, grinding her boot as hard as she could, withdrawing it with a smile of contentment.

"Bastard," she said, watching him die.

"You killed my boy, you whore-slut gaudy bitch!" Norman Mote screamed, standing at the corner of the burning building, clutching an effigy of one of the mutie rattlers that looked as if it were made from pure silver. He staggered drunkenly, and his gray hair was tilted lopsidedly across his sweating temples.

Ryan didn't hesitate.

The 9 mm round that burst from the SIG-Sauer drilled a neat hole through the angry furrow between Mote's eyes. Like an empty suit of clothes, Norman Mote, Guardian of the Shrine, slumped dead, his body rolling against his dead son's legs.

"Where's bitch-queen?" Jak asked, looking around the corner of the alley.

"Probably heard the thunder of Doc's mortar," J.B. guessed. "Two from three isn't bad."

There was a note of real concern in Krysty's voice. "Wind's come right around. We *have* to move now, Ryan. Come on!"

J.B. led the way back along the end of Main Street, followed by Lori, tottering on her high heels, Doc holding her arm. Jak jogged behind them, followed by Krysty. Ryan, bringing up the rear, suddenly realized that Rick wasn't with them.

"Keep going, lover!" he yelled. "Freezie's vanished. We'll catch up when we can!"

Richard Ginsberg was in the alley, kneeling near the two corpses. For a moment Ryan thought of Joshua Mote's turquoise nugget around his neck, but it wasn't that. The scattergun that Rick had absently picked up after Rat's shooting lay in the dirt. The freezie was picking through the pile of paper. He heard footsteps and looked around.

"These are from my time, Ryan. Porno magazines. Kiddies and animals. So much of my society blasted to kingdom come and this filth remains! There's something real . . . Look out!"

Ryan Cawdor whirled, too late. Marianne Mote had come out of the side door of the nearest house, and she was holding a small silvered machine pistol, which was aimed at Ryan's chest almost point-blank.

Her makeup was blotched and smeared, and the dense smoke had darkened her doll-like complexion. Her dress was torn down the front, revealing the pallor of her thighs. She'd aged twenty years since Ryan had last seen her. But the venom was unsullied.

"Seen what you done, outlander. You won most all of the prizes. But you lose the last hand. And I win it."

"No." The overlooked, crouching Rick Ginsberg shot her through the back with both barrels of the shotgun.

Ryan winced at the expectation of her shooting him with a dying spasm, but her long-nailed fingers opened and the blaster dropped. Her hands waved frantically, as if she were gripped by one of her religious frenzies, and her mouth opened wide. A worm of thick, blood-roped spittle oozed out over her chin. Her legs gave way, and she collapsed beside her husband and son, making a surprisingly ladylike corpse.

"Thanks."

"What?" Rick looked like a man waking after a long sleep. He stared at the empty, smoking scattergun he was holding as if he'd never seen it before.

"I said thanks for that. She'd have chilled me for sure."

"I guess she... Oh..." He closed his eyes, taking deep breaths. "I thought I was going to throw up. You know, you were wrong, Ryan."

"How's that?"

"Killing people. You said it was hard. It's not. It's too damned easy."

Chapter Thirty-Six

SNAKEFISH WAS in its final, scorching death throes. Every building in the ville was burning. Smoke soared ten miles high, shredded by the wind as it was winnowed away from the foothills of the Sierras.

At the end nobody had tried to stop the seven friends or follow them. But now the threat came from the fire that they'd initiated. It was running along the highway and beginning to nibble at the edges of the mesquite.

"Gotta go for it," Ryan said. "Keep together. You can see the higher ground. Rocks. Reach that and we're safe. We'll soon be at the redoubt and away from here. Go for it."

They saw no signs of the mutie rattlers. No doubt the explosions and the fire had sent the great reptiles to their hidden burrows, deep beneath the desert.

Ryan set a steady pace, knowing that to start off too fast would have meant stragglers within a mile. He and J.B. could have pushed on at twice the speed, as could Jak and Krysty. But Doc Tanner was an old man, and Lori insisted on wearing her high-heeled crimson boots. And Rick was sickly.

The rising ground promised safety, but the wind had turned, causing the fire to pursue them. It was gaining all the time, and the roaring and crackling flames raced nearer to their heels.

"Gonna be close," J.B. panted.

"Freezie's bushed," Krysty said.

"An' Doc," Jak added.

Ryan held up his hand to stop everyone. The brush ended a scant half mile away, but the prairie fire was less than that. Smoke filled everyone's lungs and made running even more difficult. Rick was on hands and knees, clutching his cane, fighting for breath, shoulders heaving. Doc trembled with exhaustion.

"Krysty and I'll help Rick. Jak, you help Doc, and J.B. can give Lori a hand."

The girl shook her head, close to tears. "No. Jak and J.B. can help Doc along. He's needing it better than me. I'll be real fine."

It wasn't a situation for argument. Ryan nodded his agreement and the seven friends set off again for the last lap of their desperate race.

Rick was in a state of virtual collapse, feet shuffling and kicking out, hanging between Ryan and Krysty. Doc wasn't in much better condition, flopping between the two much smaller figures of Jak and the Armorer.

The nearer to safety, the steeper the slope, the greater the effort.

"Leave me!" Rick groaned. "Let me die again."

They ignored him.

Nobody dared to pause to look back, but they could all feel the heat of the fire and catch the smell of the burning creosote bushes. The roar of the flames, fanned by the wind, was deafening. Ryan could feel even his own enormous strength beginning to falter and fade. Now he was helping both Rick and Krysty, who was sobbing with the heart-bursting effort of staying alive.

Blinded by smoke, Ryan didn't even realize that they'd reached safety. Krysty was screaming in his ear, dragging at his arm to make him stop. He blinked his eye open and saw that they stood a good fifty paces clear, on the bare rock and out of danger from the onrushing fire.

Rick rocked on his knees, vomiting. A little to their right J.B. was bent over, hands on hips, fighting for breath, his spectacles hanging over one ear. Jak supported Doc, who was beyond the edge of physical tiredness, his face drained and blank, blackened with soot.

"Made it," J.B. gasped.

Ryan was beginning to nod his agreement, when the realization struck him like a dash of iced water. They hadn't made it. Not all of them. Lori was still—

"Lori!" Krysty screamed, pointing.

The tall blond girl was silhouetted against the towering wall of yellow-orange fire as it swept toward her, barely ten paces behind. She was less than fifty yards away from Ryan and the others.

Fifty yards from safety.

As she raced forward the heel of one of her boots twisted. Fatigue had robbed her of balance, and she slithered sideways, falling awkwardly. She struggled to get up for a moment, then slumped to the ground.

"No..." Ryan said disbelievingly.

The fire seemed to hang over the girl for a moment, in hungry anticipation. Then it plunged down and overwhelmed her. Lori Quint vanished in the torrent of flames.

Doc Tanner began to weep.

Chapter Thirty-Seven

"GOT TO BE GOING somewhere better, lover," Krysty said.

The door of the gateway was closed and the disks in floor and ceiling were beginning to glow. In only a handful of seconds the six friends would be making another jump into the unknown.

Ryan gazed around the glass-walled chamber. Doc sat quietly, knees drawn up under his chin, staring blankly ahead; J.B. was at his side, glasses folded neatly and safely tucked away; Jak whistled quietly to himself. Rick lay fast asleep, curled into a fetal position.

And Lori was dead.

"Somewhere better, lover?" Ryan repeated. "Couldn't be much worse." He paused. "Could it?"

Out of the ruins of civilization emerges...

The Deathlands saga—edge-of-the-seat adventure not to be missed!